THE
SECRET
OF
RAVENS
VALLEY

THE
SECRET
OF
RAVENS
VALLEY

A LIZA and
MRS. WILKENS
MYSTERY

LINDA NORLANDER

To Librarians Everywhere

Praise for The Secret of Ravens Valley

"*The Secret of Ravens Valley* owes much of its appeal to the way author Linda Norlander uses a trio of suspenseful narrative threads to power the central mystery: a librarian's suspicious death. Book bans, corporate greed, and a corrupt police department each play a role in the escalating tension, but it's the finely drawn characters who bring all of those to life. Thirty-something Liza Johnson and eighty-four-year-old Mrs. Wilkins are the amateur sleuths who investigate murder, arson, and more in Ravens Valley, but they're helped by a raft of vividly realized allies and convincingly menacing opponents.

Perhaps the most unexpected source of help comes from Liza's long-deceased sister, who whispers ghostly advice and plays a central role in several of the laugh-out-loud scenes. Goldie, Liza's cat, is also on hand to provide comic relief in a novel that expertly handles explosive elements that converge in a memorable climactic scene.

The conclusion does what the best ones do: provide a satisfying ending as well as whet the reader's appetite for another installment of this excellent series."—**Lori Robbins**, Amazon bestselling author of the award-winning On Pointe and Master Class mystery series

Chapter One: The Librarian is Dead

Before ending our video conference call, Fannie Porter closed her eyes for a moment and rubbed her forehead. "You know, I'm in deep, and it's scaring me."

Fannie was the rural Ruston County librarian and was mentoring me in a graduate summer school class on dealing with the issues of free speech in schools. Ravens Valley, the Ruston County seat, was in the middle of conservative southern Minnesota farm country. She was under siege from a local group called "Protect Our Children," who were pushing the banning of some of the most classic books, along with those addressing gender and race issues.

"What do you mean? Is there any way I can help?"

On the laptop screen, she appeared tired with deep circles under her eyes. She shook her head. "I have to deal with it here."

Three days later, Mrs. Wilkens, my eighty-something upstairs neighbor, stood in the doorway of my apartment, waving a newspaper. "I can't believe it. This is awful! I knew she was in danger!"

I quickly closed the lid on my laptop because instead of doing class homework, I was watching cute cat videos, and I'm not a cute cat video kind of person.

"What's wrong?"

"Fannie. They found her, and they're not doing anything about it."

"You mean our Fannie? What happened?"

"Yes, our Fannie. She was hit by a car, and those cowards in Ravens Valley aren't doing anything!" Mrs. Wilkens's cheeks flushed with anger.

I knew I needed to calm her down in order to get the whole story. "Maybe we should have some tea, and you can tell me about it."

We probably should have had gin and tonics, but I was out of everything except the lime. We sat at the kitchen table, drinking tea and nibbling on stale Girl Scout cookies while Mrs. Wilkens read the article in *The Ruston County Times* to me.

"Fannie Porter, 47, Ruston County librarian, was found dead near County Road 8—a probable victim of a hit-and-run. A spokesperson for the sheriff's department stated they were investigating, and anyone with information should contact them. Porter was known in the community for her devotion to the library. Recently, she had clashed with a local group called Protect Our Children, which wanted to ban certain books from the library. Funeral arrangements are pending."

I pictured Fannie on the last video call, with her short hair and glasses too large for her face, and how she appeared to be frightened. I was stunned at the loss and asked Mrs. Wilkens to read the article again.

"Why do you think no one is doing anything about this?"

Mrs. Wilkens rubbed the back of her neck and spoke with a sigh. "Fannie told me she was afraid of someone, and when I suggested she contact the sheriff, she said his office was corrupt, and she didn't trust anyone there."

Mrs. Wilkens had introduced me to Fannie this summer. As the former Ruston County librarian, Mrs. Wilkens had known Fannie for several years. Over the next two cups of tea, she filled me in again on all she knew about Fannie Porter, the town of Ravens Valley, and the controversy with Protect Our Children. I'd heard the story before, but I let my elderly neighbor talk.

"As I've told you, I used to be the county librarian back many years ago—before we moved to the cities. I know that community, and something dark has taken over."

I remembered Fannie on the last video call telling me she was in a deep controversy. I wondered if this was the "darkness" that had taken over the town.

Mrs. Wilkens stirred her tea, "Fannie contacted me a few years ago when they were planning a hundred-year celebration of the library. The library was built in the 1920s with money from the Carnegie Foundation. Fannie needed the history of the library, and her mother suggested I could help. This was before the ugliness with the book banners."

Goldie, my cat, emerged from the bedroom and stretched. It was time to feed her. I scooped the dry food into her dish. "On our last video meeting, she looked terrible. She also told me she was scared but didn't tell me why. Do you think things had gotten worse with the book banners?"

Mrs. Wilkens closed her eyes like she was trying to put it all together. "I don't know. She only said she'd overheard some things in the library and had looked into them. But she didn't sound like herself. Fannie—well, Fannie wasn't easily scared."

"That's mysterious."

Mrs. Wilkens's hand shook as she picked up her teacup. "It's more than that. Not only did they demand that the library get rid of a whole list of books, they threatened to have her fired."

Goldie delicately ate her food and then leapt onto Mrs. Wilkens's lap. Goldie and I have a détente kind of relationship. She hardly ever spends time on my lap.

As a schoolteacher, I had experienced the craziness of the book-banning movement. Because I had a copy of *To Kill a Mockingbird* in my classroom, a parent accused me of trying to "woke" my students. I had no idea what she was talking about, and it turned out, neither did she. She'd read something on the internet and decided books were dangerous for her children. That's what Fannie was helping me with for my class. What upset the parents so much that they were afraid of the books in the library? And how do you talk with them about it?

"Is that why she was scared?" At least the anti-woke parent didn't threaten me.

"I'm not sure, but the book banners got one of their people appointed to the library board. Fannie said it has been a living hell from then on."

"What about the threat?"

"Well, she emailed me a couple of weeks ago and said someone had taken out the book *The Hate U Give*. It was returned completely defaced with a note inside claiming they'd shoot her if she let kids see any of this trash. Then someone threw cow pies onto her doorstep. It's been harassment ever since." She stroked Goldie, who purred like no one had ever shown her affection.

"Do you know if she reported it?"

"Bah! The sheriff's wife is one of the instigators. I doubt Fannie said anything. She was desperately trying to hold on to her job because she was taking care of her mother. I'm sure she would have loved to wave goodbye to Ravens Valley if she could have." Mrs. Wilkens brushed crumbs off the table with a thoughtful expression. "Something else was going on, too."

"Besides the hysteria about the book banning?"

"I think so. In her last text to me, she wrote something odd." Mrs. Wilkens took out her phone and scrolled through it. "Here it is. She said, 'Scenes from *It's a Wonderful Life*' around here. More later, but I'm worried I've heard too much.'"

"Do you think she was talking about life in Ravens Valley?"

"I don't know. At first, I thought she was referring to the Christmas movie. You know the one with Jimmie Stewart and the evil rich man. But now I can't ask her." Her eyes moistened before she lifted Goldie up and set her on the floor. "Well, of course, first we need to go to her funeral. After that, we'll do some snooping."

I felt a tingle inside my head.

Help her.

Go away.

Charlee, my dead twin sister, was ordering me around—again. She tended to show up in times of crisis. My old therapist, Dr. Slack, suggested Charlee was the result of my brain disassociating when I became overly stressed. Basically, the voice of Charlee was a figment of my imagination. Figment or not, Charlee was here now.

Go! You're good at snooping.

Mrs. Wilkens stared at me, "Are you alright? You suddenly got that look like you are miles away."

"What look?"

"That look when sometimes you talk to yourself."

"Must be the tea and the excitement." I cleared the empty cups, wondering how much I talked out loud when Charlee showed up, "Even though I never met Fannie in person, I felt like she was a friend. I'll go with you."

See, that wasn't so hard.

I'm not sure this is a good idea. You know, Mrs. Wilkens can get bullheaded.

And you can't?

Stop showing up. Mrs. Wilkens might be on to us. Next thing you know, they'll be carting me away to a locked psych unit.

Nonsense.

Mrs. Wilkens headed for the door, "I have to get home and make arrangements. We'll stay overnight, of course."

Of course.

Charlee's voice stayed in my head after Mrs. Wilkens left.

"What have you gotten me into?"

Take Goldie with you. Otherwise, she'll miss you.

"What? Have you been reading those mysteries where the cat solves the case? I think Goldie can go to the cat sitter place."

Charlee poured on the heat. *Take her!*

Goldie stared at me. I stared back, "What? You want to go to a funeral? Not only a funeral, but one two hours away for someone you've never met?"

Apparently, Goldie wanted this because she rubbed herself against my leg with a loud purr. "When did you start conspiring with Charlee?"

By the evening, all the plans were set. Mrs. Wilkens had called the Ravens Valley funeral home and gotten the service information. We'd leave in two days, attend the funeral, stay overnight in a local motel, and come home the next day.

"I'd stay longer," she told me, "Except I have a 'guns to garden tools' meeting." Then she lowered her voice, "But we might have to go back depending on what we find out."

That evening, I sat alone in the living room with a glass of wine and wondered what I'd gotten myself into with Mrs. Wilkens. My summer school program had been shortened due to budget issues, and I'd missed the chance to go on an excursion to Ireland with a couple of teacher friends because of the class schedule. Instead, I'd opted to take an online college course to increase my post-Masters credits and increase my pay. To my surprise, I liked the class on difficult communication. Maybe by the time I was done, I could have a reasonable conversation with the parents who didn't like *To Kill a Mockingbird*.

Teaching was my life. I loved the rainbow of backgrounds my students brought with them and their curiosity and enthusiasm. I did not want some narrow-minded group to tell me what books my students could read.

"Okay," I said to Goldie, who was contentedly shedding hair next to me on the couch. "I don't miss some parts of teaching—like the few kids who come in the door hell-bent on making my life miserable, or all the staff meetings and the endless paperwork. And I don't miss it when Billy or Alisha throws up in the classroom."

After I finished my wine, I googled Fannie Porter and found her obituary. There was little of note. Other than the time she spent in college, it appeared she'd lived in Ravens Valley all her life. She'd been the librarian for the last ten years. Prior to that, she'd worked a variety of jobs within the public school system. She was survived by her mother, Dora, and her good friend Alex. No other relatives were mentioned.

When I saw the name Alex as a friend, I wondered if he or she was human or a cat. People often mentioned their pets in obituaries.

I rubbed my forehead. "Did Charlee expect Goldie to make friends with Fannie's pet and find out through the dog or cat what really happened to her?"

Goldie had no opinion as she made her way back to the bedroom.

I checked social media but found no Fannie Porters on Facebook, X, or Instagram. She was in the middling age—too old for TikTok and too young for Facebook. Either that or she'd taken down her pages because of harassment.

Yawning, I did one last search, Googling Ravens Valley. I doubted I would find much except an official website listing all the reasons to live in the community. Sure enough, the page came up with vivid color photos of a scenic river and a classic downtown, complete with a town square. How many small towns in Minnesota had a town square?

I clicked around and was told about the beauty of the area, the recreational activities, and the top schools. The site boasted the state's largest organic poultry farm and processing plant and the annual Chicken Wing Festival sponsored by the Santos Brothers Farms. Nothing on the site referred to a group of enraged citizens trying to ban books in the library.

Closing the laptop, I wondered what we would find in Ravens Valley and what the darkness was that Mrs. Wilkens talked about, and what had frightened Fannie.

Chapter Two: Ravens Valley

Goldie was not happy about being put in her carrier. She hissed when I closed the door.

"Listen, cat, the alternative is the Kitty Minders, and I hear they make you clean your own litter box and only give you cheap cat food." Goldie wasn't appeased.

Due to an atmospheric inversion that held the sticky August air hostage, Minneapolis smelled like old-fashioned smog. My weather app told me that the air quality was poor and I should stay inside. I cursed the climate change deniers and hoped, by going south and west, we'd drive out of the thick air.

Mrs. Wilkens met me in the parking lot, pulling a large orange roller suitcase. "I'm ready."

I pointed to it, "Did you fit the kitchen sink inside? I thought this was going to be a quick overnight."

"You can never be too prepared."

I hefted it into the trunk, convinced she really had put the kitchen sink inside. I'd packed a pair of jeans, a pair of shorts, and a University of Minnesota Gophers sweatshirt in case it cooled down at night. Today I wore black slacks and a plain white blouse suitable for a funeral.

It was early enough during the day that most of the traffic was coming into Minneapolis. We made good time taking Highway 169 southwest. Mrs. Wilkens had an app on her phone that she followed, letting me know where traffic was backed up. On the floor of the backseat, Goldie remained silent, probably thinking up ways to make me miserable once we arrived.

It didn't take long to be out of the suburbs and into the rolling landscape.

Rounded bales of hay dotted the fields, and cattle grazed, huddling together under trees for the early morning shade. A two-year drought had left some of the land fallow after the farmers plowed under the stressed crops. Other fields looked green and healthy from the irrigation systems.

"Weird," I commented when we drove by another field of soybeans looking green and healthy. "This is the land of 10,000 lakes, and yet the farmers have to water. Who knew?"

We passed a grove of mature oaks and a herd of cows taking in the shade. "It's beautiful, don't you think?"

Mrs. Wilkens glanced out the window. "So short-lived. With climate change next thing you know, this will be a desert."

"Well, that's a day brightener."

Mrs. Wilkens rifled through a folder on her lap, ignoring the beauty of the countryside. "They're evil. Harassing that poor girl like they did. It's happening all over the United States—librarians under siege from stupid people."

"I heard some of the librarians in the Southern states are sleeping with guns under their pillows."

I slowed as we approached a small town. A crudely painted sign by the side of the road read, "Proud of Our Guns, God and Country."

Mrs. Wilkens shook her head. "Whatever happened to peace, love, and 1,000 points of light?"

We made our way through the town. It looked bedraggled with unpainted empty storefronts. A few cars were angle-parked in front of a restaurant, but otherwise the street was quiet.

Once out of town, I asked Mrs. Wilkens for more information about Ravens Valley.

"Did you grow up there? I read the obituary for Fannie, and it looked like she was a lifelong resident. What was her family like?"

"We moved around when I was young. My father was a linotype operator. Back then, every county had its own newspaper, and some of the small towns had two. We moved to Ravens Valley when I was in high school. That made me an 'outsider' even though I married a local boy. Mr. Wilkens's family farmed for several generations in the area, and we thought it was a good place to raise our son." Her voice drifted off.

I knew her son Peter had gone into the army after high school and struggled when he came back. He'd died in his late thirties after a rough life. She didn't talk about him much.

"Back when I lived in small towns like Ravens Valley, most of the farms were owned by families. Usually eighty to one-hundred sixty acres. Now you can't survive unless you have at least a thousand acres. The small family farm is a myth." She stared out the window. "It's all corporate farming. Towns like Ravens Valley are barely hanging on."

I pictured the website with its glossy photos. "At least on the internet, the town looks prosperous."

"Hah! It's run by the Santos Brothers. They are the definition of corporate farming."

"You mean the organic people?"

"You'll see." Mrs. Wilkens nodded with emphasis.

We reached Ravens Valley with just enough time to check in at the Ravens Nest Inn, the little motel on the highway. When we walked in the motel clerk was leaning on the counter, talking with a man wearing a clerical collar. They both stared at us like the aliens had invaded. A young teenaged boy with red hair sat in a plastic chair working his phone.

Mrs. Wilkens walked up to the counter and introduced herself. "We're here for the Fannie Porter funeral. Did you know her?"

The minister backed away from the counter, studying the two of us. He was pale-skinned and freckled in a not-good-looking kind of way. "You from out of town?"

I didn't like his tone, so I did what I would do with hostile parents. I stepped over to him and held out my hand. "Liza Johnson. I'm a schoolteacher. Nice to meet you, Reverend."

For a moment, he peered at my hand before taking it limply in his. "Reverend Vogel from the church on the hill."

I fought the urge to pull my hand away and wipe it on my pants. Vogel was one of the names Fannie had mentioned as part of the "Protect Our

Children."

I looked at the teenager with the phone. "That must be your son. You look so much alike."

"Jasper, say 'hello.'"

Jasper didn't look up as he mumbled something like "Lo."

As I filled out the reservation card, Mrs. Wilkens tried to engage the clerk and the minister in a conversation about Fannie. "Such a shame. I heard it was a hit-and-run. Did they catch the person?"

The clerk shook his head. "Probably one of those workers from Pottersville. Driving old wrecks of cars and acting high and mighty."

"Pottersville?"

Before he could answer, a boy about the same age as Jasper limped in from the back. He had dark, Hispanic features and scarring along the side of his neck. "Big Mike, I have cleaned 12 and 14. I can go now?" He spoke with a thick accent.

The clerk nodded. "Good work."

I took out my credit card to pay. "I have a cat with me. I hope that's not a problem."

"Cost you ten dollars extra a night."

Reverend Vogel and Jasper left while I was signing the credit card slip.

As we were leaving for our room, the door opened, and a man of medium height and a paunch wearing bib overalls walked in. He looked to be in his early sixties with white, flyaway hair and bushy eyebrows. Mrs. Wilkens turned and peered at him. "Lorrie Schott?"

The man squinted at her for a moment before walking up to her with open arms. "Mrs. Wilkens? Peter's mom?"

Big Mike, the clerk, and I watched in fascination as he bear-hugged my neighbor, lifting her off the ground. She patted him and said firmly, "Nice to see you. Now put me down!"

He set her down and stepped back with a wide grin. "Well, I'll be. Henry said you'd come."

"Henry?"

He nodded with enthusiasm. "My cat."

Big Mike interrupted the reunion. "Remember, you're here to fix the window in unit six."

"Always happy to be of service."

He beamed at Mrs. Wilkens. "So nice to see you. I'll tell Henry you're here. Came for the funeral, I bet. I don't think many people will go. Henry said some people are afraid to be seen at the funeral. Fannie was real nice to me."

As soon as he was gone, Big Mike apologized. "Lorrie isn't right in the head. I give him little jobs—you know, to help him out. He's a good handyman when he isn't drinking."

I noticed how Mrs. Wilkens's shoulders sagged as she watched him leave. "He was a friend of my son. They went into the army together, and both came out," she paused searching for the word, "damaged."

We brought our luggage into the motel room. The room was shabby enough that the ten-dollars-a-night pet surcharge seemed excessive. When I opened the cat carrier, Goldie refused to come out. Maybe she was offended that we'd locked her up for several hours only to bring her to a room that was a few steps above the Bates Motel. I closed the carrier door. "You'll have to stay inside until we get back."

Mrs. Wilkens spent time in the bathroom. I wasn't sure over the rattle of the bathroom fan, but I thought I heard her weeping. Perhaps coming back to this town with memories of her son wasn't necessarily a good idea.

When she emerged, however, she looked fine. Not only fine, but she had a glint in her eyes. "I don't like the feel of this town already. Let's get to that funeral."

Chapter Three: The Funeral

Mrs. Wilkens directed me into the downtown area. True to the city website, Ravens Valley had a town square. In the middle of the square was a 19th-century brick courthouse. I slowed to get a better view of it.

"That's classic and in amazingly good shape." It was two stories high with a cupola on one side and a tower with a domed top in the middle. The grounds around it were manicured with flower beds in bright colors. The grass was a deep green and lush.

Mrs. Wilkens peered at the square. "It was falling down when I lived here. More an eyesore than anything else. They were talking about bulldozing it. I had a friend who worked in the Clerk of Court's office. Freezing in the winter and suffocating in the summer."

A sign on the lawn read, "Ruston County Santos History Center."

A banner across the street in front of the old courthouse announced the Tenth Annual Chicken Wing Festival. I noted the festival started the day after tomorrow and wasn't sorry we'd be home by then.

Behind us, a car honked. I sped up as Mrs. Wilkens pointed beyond the square to a little white church. "That's where the funeral is."

A silver hearse was parked directly in front of the entrance to the church. Cars lined the street. I parked a half-block away in front of a neat little playground. The colorful equipment appeared to be new, nestled on top of a bed of fresh woodchips. A crafted wooden sign by the sidewalk into the playground read, "Santos Memorial Park and Playground."

"Well, I guess the Santos brothers have made their mark in town."

The smog-like haze had dissipated, replaced by bright sunshine and blue skies. I took a deep breath of the clear air and the fresh smell of the woodchips. At that moment, Ravens Valley didn't strike me as a dark or foreboding place.

Mrs. Wilkens looked at her watch and tapped it. "We'll be late. Things start on time here." She hurried ahead of me, her white purse swinging in the crook of her elbow.

The church door was open, and sorrowful organ music wafted outside as we approached. I straightened up to my full height of five-foot-eight and girded myself for the service. Funerals were not my favorite form of entertainment.

The small church was about three-quarters full. Mourners were scattered among the rows of pews. The minister, a woman with short curly hair, sat behind the lectern as people filed in. Another minister, an older man with silver hair and a clerical collar, turned to look at us from the front pew. It appeared he was a mourner rather than an officiant.

We sat three rows from the back and were perusing the funeral program when a flurry of activity happened behind us. A short woman about my age with long blonde hair pulled back into a careless bun hurried in. She tapped on a phone as she swept by.

Mrs. Wilkens stared at the woman with a frown. "I feel like I know her," she whispered.

The minister stood as soon as the blonde woman had settled in. She read in a clear alto voice. "Neither death, nor life, nor angels, nor principalities, nor things present, nor things to come, nor powers, nor height, nor depth, nor anything else in all creation, will be able to separate us from the love of God in Christ Jesus our Lord."

I wondered how many of the citizens of Ravens Valley believed these words. It sounded like Fannie had been hounded and harassed and possibly murdered. Had she been separated from the love of God?

While I mused, I tuned out the words and tried to get a sense of the crowd. From the back, I saw a lot of gray and white hair. It was clearly an older group of people mourning the loss of the librarian. Perhaps these were friends of Fannie's mother.

Two teenagers huddled at the end of the pew where we sat. One had been crying, and her thick mascara ran down her cheeks. The other held a piece of paper and was studying it. Her lips moved in silence.

At last, the minister read the eulogy. It was standard noting when Fannie was born, where and who her parents were. Little was said about her life beyond her service as a public employee. The minister made no mention of the mysterious Alex but did acknowledge Fannie's mother. She sat in a wheelchair next to the front pew.

When the minister asked if anyone would like to share something about Fannie, the room took on a brittle silence. The only sound was the occasional cough until the girl in our pew stood up.

"I would like to say something." Her voice shook as she spoke.

Everyone turned to her. The paper she held rattled as she cleared her throat and read, "Miss Porter was a wonderful librarian. She introduced me to a whole world I didn't know existed. We were lucky to have her, and I—we will miss her." She lowered the paper, peering at the people in the church. "And many of you should be ashamed of the way you treated her." With that, she burst into tears and fled the church, followed by her friend.

The minister stood with her mouth open.

Go after her! She knows something and needs you.

This was not the time to argue with Charlee. Next to me, Mrs. Wilkens fanned her face as I picked up my bag and whispered, "I'm going to try to talk with the girls."

As I rushed out, the minister hastily announced the hymn number. The organist must have been as nonplussed by the girl as the minister because she hit the wrong cord. I hurried out the door to a great organ blat followed by murmurings from the crowd.

I found the two girls standing by the swing set in the little park. They were hugging each other. When I approached, they pulled apart and stared at me. I couldn't tell if the stare was one of defiance or fright. Holding up my hands in a surrendering gesture, I chose my words carefully.

"That was a nice tribute to Fannie. Thank you."

The one who had given the brief eulogy wrinkled her brow as she studied me. "Who are you?"

Who was I? A schoolteacher who liked Fannie and appreciated her help. And the friend of a snooping, suspicious little old lady. I decided that explanation wouldn't work. "I'm a relative." It wasn't a lie since I was a relative of somebody.

"Oh? Do you live around here?" The girl's voice carried a note of suspicion.

"No, I drove from the Cities. I've actually never visited here before." I pointed to the bench by the side of the playground. "Could we sit a while? I'd like to talk with you. You're the first person who has said anything nice about my…cousin."

The girls looked at each other, and the one who had spoken nodded. "Okay. But you'd better not be recording this."

Recording? I pulled the phone out of my bag and showed it to them. "I just want to talk."

Once the girls sat down, I introduced myself. "I'm Liza."

"Jules, and this is my friend Rochelle." In the sunlight, Jules's complexion was pale, almost ashen, against her dark hair and fading pink highlights.

Rochelle, in contrast, had a rosy complexion and long blonde hair falling to her shoulders. Neither of them had a conventional beauty, but both had a uniqueness about them that I appreciated.

I started the conversion, "I thought it was brave of you to speak up. I know my…cousin was having problems here because people wanted to ban books."

Both nodded. "Like bigtime." Jules pressed her lips together. "Poor Miss Porter. Those people—that stupid Protect Our Children group were awful to her."

"Yeah," Rochelle spoke up. She had a high squeaky voice, but I heard the anger behind it. "Like when they started having those monitors in the library looking at what people checked out. Poor Miss Porter tried to have them thrown out, but no one wanted to go up against them."

Jules pointed in the direction of the other side of the town square, where the land rose. From the park I saw a steeple. "They mostly come from the church on the hill. It used to be a nice church when Reverend Christianson had it. But *they* threw him out and got that awful Vogel and his weird son. Vogel uses the word 'woke' like he knows what it means. He said some of the books in the library were works of the devil."

I guessed they were the same books being banned in other parts of the country.

"He said those books could turn you gay. As if…" Jules' voice dropped away. "My mother says Pru Santos gave them a lot of money."

I raised my eyebrows. "You mean from the Santos Brothers Farms?"

"Like they run things around here, and Pru is head of the 'Protect' group."

I guided them back to the problems with the library. "You said people would come in and monitor what you checked out?" I was beginning to feel the darkness that Mrs. Wilkens talked about, even on this sunny day.

Jules watched a young woman enter the playground with a stroller. As she lifted the baby out to put him in the swing, Jules dropped her voice to a whisper. "Once I took out a book that was about a girl who thought maybe she was—you know—lesbian, and that night my mother got an anonymous phone call about it. Mom was so flustered, she told me to take it back."

"Wow," I shook my head. "That's bad."

They were silent long enough that I thought they might not tell me more. The baby on the swing started to wail. The mother put him back in the stroller and walked away. Once she was gone, Rochelle spoke. "Promise you won't tell anybody?"

That's a promise a person should never make. "I can't promise. But I'd like to know what happened to Fannie."

Rochelle regarded me for a moment, chewing her lower lip. "Okay. After that started happening, some of us kids got together and made a banned book club. Miss Porter snuck us books to read without checking them out of the library. She could have gotten into a lot of trouble."

Leave it to kids to figure out a way around the meddling Protect Our Children terrorists.

Jules's eyes flashed in anger when she spoke. "Then Josh Santos ratted us out."

"What happened?" I leaned closer to them.

"That's when things got really bad for Miss Porter. Someone slashed the tires on her car, and someone painted graffiti on her porch."

"She was so good. She even wanted to set up a mobile library for the kids in Pottersville."

This was the second time I'd heard that word. "What is Pottersville?"

"You know that trailer park for the workers at the chicken plant."

As a car drove by the driver, slowed to stare at us. Jules gave her the finger. "She's one of them! The old bat. I bet she's going to call my mom."

The woman drove away, looking straight ahead.

"Does everyone feel the same way as this Protect Our Children group?"

Both the girls stared at their laps. "People are afraid. Like my dad said, we couldn't afford to get our tires slashed—or worse—lose his job."

Suddenly, it sounded like Ravens Valley was in the middle of Russia.

"Miss Porter was the only one to stand up to them. And I don't think it was an accidental hit-and-run. Someone killed her." Jules tightened her hands into fists as she fought off the tears. "They knew she always jogged in the morning out on County Road 8. But nobody will do anything."

Rochelle put her arm around her friend. "We're both out of here as soon as we graduate."

Mrs. Wilkens approached with a determined set to her jaw.

Rochelle immediately pulled her arm away from Jules. "Ah, we have to go."

"It's okay. This is my friend Mrs. Wilkens. She used to live here and was the librarian for a while. She knew about the problems Fannie was having with the book banning people."

I introduced them and told her these two were part of a banned book group that Fannie had helped. She smiled in a grandmotherly way. "You are a credit to this sad little town—both of you."

Before they left, I held my hand up. "Wait, one more thing. Do you know what Fannie meant by, 'it's a wonderful life?'"

Jules frowned. "You mean like the movie?"

I shrugged, "I'm not sure."

"She never said anything like that to us, but I know she was worried in the last couple of weeks."

"Yeah, she said she always locked her car when she drove."

I gave them my phone number. "If you'd like to talk, or you think of anything, let me know."

We watched them as they headed down the sidewalk. Their shoulders bumped, and it looked like they hooked their pinky fingers together.

Mrs. Wilkens plopped down on the bench with a distressed expression. "I talked with a few people who stayed for coffee after the service. I knew a couple of them from my days here. They said things were not good despite how prosperous the town looks. A big change came when the Santos brothers built the processing plant for their chickens."

"They definitely have a presence here."

She put her hand on my thigh and squeezed. "There's more to the story. The woman who came in after us? The one with the phone? She's from the Santos family. Her name is Annalisa, and they say she's the one who does all the PR for the brothers."

"Do you think she knew Fannie?"

"Or maybe she was checking things out to see who attended the funeral. As we were chatting, she came around, and suddenly everyone got quiet." She took a deep breath, "We have to get to the bottom of this."

I didn't want to pour cold water on her, but I doubted we would be learning anything before we had to leave tomorrow.

Don't be too sure.

I refrained from replying to the imaginary voice in my head.

Chapter Four: Goldie's Disappearance

We ate a late lunch at Ike's Diner on the highway. Judging by the busyness of the parking lot, this was the place to go in Ravens Valley. We sat at a booth by the window where we could watch all the traffic rolling down the highway. Two delivery trucks from Santos Brothers Farms sped by while we waited for the server. A painting of a young girl holding a basket of eggs covered the side of the trucks. The advertisement said, "Santos Brothers All Natural Products: Fresh from Our Farm to Your Table."

Ike's menu had standard diner fare, including hamburgers and french fries, but Ike's specialty was broasted chicken.

I pointed to it. "What does 'broasted' mean?"

Mrs. Wilkens smiled. "Ike's has been making that for seventy years, I'll bet. They marinate the chicken in Ike's special seasoning, cook it in a pressure cooker to keep it moist, and then fry it. I used to love the taste of it. Probably took ten years off my life."

"Do you suppose they use Santos Farm's organic natural chickens for this?"

When the server came around, I asked her. She rubbed her arm and lowered her voice. "Don't tell anyone, but the new owner doesn't buy them Santos chickens. Says he doesn't like their taste and they're too expensive." She glanced at the door. "But if Heck or Vince Santos walk in the door, I always tell my customers Santos has the best chickens."

I ordered a chef salad, and Mrs. Wilkens ordered a cheeseburger.

I filled her in on what the girls told me about the monitoring of the library and the banned books group. She said one of the women at the funeral used to work as a library aide for her years ago.

"Imagine. Jessica was in high school when she was an aide, and now she's the assistant librarian. Time does fly."

"Did she have anything interesting to say?"

In the booth behind me, two people suddenly stopped talking. I wondered if they wanted to hear what she had to say.

Perhaps Mrs. Wilkens thought the same thing. Mrs. Wilkens gazed up at the ceiling for a moment. When she spoke, she raised her voice. "She said Fannie shouldn't have been running on that road so early in the morning with the sun just coming up. Poor driver probably didn't even see her."

Mrs. Wilkens was not a good liar. I saw the little twitch of her lips when she spoke.

"Very sad to lose such an asset to the community," I added, raising my voice, too.

The server set two coffees down on the table and hurried to another customer. I took a sip, expecting it to be weak and tasteless. Instead, it was better than the coffee at the shop down the street from my apartment. When the server came back, I asked her what kind of coffee they used.

"Just the normal stuff from a can, Hills Brothers, I think. Nothing special."

And I'd been paying twice the price for half the flavor.

For the rest of lunch, we confined our conversation to comments on the weather and otherwise ate in silence. When the couple seated behind me got up to leave, I recognized them as attending the funeral. They stood out because they were younger, maybe in their late thirties, and had an air of smugness about them.

One of them stopped at our table. "I saw you go after that Jules. She a friend of yours?"

I peered at her before I spoke in a honeyed voice, "Well, of course, that's none of your business. But I was surprised that no one at the funeral seemed willing to show her either kindness or compassion."

The woman opened her mouth as if to retort when her friend grabbed her by the elbow and ushered her out.

Mrs. Wilkens smiled at me. "I don't think you made a friend."

I looked out the window to see the two of them in the parking lot. One of them pointed at me and shook her head. Remembering the sign about guns and God in the other town, I hoped people around here weren't armed.

By the time we got back to the Ravens Nest Inn, the sky had darkened, threatening rain. Goldie had been crated for several hours. I hoped she would forgive me.

When I approached the door, it was slightly open. "Did we forget to close the door when we left?"

"I don't think so."

At least Goldie was in her carrier, so she couldn't get out. Except when I walked in, the carrier door was open. "Goldie?" I quickly looked through the room, including the bathroom. No cat.

Mrs. Wilkens peeked under the bed. "Well, that's a problem."

The room had a musty odor, like unwashed teen. I looked around. Our bags seemed to be intact. "Mrs. Wilkens, I think someone was in here and let Goldie out."

She put her hands on her hips. "Now, why would they do that?"

I pictured the women in the parking lot at Ike's. "Maybe I really did make some enemies. We'd better check with the office."

The office was deserted when we walked in. I rang the bell and the boy with the scarred neck came out holding a book.

"We think someone has been in our room. The door was open, and the cat was gone."

"What?"

"My cat got out."

He blinked. "No one has been in the room."

"Are you sure?"

He looked over his shoulder. "Big Mike is not here. I can ask when he comes back." The boy fingered nervously at his book. It was a middle-grade science fiction novel.

I pointed to it. "That's a good book."

"Miss Porter, she said so too."

"Oh, you knew Fannie?"

The boy's eyes widened as Big Mike strode in from outside. "Is there a problem, Paulie?" His voice had an accusing tone to it.

I jumped in. "My cat is missing. Do you know who was in our room?"

Slow down, sis. Remember, you get more with honey than with vinegar.

I'd get more done if you didn't show up all the time.

Big Mike stared at me. "You okay?"

"Sorry, zoned out for a minute. Do you know what happened to my cat?"

He shrugged. "I'm guessing your cat went for a stroll and will be back as soon as it gets hungry."

He had a smugness about him that made me want to punch him in his bulbous nose.

No punching!

This was getting us nowhere. Mrs. Wilkens touched my arm. "Maybe we should look around. Goldie couldn't have gotten far."

I walked to the back of the motel and called for the cat. Of course, she didn't come running. Behind the motel was a vacant lot filled with dying weeds, stray plastic bags, and a few old tires.

Mrs. Wilkens called me back. "I'm sure Goldie will be okay. Remember, she was once a street cat."

True, Goldie had been rescued from the streets of Minneapolis. In her wild youth, she'd managed to lose part of her ear. But nowadays, she seemed content to live in luxury and leave hairballs on my carpet.

"We have to go." Mrs. Wilkens's voice had an urgency to it. "I made arrangements to meet Jessica from the library."

"Where?"

"There's a little county park about five miles from here. If I recall right, it has a picnic shelter. I said we'd be there at 3:15. We'll be away from prying eyes and ears."

I stared at the weedy lot in hopes of seeing Goldie, but nothing moved except a bread bag swaying in the breeze.

Damn you, Charlee, I thought. Whatever possessed you to suggest bringing Goldie? Now I had to worry about a lost cat.

You shouldn't be hasty in your judgment.

Pah! You're making my life a nightmare.

Nightmare? Oh come on!

Go tell my cat to either come back or find a new home.

Have patience. I'm sure she has a role to play.

I took one last survey of the vacant lot. I couldn't imagine what kind of role Goldie had in this misadventure.

Mrs. Wilkens called back to me, "Come on, or we'll be late!"

"I hope you can find your way back," I muttered to my absent cat as Mrs. Wilkens tugged on my sleeve.

When we pulled out onto the highway, a Santos truck with its happy little girl and her basket of eggs whisked by. As I drove, I thought about somebody opening the door on Goldie's carrier and then leaving the door to our motel room open. Who would want to do that?

Chapter Five: Jessica, the Assistant Librarian

Mrs. Wilkens directed me to a gravel county road. "We used to picnic with Peter at this park. It has one of the only decent beaches on Grass Lake, so it was always busy in the summer. I hope no one is there today."

The air had a heaviness to it as the clouds grayed out the sun. I prayed it wouldn't rain on my cat. Dust and gravel made a thrumming rhythm beneath the car as we drove. Fields surrounded us until we approached a wooded area dappled with a variety of colors from the various trees. A few appeared to be stressed, bare-branched as if ready for the bleak winter. I almost missed the turn-off to the park because the green metal sign pointing to it was so riddled with bullet holes. I could barely make out "Grass Lake County Park."

"Rural vandals. In my day, the county kept this area clean because all the families used it."

We bumped down a rutted road toward the lake and parked in a small, deserted parking lot. Near the end of the lot stood a wooden building housing old-fashioned pit toilets. The door to the men's side hung askew as if someone had tried to rip it off its hinges. The door to the women's side was padlocked shut.

I was glad I'd used the bathroom at the motel before leaving. The men's room hardly looked or smelled attractive.

Mrs. Wilkens stood with her hands on her hips. "My, it has gone downhill."

Since Jessica, the person we were meeting, hadn't arrived, we walked down a path to the lake. The first thing I noticed before we got to the water was the odor. It had a rotting smell to it.

"You swam in this?" The water was thick with green algae and weeds. A dead fish floated atop the muck.

Mrs. Wilkens pressed her lips into a tense line. "I'd heard rumors about Grass Lake, but I find it hard to believe. They've spoiled it."

"Who?"

"The corporate farmers—they use a lot of fertilizer, and it runs off from their fields into the lake. That increases the growth of algae, and too much algae chokes off everything else in the lake. A lake is a delicate ecosystem; mess with it, and you'll get this."

"I wonder what the Santos Brothers think about this. If they are raising organic chickens and supposedly using organic feed..."

A voice from above interrupted us. "Ginny? Is that you?"

While I could never bring myself to call my neighbor anything but Mrs. Wilkens, others felt more comfortable using her first name. We both turned at once as a large woman wearing a purple Vikings t-shirt and black leggings stood at the head of the trail.

As we joined her, rain began to fall in gentle sprinkles. Mrs. Wilkens pointed to a clearing behind the toilets. A ramshackle picnic shelter with a mossy roof protected us from the rain. We sat at a wooden picnic table that hadn't been stained or painted in years.

Mrs. Wilkens introduced me. "This is my neighbor, Liza. Fannie was helping her with a school project."

Jessica nodded, "She told me about it. I hope you can figure out how to talk with people about banning books because we certainly haven't been successful."

"Nice to meet you. Librarians are some of my favorite people."

Jessica smiled. "Ginny and I go back a long way. I think I was a sophomore in high school when she took me on at the library."

"Well, I had to. You were such a pest."

"And you were a grump." Jessica's eyes sparkled.

It was clear the two enjoyed each other's company.

"The real reason I hung around the library all the time was that I had a crush on Peter. He was so cute." She stopped talking, and I noted how Mrs. Wilkens tensed up.

Around us, the sky darkened. Mrs. Wilkens saved Jessica from more embarrassment. With a half-smile, she said. "Peter was good around the girls. That's for sure. But he only had eyes for one. Got his heart crushed the summer after he graduated when Lily broke up with him."

Jessica wrinkled her brow. "I remember how you worried about him."

Mrs. Wilkens took a deep breath. "Lily was the reason he didn't go off to college that fall like he'd planned. He enlisted in the army, and things were never right with him after that." She looked away. The wind had picked up and brought a chill with it.

"I remember that she went to college somewhere out of state. Came back divorced with a little boy and taught school for a while. We were surprised when she moved back, but her mother was getting bad by then." Jessica absently tapped her fingers on the rough wood of the table. "She married Heck Santos."

"Of the Santos Brothers?" I shivered as raindrops splatted on the roof of the shelter.

She gazed beyond me. "There was some story about that first marriage, but I don't remember it. They have two kids—or I should say—adults. Alex is her son from her first marriage; he's the local veterinarian, and his half-sister Annalisa works for the Santos Brothers."

I wondered if this was the Alex from the obituary. I was about to ask when Mrs. Wilkens leaned toward Jessica with a serious set to her mouth.

"I'd love to hear more, some other time. As I said at the funeral, I have questions about Fannie's death. And clearly, you aren't comfortable talking about it where someone can hear you."

Jessica stopped drumming her fingers and sat up straighter. "Ravens Valley used to be a safe place. You know, comfortable and all, but something has happened in the past couple of years, and things have gotten nasty."

"You mean like the way Fannie was harassed?" I asked.

"And other things. People are afraid they might lose their jobs if they say anything negative about the town or the Santos Brothers." She paused as if looking for the right words. "It's like in the old days when the coal companies owned the stores. The Santos have their fingers in so many of the businesses now."

Mrs. Wilkens scowled. "Sounds like it's time for the union to step in."

Jessica pressed her lips into a grim line. "People watch Fox News here. That tells you a lot. Union is a bad word. They're anti-abortion, anti-immigration, anti-gay. It wasn't always like that. If it had been, maybe I would have gone elsewhere. I know the kids can't wait to get out of here."

As the rain continued to tap on the roof of the shelter, I prompted Jessica about Fannie. "I get the sense Fannie wasn't very popular."

When she spoke, it was in a low tone as if the shelter was bugged. "She wasn't an easy person to work with or to like, I'm afraid. Prickly is the word I'd use. And a stickler for detail. I'd worked at the library for years, and when she came in, she upended everything."

A gust of wind swept through the shelter. I wished I'd worn my sweatshirt as the air cooled with the rain.

Jessica didn't notice the drop in temperature, "I almost quit, except jobs are hard to come by here unless you want to pluck chickens." She said it with no hint of amusement.

"You stuck with it," Mrs. Wilkens nodded at her.

"Yes, and I'm glad I did. She brought the library out of the stone ages," She blushed looking at Mrs. Wilkens, "I mean, you did your best."

Mrs. Wilkens chuckled. "No need to apologize. When I left, computers were those giant machines hidden inside big businesses. I worked with the card catalogue and an electric typewriter. I'd stepped on enough toes with my campaign to get a decent family planning clinic that the county commissioners weren't about to fund any innovations. I barely got enough funds to buy a few books every year."

Jessica nodded.

The rising wind blew rain into the shelter, wetting the concrete floor but missing us. At this rate, we wouldn't be able to stay here long. I hurried the discussion along. "Do you think Fannie's death was anything besides an accident? I understand she'd upset a lot of people and was under attack by a group of book banners."

Jessica rubbed her cheeks before she spoke. "I heard rumors. It's amazing what people whisper in the library stacks. As if we employees don't have ears."

Mrs. Wilkens nodded. "You are so right. I tried not to listen, but sometimes…"

I interrupted as more rain came down. "What did you hear?"

"It was just whispering, but two weeks ago, as I was shelving books, one of the volunteer monitors—we staff call them the KGB—was talking to someone in the young adult section. That's where they like to hang out. She said, 'I heard Fannie knows something they don't like. She could end up in big trouble.'"

"Do you know who 'they' are? Or anything about what Fannie was onto?"

Through the pelting sound of the rain on the roof of the shelter, I thought I heard the rumble of a car. Jessica glanced over her shoulder. "If someone finds me here, I might be in trouble. I should probably leave."

Mrs. Wilkens held up her hand. "Wait. I know you're scared of something. Who is in charge of these volunteers? Who would they talk to?"

"That's the thing. It's Pru Santos—Vince Santos's wife. And she's on the library board. You don't want to get in trouble with her. She's a bitch and worse."

She stood up to leave. The sound of the car grew louder. "I really should go."

"Do you think you're in danger?"

Jessica didn't answer, but the frown on her face said everything.

Mrs. Wilkens said in a quiet voice, "Take care. Something is very wrong here."

I guess Charlee was right to send me on this mission. I had no intention of telling her, however.

I know I'm right. Now go back to the motel and find your cat.

Mrs. Wilkens and I made a dash for the car. The rain came pouring down in sheets, and by the time I slid behind the wheel, water dripped down my face. Mrs. Wilkens sat with a grim expression.

"We have to get to the bottom of this," she growled.

At that moment, I didn't care about anything but finding my cat and warming up. Inside my head, I swore at Charlee, who didn't bother to answer. As we drove away, we were met by a black SUV heading to the park. The windows were tinted, and the rain was coming hard enough that I couldn't see who was inside as the car passed by.

"Quick, look back and see if you can read the license plate."

Mrs. Wilkens turned her head and squinted. "Sorry, I can't see it."

On the deserted gravel road back to town, I felt vulnerable in my little Toyota Corolla. Was the SUV sent to spy on us, or was my imagination running away with me? Just when I decided I'd watched too many crime shows on television, I saw through the rain that headlights were closely following my car.

Chapter Six: Trey the Stupid

Behind me, I heard a "whoop" sound like the beginning of a siren. In the rearview mirror, I saw the red flashing lights.

Mrs. Wilkens twisted to look. "Oh, my. It's the fuzz."

"Fuzz? Really?" I didn't have a good feeling about this.

Mrs. Wilkens did not reply.

I pulled over as far as I thought I could without going into the ditch. After reading about traffic stops that ended with the driver being shot by the police, I sat still with my hands on the steering wheel. The police car stopped behind me and sat while the heavens opened, and the rain poured.

"What are they waiting for?" My hands started to sweat, and the windows steamed up.

"This is ridiculous. I'm going to find out." Mrs. Wilkens reached over to take off her seat belt. "Who do they think they are?"

I grabbed her arm. "Wait." My brain filled with doubts. What if this was someone impersonating a policeman and was out to rob and murder? Here we were on a deserted gravel road, not close to anything. My fingers tensed as we waited for something to happen.

Meanwhile, Mrs. Wilkens repeated, "This is ridiculous." She glanced back at the patrol car. "You weren't speeding, were you?"

"How would I know? Have you seen a speed limit sign anywhere?"

She dug in her bag and took out her cell phone. "If he doesn't hurry up, I'm calling 911."

I squinted at the rearview mirror, hoping to see if the car had one of the special license plates used by law enforcement vehicles. I couldn't read it.

However, the flashing cherry top was reassuring that the car was official.

Within a minute or two, the rain let up enough for the officer to finally step out of his cruiser and approach my side of the car. I could hardly see him; the window was so steamed by the time he tapped. I rolled it down, appreciating the fresh air that wafted in.

He studied us for a moment before Mrs. Wilkens spoke up. "Young man, what are you doing out in the rain like this?"

The officer wore a hooded rain jacket. The hood emphasized his large face with small eyes. It gave him a piggish look. Water dripped off the jacket and beaded down his chest.

"License, please." He commanded in a terse voice.

I reached in my bag and pulled out my license. He studied it, his lips moving. "You're a long way from home."

My shoulders tensed. "Could you tell us why you stopped us?"

He wrinkled his brow as if he was thinking up the answer. "Uh…Report of a stolen car. Kids take them and like to party at the park."

Bullshit, I thought. Partying in the middle of a weekday afternoon in the rain. Hardly. I clenched my teeth. "I assure you, as beat up as this car is, it's mine, and it's paid for."

The officer apparently didn't notice the squeak in my voice. He simply grunted as he stared at the license.

Mrs. Wilkens opened her mouth to speak. I shook my head at her. I'd read enough pulp thrillers to know about bent cops in rural areas. I didn't want to find myself face down in Green Lake. Goldie and Charlee would never forgive me.

In as polite a voice as I could muster, I asked, "Would you like to see the car registration?"

"Could you open the trunk, please?"

Mrs. Wilkens could not hold herself back. "I know the law. We don't have to show you anything."

Again, I touched her arm. "It's okay. I'll open it for you." I reached down and pulled the latch on the trunk. When he moved to the back, I got out of the car and followed him. The rain had stopped, and I expected a fresh smell. Instead, the air was filled with an aroma that reminded me of a wet dog. In fact, a very old wet dog.

The trunk was empty except for a few reusable grocery bags. The officer appeared to be disappointed.

"Can you tell me what you're looking for? Maybe I can help."

The passenger side door slammed, and Mrs. Wilkens strode back to us. "What is this? Some kind of shakedown?"

I stared at her. Where was she getting these words?

The officer looked at her with a puzzled expression. "Ma'am, I'm looking for contraband."

I watched the color rise on Mrs. Wilkens's cheeks. Time to intervene. With my best teacher-meeting-parents voice, I extended my hand. "I'm Liza Johnson. Nice to meet you…ah…what did you say your name was?" If he had a name tag, it was hidden under his rain jacket.

"Ah, I'm Deputy Trey of the Ruston Sheriff's Department."

Trey the Stupid came to mind, but I held my tongue.

Ask him what he's really looking for. Be nice, though.

I'm always nice.

In the sweetest voice I could muster, I used his name. "Deputy Trey, can you tell us what you are looking for? We were just at the county park. Maybe we saw something that could help you?"

Mrs. Wilkens glared at me.

"Ah…well…we've had some problems with those tree-hugger types from the Cities. They're after the farmers around here. Trespassing on private land and all that. The farmers are getting tired of it."

It took me a minute to understand what he was trying to say. "Oh, I get it. People from the Cities trying to get water samples and stuff."

"Yeah, like that. Anyway, they're a nuisance. I was just checking to make sure you weren't one of them."

I thought Mrs. Wilkens might have a stroke. Her eyes widened. "Young man, I thought you were checking to see if we were driving a stolen car. Maybe you should get your story straight."

It had been going so nicely until now. Trey blinked his little piggy eyes.

"What did you say?"

Mrs. Wilkens could hold her own in an argument, but this wasn't the time. Especially arguing with an armed man with a badge. I needed to get back to the motel to find Goldie. I didn't want to spend the next 24 hours in the Ruston County jail.

I jumped in as quickly as I could, "Please. Mrs. Wilkens here was just showing me around. We came for a funeral, and I said it was a pretty area, so she said I should see the lake." I smiled in the most insincere way. "She told me it had changed from when she lived here a hundred years ago or whenever."

Mrs. Wilkens glared at me but stayed silent.

Trey shifted his weight from one foot to another like he wasn't sure how to handle us. Finally, he clicked his tongue and said, "I guess you can go. Looks like the car belongs to you."

After we got back on the road and headed to town, I took a deep breath. "I can't believe that just happened. Did I dream it?"

"You told him I lived here a hundred years ago?"

"I'm not sure he caught that. Trey didn't strike me as an A student."

"Humph. Ravens Valley has turned into Russia, complete with police and the KGB."

I noted Mrs. Wilkens "humphed" a lot on this trip.

It started to rain again when we crossed into the city limits. I took it as an omen that as soon as we found Goldie, we needed to get back to the noisy, polluted city and away from Trey the Stupid, the monitors, and the book banners.

Chapter Seven: The Lily

By the time we reached the motel, the wet pavement glittered as the sun broke out from behind the clouds. The air had chilled with the rainstorm, and as I walked to the room, I shivered. I wondered if Goldie had gotten cold and wet on her adventure. I half expected her to be waiting at the door with a sour expression.

A stargazer lily in a plastic vase and an envelope were propped by the door. Mrs. Wilkens and I stared at it.

The lily had a sweet fragrance as if it had been newly cut. The envelope didn't have a name on it and was the size of a standard greeting card. "Who would know we were here?"

"Only about half the town." Mrs. Wilkens nudged me in the door. "Let's see what the card says." She glanced around, "In private."

I set the vase on the bedside table and slipped open the envelope. It was a sympathy card, "May You Find Peace and Comfort" on the front with a drawing of a bird holding a flower. Inside, carefully hand-printed in blue ink were the words, "I'm sorry this is too little, too late." Next to the writing was a hand-sketched bouquet of lilies.

"Curious." I examined the back of the card. It came from a charitable organization concerned about the environment and was printed on recycled paper. I had gotten these same cards after making a donation last year.

Mrs. Wilkens took it from me and studied it. When she handed the card back, it was with a thoughtful expression. "Maybe someone heard we were here for the funeral and wanted to express condolences."

"But why would they send it to us? As far as Ravens Valley knows, we were only acquaintances."

As I took the card and put it back in the envelope, I remembered telling the girls from the funeral that Fannie was my cousin. "Maybe it's from Jules and Rochelle." Except I doubted the two teenagers would be sending me flowers.

Mrs. Wilkens sat quietly, her hands clasped as in prayer. "Curious."

I agreed about the curious part, but was more concerned about Goldie. "We need to find my cat before she decides to hitch a ride with a van full of frozen free-range organic chickens."

"Let's see if Big Mike knows anything. Maybe he's seen Goldie."

I followed her to the office. No one was at the desk. Mrs. Wilkens tapped the bell three times before Paulie appeared. He pulled off a pair of yellow vinyl gloves that smelled like bleach.

"Yes?"

Mrs. Wilkens held the envelope up. "Do you know who left this at our door?"

"Sorry. I don't know."

I thought he answered the question too quickly. "Are you sure? Maybe you saw someone in the parking lot?"

He flinched as he glanced behind him. "I don't know anything."

Mrs. Wilkens pointed to a camera mounted on the wall behind the desk. "Don't you have security cameras? Maybe we can look at them. You see, the card wasn't signed, and I'd like to thank whoever left it."

"Uh…the camera isn't real. Big Mike put it in, thinking a thief would see it and leave."

"Do you have problems with being robbed?" It hadn't occurred to me that the motel might be vulnerable to thieves. Yet it stood on the highway with little business around it. I felt sympathy for Paulie, who couldn't have been older than fourteen, manning the reception desk alone.

He shrugged. "Once someone tried. But we don't have much cash. Mostly, it's all credit cards now. And the police watch out for us."

Something in the way he said "watch out for us" struck me as odd. "Do the police patrol here a lot?" I thought about Trey the Stupid and wondered if they kept an eye on the motel to discourage the environmentalists.

"Uh, we have no crime here in Ravens Valley." He shuffled his feet and gazed at the floor.

I didn't believe him, but I wasn't there to argue with the poor kid. "I'm still looking for my cat. Has anyone seen her?"

"No, I haven't seen a cat. I can ask Lorrie to look out for it. He's good with animals."

On the way back to our room, I surveyed the parking lot. Other than my car, the only other guest drove a beat-up SUV with California license plates. "I wonder how they can stay in business?"

Mrs. Wilkens did not answer as she gripped the envelope. "Something about this card," she muttered. "Maybe it's a warning."

While Mrs. Wilkens returned to the room, I walked around the outside of the motel calling softly, "Come on, Goldie. You know I have the best canned liver money can buy. Show your raggedy ears and come back."

If I thought this would lure my cat from wherever she'd gone, I was wrong. I saw no evidence of her in the weedy lot. I even checked the dumpster. Perhaps she'd jumped in and couldn't get out. It was filled with black plastic bags and the odor of rotting food. No cat.

When I returned to the room, Mrs. Wilkens was staring at the card and pacing.

"The more I think of it, the more this feels like a warning." She tapped it against her head. "If only I could figure it out."

"It seems to have a lily theme. Do you know anyone who is into lilies from around here?"

Mrs. Wilkens shook her head. "I've lost contact with almost everyone."

"Your son's girlfriend was named Lily. Could it be from her?"

She stared out the window but said nothing.

Chapter Eight: Lorrie and the Cat

I went to the Subway Sandwich shop and picked up take-out supper. Neither of us had the energy to sit in a restaurant. I was filled with angst about Goldie and angst about Fannie and even more angst about what we had gotten ourselves into.

We sat in our dingy motel room with the aroma of Subway Sandwich pickles and onions and talked about what we'd learned today.

"There's more to this than meets the eye," Mrs. Wilkens pulled at a bit of the sandwich bread. "Fannie had discovered something. I'm sure of it."

"One thing we do know, judging by the sparse attendance at the funeral and what Jessica said, people around here are afraid." I finished the sandwich. "But before we solve the problems of Ravens Valley, I need to make one more round to see if Goldie has found her way back."

The air was filled with the smell of fallen leaves from the line of trees behind the motel. Several more cars had joined the SUV from California in the parking lot. It looked like Ravens Nest Inn was filling up. Darkness covered the back of the motel, and I felt an eerie sensation as I called for Goldie that someone was watching me. A car with a broken muffler roared down the highway, leaving the acrid odor of exhaust. I longed for my garden-level apartment and my online class with its twenty-page final paper.

Perhaps it was the loneliness of the evening twilight, but I found myself reflecting on my sad love life and my almost love affair with a middle-aged neurology nurse practitioner. He was everything a person could want—kind, funny, smart, and caring. Goldie even liked him much better than she liked me. Unfortunately, he was also divorced with a child and a demanding ex. We hadn't talked in a month since he told me his ex was moving to Sioux Falls, South Dakota, and he was considering moving there to be with his daughter. I realized the competition for his attention was more than I wanted to deal with. We'd ended without really agreeing to either break up or try a long-distance relationship.

In love relationships, I was in limbo again.

Unfinished business, eh?

"Just like you're unfinished business," I spoke aloud as I rounded the corner of the motel.

Tut. You have enough to keep you busy here.

"No kidding. You've caused me to lose my cat. Now what!" My voice rose in irritation.

A couple leaving the corner room of the motel glanced at me. There was a time in our lives when people talking out loud to themselves was an unusual sight reserved for those who were hallucinating. Now with smartphones, everyone chattered to the air.

I held up my phone and waved at them.

Pay attention to the cat. She'll take you places.

"Oh, stop talking in riddles! Perhaps you could help me find her." I hissed. "And maybe find who let her out." The thought that someone had been in our motel room and deliberately let Goldie out sent a shiver down my spine. This was not a friendly town.

The voice disappeared, and I felt a little sad that she'd gone.

"Damn evil twin!" I muttered before letting myself back into the room.

Mrs. Wilkens sat on her bed watching a cooking show. I would never admit it to either my elderly neighbor or my school colleagues, but I loved cooking shows. No, I didn't love to cook, but I appreciated the creativity and artistry. Really, how could someone make macaroni and cheese into a five-star meal?

"Any luck?"

I shook my head. "The good news is that Goldie was once a street cat. Hopefully, she knows her way around cars." Damned cat. We didn't like each other, and yet I missed her already.

I sat on the bed with Mrs. Wilkens and stared at the television. In the middle of the taste test, someone pounded on the door. I found myself being irritated that I would be interrupted when we were about to find out whether the creamy or the crispy mac and cheese would win.

When I opened the door, Lorrie stood holding a threadbare towel with something wrapped in it.

"Found your cat, I think."

I stared at the towel, afraid to ask if it held a living creature.

Mrs. Wilkens saved me. "Come in. Is she hurt?"

He carefully set the towel down on the bed and unwrapped it. Goldie lay limp on her side, eyes open, breathing heavily. "Henry thinks she might have been poisoned."

"Poisoned?" My knees felt weak.

"Someone around here has been after cats. That's why Henry stays in the house."

I gently touched her fur. She moved a little and made a mewling sound. I was flooded with remorse for all the times I'd threatened to send her to Cat Haven for adoption. "We have to get her to a vet. Is there one here?"

"Dr. Alex. He's good. You hold your kitty, and I will take you."

Lorrie led us out to his car. It was parked under a streetlight and looked like it had been assembled from parts found in a junkyard. I didn't care as long as it could get me to the vet. I slid into the backseat, cradling Goldie and silently cursing Charlee for insisting I bring the cat.

Mrs. Wilkens sat next to Lorrie in the front. The junkyard car smelled surprisingly clean and fresh.

Lorrie talked with Mrs. Wilkens while I stroked Goldie.

"Where did you find her?"

"Paulie from the motel called me to ask if I'd seen a cat. He's a good kid, you know. I decided to look around, and she was lying by that abandoned shed over there." He pointed in the direction of the weed-infested vacant lot next to the motel. "Doesn't look like she got too far. Maybe was trying to get back to you."

Now I felt even worse.

Lorrie drove carefully through town, glancing frequently at the rearview mirror.

"Can we go a little faster?" Goldie shivered beneath my touch.

"Nope. The town cop is always sneaking around. People don't speed in this town."

Although it took less than ten minutes to get to the veterinary clinic, I felt like it had been hours. The muscles in my shoulders were so tense, the back of my head pounded with every beat of my heart.

The clinic was next to a dilapidated old Victorian-style house with a large porch. All the windows were dark and unwelcoming. Lorrie parked in front of a newer building that held the clinic.

"He sees his patients here."

As soon as he stopped the car, I slid out, cradling Goldie close to me to keep her warm. Her breathing continued to be labored, and a little drool mixed with blood stained the towel.

Mrs. Wilkens and Lorrie followed me as I raced to the door. Even though the lights were on, the door was locked. I jammed my finger into the doorbell below a sign announcing Dr. Alex Santos, DVM. I held it until Mrs. Wilkens gently pried it away. "If he's in, he will have heard the bell."

"Where is he?" I shifted my weight from one foot to the other, straining for the sound of footsteps. Somewhere in the woods behind the house and clinic, an owl hooted. I stiffened. Was this a bad omen?

We huddled in front of the door waiting. "We should call him." Holding Goldie against my chest, I reached into my pocket for my phone. Of course, it wasn't there because in my haste, I'd left everything back in the motel room.

"Someone call him!" My voice rose.

"Sorry, dead phone. That's why I came to the motel instead of taking her right to Dr. Alex. Henry said I should."

Mrs. Wilkens shrugged. "Left it in the motel room."

"Damn it!" I reached over and pushed the doorbell again. Just as I pulled my finger back, a van drove in, throwing us into the glare of its headlights.

A man wearing a long-sleeved denim shirt and jeans slipped out and hurried to us. "Trouble?"

"My cat Goldie, I think she's been poisoned." I told him about how she'd gone missing, and Lorrie had found her near the motel.

He unlocked the door and beckoned us in. "How about if you give Goldie to me and wait here?" He had a deep and reassuring voice that didn't match his thin, marathon runner's body.

I reluctantly put her in his hands. He talked to Goldie in a gentle voice. "Not having a good day, are you? Let's see what we can find out."

As he took her to his surgery, he motioned to the seats in the little waiting area. "I'll be out as soon as I know something."

The next half-hour ticked by in slow motion. My throat was dry and tight as I thought back about my life with Goldie. I hadn't wanted her, and she hadn't wanted me after her true mistress died. I agreed to take her for two days until a decent home could be found. That was over two years ago. Now we lived like an old married couple who had grown used to each other and had called a truce from all the hostilities. In truth, I couldn't imagine coming home from teaching and not having her accuse me of not feeding her enough.

Mrs. Wilkens and Lorrie spoke in low voices. I ignored them as I paced back and forth. She finally glared at me. "Why don't you go outside and get some fresh air?"

She was right. I needed fresh air. Outside, I was immediately hit by a chill ripple of wind. The owl had stopped hooting, and a darkness so different than nighttime in the city enveloped me. I resolved that as soon as Dr. Alex performed a miracle, I would take Goldie and go back home. The Ravens Valley intrigue or horror, or whatever you wanted to call it, could stay here. I was done.

Hey sis, you'll get through this. You still have work to do here.

"It's not my problem. Whatever happened to Fannie and whatever is happening here in this godawful town is someone else's problem." My voice was tight as the leaves fluttered in an evening breeze.

You need to fight for the library and those girls. They deserve better.

"What are you? My conscience? I blame you for all of this." I waved my arms at the clinic.

I didn't notice Dr. Alex in his lab coat standing in the doorway until he called out, "Excuse me? I'm ready."

He must have thought I was a madwoman shouting at the air and waving my arms. "See? Now you've made me look like a fool!" I whispered this time.

Pah! Go find out about your cat.

"And you leave me alone. You're supposed to keep me out of trouble, not put me in it."

I hurried to the clinic door and the doctor who held my cat's life in his hands.

Chapter Nine: Dr. Alex

Dr. Alex motioned to a chair next to Mrs. Wilkens and Lorrie. "Have a seat."

I was sure he was going to tell me Goldie was gone and was trying to soften the blow. A clock in the waiting room ticked away the seconds.

He cleared his throat. "Uh, I like to have people sit down when I talk to them. They remember better when they're sitting.

"She's dead, isn't she?" I tried to bite back the note of hysteria in my voice.

He smiled at me. "Well, no. She's a strong cat. I think she'll pull through."

The relief in the room was palpable.

"I think we should introduce ourselves now that we know Goldie is stable. I'm guessing you're not from around here." He first looked at me. He had hazel eyes. The same color as my high school boyfriend.

"Liza Johnson. I'm here with my friend and neighbor, Mrs. Wilkens."

He reached over and shook my hand. "Nice to meet you."

Mrs. Wilkens studied him with a puzzled expression until I nudged her. "Oh," she blinked. "Sorry, I'm Ginny Wilkens. I used to be the librarian here long before your time."

He smiled at her. Suddenly, this had the feel of a business meeting. Next, he'd bring out the agenda and the whiteboard. Meanwhile, Goldie was in the back room, surviving a possible poisoning.

Dr. Alex nodded at Lorrie. "We know each other."

"Yup." Lorrie turned to us, "He's a good vet, and when he was in high school, he used to run track. Got to the state tournament, didn't you?"

Alex smiled and nodded. "Lorrie helps me out sometimes with the clinic."

I quickly grew tired of the niceties. "Dr. Alex, what about this poisoning? How did it happen?"

His expression darkened. For the first time, I noticed him beyond his white lab coat. He was a little taller than me with a thin build. I guessed he was in his early forties with thick, light brown hair. He had that fresh Nordic look of a Scandinavian descendant.

"I've seen several cats in the last couple of weeks who have been poisoned like this. The experts at the Vet school at the University of Minnesota think it might be a rat poison that's long been banned in the state."

"Them old barns, they have stuff like that stored from years ago." Lorrie scratched his head. "But I don't get why someone would go after cats."

Alex grimaced. "Hard to tell sometimes what's inside a person's head." He turned to Mrs. Wilkens and me. "What brings you here?"

"Fannie's funeral." My voice had a flatness to it that reflected a sudden exhaustion.

He raised his eyebrows. "You knew her?"

"Mrs. Wilkens knew her and introduced me to her. She was helping me with a school project."

Mrs. Wilkens narrowed her eyes. "Book banning. What a crock! Liza was working on a paper on how to talk with those people."

Alex sat up straight. "You know, not everyone is in line with that group. I think we have a large silent majority here who are simply minding their own business."

Mrs. Wilkens clenched her jaw. "Well, it's time they spoke out!"

I interrupted before she could work up to a rant. "Uh, what's going to happen to Goldie? Can I take her?"

"I'd like to keep her for twenty-four hours and run fluids through her to make sure we've washed out the toxins."

I thought about being stuck in that moldy motel room for another night and shivered inwardly.

You need to stay and find the answers. Ask him about Fannie.

I swallowed back a silent retort. Who was Charlee to tell me to stay or go?

You know I'm right.

"Hah!" It came out before I could stop it.

Dr. Alex stared at me. "Did you say something?"

"No…uh sorry…trying to keep down a sneeze." I knew as soon as I said it how silly it sounded.

Mrs. Wilkens saved the situation. She raised her voice, "Did you know Fannie?"

He pressed his lips in a grim line. "She was my running partner. We were practicing for the annual Chicken Wing 10K." He shook his head. "In fact, we were supposed to meet the morning she was hit. I had to cancel my run because of an emergency." His shoulders tensed. "Maybe it wouldn't have happened if I'd been there."

Mrs. Wilkens reached over and patted his leg. "You shouldn't feel guilty."

Outside, a couple of motorcycles roared by, the noise disappearing down the road. Alex glanced at the door as if he expected them to stop here. "We always have more activity when the Wing Festival is on. Draws from all over the place, including motorcycle clubs."

Lorrie nodded. "Sure can get wild around here."

I wasn't interested in the festival or in chicken wings. I guided the conversation back to Fannie, "What do you think happened? We read it was a hit-and-run. Have they found who did it?"

Alex rubbed his chin before replying. "I don't know anything more than you do. It was sunrise, and I know people can get blinded. But I don't understand why they didn't stop."

"Is the sheriff looking for the car?" I pictured Trey the Stupid and doubted he was much of an investigator.

Alex continued to work on his shoe. "Um…Fannie wasn't real popular around here. I doubt the sheriff is putting a lot of manpower into it."

Mrs. Wilkens frowned and shook her head. "Humph…you'd think we were in the deep south with a corrupt sheriff. Something bad is happening to this town. I can feel it. And Fannie was worried. Do you think she was murdered?"

Alex stared at her. "Uh…"

Another motorcycle roared by, and the room lapsed into an uncomfortable silence. I noted how loud the clock ticked and how the leaves rustled outside the clinic.

Finally, Lorrie, who didn't appear to pick up the vibes in the room, spoke up. "Alex and Fannie won their divisions last year. I remember you broke a Chicken Wing record."

The tension in the room broke. To me, a "chicken wing record" had to do with how many you could eat in five minutes.

Alex smiled before looking at his watch. "Sorry, I don't have answers. But I need to get back to my patients." He turned to me, "I'm sure Goldie will be all right. Why don't you come tomorrow afternoon, and we'll see if she's ready for discharge."

We all stood and watched as Alex disappeared into the dispensary.

Once outside, Lorrie was the first to speak. "Nice guy. I always wondered why he came back here. Didn't get along much with his family."

I was less interested in the doctor's history than in his reaction to our questions about Fannie. I needed to talk with Mrs. Wilkens without Lorrie present.

On the ride back to the motel, she chatted in a high-pitched voice—so unlike her. "You say Alex didn't get along with his family? He seems like a nice man."

Lorrie turned out of the driveway onto the road. I noticed a car parked near the driveway. It pulled out behind us without its lights on.

"He's Lily's boy, you know. I remember her from high school. She and Peter were tight. Always wondered why they split up."

Mrs. Wilkens sighed. "It was a sad breakup. Peter never told me the whole story."

"Yup. Didn't talk to me about it either. He just said, 'Let's sign up for the army and see the world.'"

I glanced in the rearview mirror to see the car behind us like a dark shadow. "Someone is following us."

Mrs. Wilkens turned to look. "I don't see anything."

She was right, the car without headlights had disappeared. Maybe this town was getting to me.

Lorrie continued to talk about Alex. "Wouldn't you know, Lily turned up several years later with Alex. Next thing you know, she up and married Heck Santos. The Santos Brothers were just getting started with the chicken thing. Heck must have adopted him because he took the Santos name."

"Does he do vet work for his father?" I looked back to see if another car was following, but the road behind us was empty.

"I heard the Santos brothers have their own full-time vet—you know, to keep those chickens healthy and deal with the bird flu and stuff. I don't think Dr. Alex is all that interested in chickens. I heard he had a practice over in the cities and came back here after the breakup with his wife. I heard she took him for a lot of money."

I didn't care about Alex's history. I cared that he knew what he was doing with Goldie, and I cared that she would recover and we could get out of this town as soon as possible.

Once we were settled in our motel room, I stared at Goldie's empty carrier. "Why would someone poison my cat? And why would someone let her out in the first place?"

I glanced at Mrs. Wilkens, who was propped up on the bed, staring at the window. It appeared that she hadn't heard me.

I raised my voice. "Are you alright?"

She blinked. "Oh? Did you say something?"

"I said…"

Again, she appeared to have tuned me out. I decided to brush my teeth and crawl under the covers. It was clear she didn't want to talk. Yet, I did. Something was off with Alex when we brought up Fannie. I couldn't put my finger on it, but I sensed he was holding something back. If I were at home in my own apartment, I would have mixed a gin and tonic for the both of us and insisted that Mrs. Wilkens tell me what was on her mind. Instead, I was stuck in this motel with a roommate who had mentally checked out.

"I'd like to check out, too."

Mrs. Wilkens didn't respond.

"With my cat," I added.

Chapter Ten: Mrs. Wilkens is Missing

Considering all the activity and stress of the day, I thought I'd toss and turn and have a bad night. I fell immediately into a deep sleep. I woke up to the sun sneaking through the crack in the dark curtains and the sound of my car starting and the crunch of the gravel as it backed out.

"What!?" Maybe I was dreaming, but car owners know the tapping and growls of their cars. Just like pet owners know the difference between their cat's yowl and the neighbor's cat's yowl.

I stumbled to the window in time to see Mrs. Wilkens pull out on the highway just in front of a semi. If I hadn't already been awake, the blast of the semi's horn would have done it. I squeezed my eyes shut, waiting for the crash, but nothing happened.

Mrs. Wilkens's bed was made as if she hadn't slept in it. Her orange suitcase was still in the room, although it was shut like she'd packed everything up. Maybe she was just going out to get us coffee.

I dragged myself to the bathroom to shower, hoping to step out of the room to the aroma of fresh coffee. When I was finished and toweled off, I opened the bathroom door to silence and the musty smell of the worn carpet. No Mrs. Wilkens.

My phone said it was 9:00 a.m. She'd been gone for at least a half an hour. Time to text her and find out what she was up to.

Where r u?

The bing of a text chimed in the room. I looked around and spied her phone on the bedside table. The lily from last night sat in its vase, but the card that went with it was gone.

"Alright, Charlee, what's she up to?" My head remained quiet. It occurred to me that at long last, I was completely alone. No cat demanding cans of meat by-products, no elderly neighbor getting me into trouble, and no Charlee telling me what to do. I should have crawled back in bed and enjoyed the moment of peace.

Except, Mrs. Wilkens was missing.

I started by going to the motel office. Maybe she'd left a message. Paulie sat behind the desk, head down, fingers flying on his phone.

"Excuse me?"

He looked up, startled. "Oh, I didn't see you."

In the morning light, the scarring on his neck appeared to be redder against the light blue of his t-shirt. I told him my roommate had "borrowed" my car, and I wondered if she had left a message.

He tapped some keys on the computer and shrugged. "I don't see anything." He tapped a few more and added, "You need to check out by 11:00. The room is reserved for the rest of the week."

"No problem. We should be leaving today."

I noticed that he had another book sitting on the desk beside him. "That's a good book, too. You must be a fast reader."

He mumbled something I couldn't understand.

"Hey," I waved at him. "I'm a schoolteacher. I love to have students read."

"You won't tell Big Mike, will you? He doesn't like me reading at the desk."

"Of course not." I wondered if he was afraid to show people he read books or if he was in trouble for reading on the job. "Did you get the book from the library?"

A shadow seemed to pass his face, but he said nothing.

"We came for Fannie Porter's funeral. I heard she was a great librarian, but some people weren't happy with the books she had in the library."

He stayed quiet.

"Listen, I think they're wrong. You have a right to freedom of speech." I was ready to launch into a lecture about the harm of book banning when Big Mike walked to the doorway behind the desk. The boy swept the book onto his lap.

"Are you helping this lady, Paulie?"

"I told her she needs to check out by eleven."

He nodded and walked back inside.

Paulie shrugged. "He doesn't want any trouble."

I would have asked him to clarify, except a sports car pulled up and a tall, tanned man with dark hair pulled back in a ponytail walked in. He smiled at me with perfectly straight teeth.

"Hey, Paulie. What's up? Big Mike in?" He spoke with a slight drawl that I couldn't place.

Strangely, the greeting didn't appear to me to be very friendly.

Paulie motioned to the back, and the man skirted around the counter and into the back room.

Paulie whispered to me. "Don't talk out loud about books. Okay?"

I stepped a bit closer. "Who is he?"

Paulie whispered. "Elvis. He kinda owns part of this place."

"Oh."

He raised his voice, "Just make sure you check out by eleven. We got lots of guests coming this afternoon, and we gotta get the rooms cleaned."

Puzzled by the interchange, I walked back to the room. I noted a slight headache growing behind my eyes. I needed my morning dose of caffeine.

The diner with the broasted chicken was about a half mile down the highway. I grabbed my purse and threw Mrs. Wilkens's phone in it. Perhaps someone would call who knew where she'd gone.

I walked on the shoulder of the highway facing the traffic. Cars, trucks, and vans zipped by, leaving road dust in their wake. The day was already beginning to heat up, and by the time I reached the diner, my t-shirt was damp with sweat.

Inside the booths were full. I found one stool at the counter and slipped onto it. When the harried server finally got to me, she squinted, shaking her head. "You're not from around here, are you?"

"Twin Cities. How did you guess?"

She pointed down with her chin. "No one here would wear that t-shirt in public."

Confused, I looked down at the shirt. I'd gotten it earlier in the summer when I marched with a group that Mrs. Wilkens was involved with. The t-shirt simply had an automatic weapon with a line through it, and the website for GGAAW—Grandmas and Grandpas Against Automatic Weapons.

"Strong support for guns here?"

She blinked. "You best change when you can. We don't like trouble."

A bell rang in the kitchen, and a voice called out, "Stacy, order up!"

"Gotta go. What can I get you?"

I ordered two coffees and two cinnamon rolls to go. When she brought my order, she leaned close. I expected she was going to tell me to get out of town. She spoke in a low whisper, "You didn't hear it from me, but a lot of bad things are happening here, and most of us don't like it."

Before I could ask her what she was talking about, she was gone.

Did bad things…meaning the book banning? Or the swampy green lake? Cat poisonings? For a moment, I felt like I'd been dropped into the middle of a black-and-white Western movie, complete with a bad sheriff and the need for someone to ride in on a white stallion and clean up the place.

Outside with my paper bag of rolls and the cardboard tray with coffee, I headed back to the motel. Halfway there, as I was musing about the state of Ravens Valley, I heard a vehicle accelerate. When I looked up, a white van was careening toward me, its wheels kicking up gravel as it drove half on and half off the pavement.

For one moment, I understood the phrase "deer in the headlights" as I stopped dead to stare as the van bore down on me.

Chapter Eleven: The Trouble with Ravens Valley

"What the...?" Before the van could reach me and send me to the great beyond, survival instincts kicked in. I threw myself into the weedy ditch, landing on a black plastic garbage bag reeking of dead meat. The van screeched to a halt, kicking up enough dust and gravel to pelt my face. The coffee landed upside down next to me, leaking hot liquid into the ground and onto my shorts. The rolls ended up in a puddle of oily standing water in the ditch.

I groaned, pushing myself onto my knees. Carefully, I moved my shoulder. Fortunately, it was the healthy one, not the one that tended to dislocate whenever someone looked at it funny. For an irrational post-trauma moment, I heard the words of Mrs. Wilkens pestering me to get my bad shoulder fixed. "You know, dear, those surgeons can repair almost everything."

A man jumped out of the van as I was wiping the grit from my eyes, "You okay? Geeze, I'm so sorry. It was a wasp. Got me in the neck." He rubbed the area. "Ouch."

"I...uh...think so." I wobbled to a stand, blinked the road dust out of my eyes, and saw that the man who had pulled over was Dr. Alex. He wore a t-shirt and running shorts, and his forehead was damp with sweat.

He steadied me as I moved my arm up and down, hoping I hadn't broken my good shoulder.

"Here, let me check it out." He probed my shoulder and had me move it around. "Looks okay." Smiling, he added, "At least, I think so. I'm better with horses than humans."

I winced as I tried to brush some of the weeds off my coffee-soaked shorts.

"I should get you to the clinic to be checked out."

The last thing I wanted was to sit in a clinic waiting room. I shook my head, "I'm fine. I just need to shower off and change my clothes." Of course, I hadn't brought a change of clothes other than what I wore for the funeral yesterday because we were going back home this morning.

I immediately thought of Mrs. Wilkens. Where could she have gone? And why did she leave me to almost get killed bringing her coffee? Then I thought about Goldie.

"What about my cat? Is someone watching her?"

He chuckled. "You almost get killed, and you are worried about your cat. She's fine. I have an assistant who comes in if I have a patient in the clinic. I checked her before I went for my run. She's a tough cat. I think she can go home after the next round of antibiotics."

I took a deep breath. "Thank you." I had to admit that despite the nuisance, I'd become attached to my ratty furball—not that I'd ever tell her that.

Alex guided me up the incline to his van. "Let me take you to your motel."

I started to shake as soon as I was buckled into the van. Alex touched my shoulder for an instant. "Sure you don't want to go to the clinic?"

I shook my head. "Positive. I just need dry clothes and some coffee." And my cat, and elderly neighbor, and a car to get me out of town.

He pulled up to the motel. He had an uncertain expression on his face like he wasn't sure what to do with me now.

Ask him for coffee.

"I was going to." I spoke out loud.

"Pardon me?" Alex wiped his brow.

"Sorry, I was mumbling. If you'd like to wait about fifteen minutes while I wash off the coffee and muck, maybe you could buy me a a coffee?

Not that I really wanted to spend time in a café with a sweaty veterinarian who had almost sent me to my eternal reward.

He hesitated for a moment. "Sure. I guess I owe you. How about if I dash home, take a quick shower, and come back and pick you up?"

"Sure." Too bad I didn't have any clean clothes to wear.

I let myself into the room, trying not to mutter out loud. "Charlee, I can handle things without you."

I doubt it. At least he didn't kill you. Besides, he lives here and might tell you more about Fannie.

I closed the door. "Speaking of knowing things. Where is Mrs. Wilkens?"

Charlee, in her usual manner, had disappeared. "What good are you?" I muttered to the empty room.

After a quick shower, I changed back into my funeral clothes and stuffed the shorts and t-shirt into my duffle bag. I checked my phone to see if Mrs. Wilkens had somehow contacted me, but found no messages. I picked up her phone. No one had called or texted. Radio silence from the old lady.

When a knock came on the door, I was surprised that Alex could get home and showered so quickly.

Paulie stood at the door staring at his feet. "Big Mike says you have to check out. Now."

My phone told me it was 10:15 am. "I thought I had until 11:00, and I was actually going to find out if I could stay until noon."

By the anxious way Paulie shuffled from one foot to the other, I knew I had to pack up. "Do you know why he wants the room so quickly?"

He shook his head.

I pictured the man named Elvis with his drawl and sports car. Would he have "suggested" Mrs. Wilkens and I leave early? If so, why?

"Um, my roommate has stepped out. I'm not sure when she will be back."

Paulie stood firm. "You can leave your bags in the office, if you'd like." He turned and walked toward the office.

"Okay." As he walked away, I noticed for the first time how badly he limped, favoring the scarred side of his body. I wondered what had happened to him.

I gathered our few possessions, including the toothbrushes, and threw them in my duffle. Mrs. Wilkens would have to sort hers out later.

When the knock came again, I was packed and ready to haul everything to the office. Alex stood at the door wearing a green polo with *Dr. Alex* embroidered beneath the pocket.

"I stopped to pick up coffee and pastries." He frowned when I held the door with my foot so I could get Mrs. Wilkens roller bag out the door.

"I've been evicted." I felt a little quiver in my lips and hoped he hadn't seen it. Being asked to check out a little early was hardly an earth-shattering event. However, almost being run over by a van was.

"Here, let me take that. I can put it in your car," He took the luggage handle from me. I picked up Goldie's carrier and kicked the duffle out the door with my foot.

"Um. My car seems to be missing, along with my roommate." I told him briefly about Mrs. Wilkens's early departure. "I don't know where she is or when she'll get back. Worse, she forgot her phone."

He took a deep breath. "Well, how about if you store your luggage in my van. We can have the coffee in the park by the river and then figure out what to do next."

At this moment in my life, it was nice to have someone do the problem-solving. Young Paulie looked relieved when I brought the room key to the office.

Alex followed me and greeted him. "Well, Paulie. When can you make rounds with me again?"

Paulie relaxed as he grinned at Alex. "Hey, doc. Helping Big Mike this week because of the Wing Festival, but maybe next week?"

"Deal."

I settled the bill and made sure they charged me for Goldie being in the room. I didn't want Big Mike to come after me for a pet fee, even if Goldie had spent the night in the animal hospital.

Alex drove by the square on the way to the park. One of the streets was blocked off, and people were busy setting up a carnival. I noted the banner across the main street advertising the Chicken Wing Festival sponsored by Santos Brothers Farms.

I pointed to it. "Are you involved in it?"

Alex's jaw tightened before he spoke. "Only to run the 10K. I'm…ah…kind of an outsider with the Santos clan right now."

On the outskirts of town, he pulled into the parking area of the Swanson Memorial Park on the banks of the Rabbit River. "Nice," I pointed to the sign, "at least everything isn't named after the Santos family."

"My great-grandfather donated the land for this park well before the Santos Brothers moved in."

Once out of the van and seated at a picnic table under a large oak tree, I sipped the coffee and closed my eyes. The storm racing through my brain eased. Alex had the sense to let me sit for a while, and I had the sense not to ask why he was on the outs with his family. Beyond the picnic table, the river meandered with a family of ducks paddling close to shore. Leaves on the trees shimmered in the breeze, and in the moment, Ravens Valley didn't seem so dark and foreboding.

The serenity was broken by the sound of a police car speeding across the bridge with all its lights flashing.

I told Alex about Trey and how he stopped us, looking for supposed environmentalists.

Alex sighed. "I don't know what to say. Trey isn't the brightest, but he's loyal. I think the sheriff is in Vince Santos' pocket. Uncle Vince doesn't like people coming to town and asking questions. I'm guessing you and your friend asked the wrong question to the wrong people."

I stared at him. "Oh, come on. A little old lady and her schoolteacher driver? What kind of a threat are we?"

He raised his hands in surrender. "I have to agree, but I'm just saying Sheriff Wayne is corrupt and lazy."

"Not much of an endorsement for your community."

Alex waved at a fly that was buzzing around the table. "My grandfather used to talk about Ravens Valley BS and AS. Before Santos and after Santos. He wasn't a fan, particularly when they hired their own vets to deal with the poultry."

"Your grandfather was the veterinarian?"

"And his father before him."

I creased my paper napkin aimlessly before speaking again. "But your last name is Santos. I am very confused." I wasn't really confused; I just wanted to hear how Alex would respond.

For the first time since we sat down, Alex laughed. "You can imagine how disgusted Grampa Seth was when Mom married Heck Santos. Heck adopted me, but I never fit in with the clan."

"So, you have no love for your adoptive father?"

He shrugged. "I think I've said too much. Heck isn't a bad guy, but he does whatever Uncle Vince tells him to do. And he's politically ambitious."

None of this was answering questions about Fannie, or the poisoning of my cat, or where Mrs. Wilkens went. Nevertheless, I was enjoying the conversation.

I looked around the well-kept park with its green grass and newly painted picnic tables. "I get the feeling, though, that the Santos Brothers have contributed a lot to the community."

Alex didn't answer. Instead, he glanced at his watch. "Listen, I have to check out a swine herd in the northern part of the county. Where should I drop you off?"

I held up my hand like a school child. "Wait, before we go, I have another question."

Alex raised his eyebrows, "Yes?"

"Do you think something happened to Fannie?" I stumbled to try to find the words and finally simply said, "Like she was murdered?"

Without answering, Alex stood up. "Sorry, I really am late. I know pigs can't tell time, but their owners can." He wasn't smiling when he again asked, "Where would you like me to drop you off?"

A cloud drifted over the sun, and I felt a chill coming off the river. "Take me back to the motel."

He said nothing as we drove back. I sensed he knew more than he was saying.

Strange reaction, sis. Don't you think?

"I agree."

Dr. Alex raised his eyebrows. "Did you say something?"

I scrambled for an explanation. Telling him I heard voices in my head was probably not prudent. "Ah…I thought you said something about how nice the weather was."

Lame.

Dr. Alex did not reply.

Chapter Twelve: The Library

After Alex dropped me off, I paced the small office of the motel for ten minutes trying to figure out what to do. Paulie stared at me with an almost frightened expression. Finally, after checking my phone and Mrs. Wilkens's phone once again, I turned to him. "Is the library close enough that I can walk to it?"

"It's just off the square. Not too far."

"I'm going to check to see if Mrs. Wilkens is there. If she comes back, tell her to call me. I'll be back soon." I wrote my cell number down for him.

At least I didn't have to walk along the shoulder of the road to get into town. Ravens Valley had sidewalks.

Workmen in white t-shirts were setting up a Ferris wheel. I gazed at the skeleton of the ride and remembered my first time being swept up in the rocking seats. Junior high school with a boy whose name I'd now forgotten, sitting nervously next to me. When we reached the top, the wheel stopped, and for a moment, I felt a sense of complete freedom as I looked down over the grounds of the State Fair. Then what's-his-name decided this was the appropriate time to try to feel me up. He had hot dog breath, and I pushed him away, rocking the seat harder. Suddenly, I was scared. Charlee showed up and whispered in my ear, *He's more scared than you. Relax.*

Sometimes, Charlee could be helpful. Other times, simply irritating.

The banner announcing The Wing Festival said it would start tomorrow.

I stopped at the drugstore and read a colorful poster in the window. Day one of the festival included the first round of the National Chicken Wing barbecue competition. Should be great fun for someone other than me. I wanted to get out of town as soon as Goldie was released from the clinic.

Assuming Mrs. Wilkens ever appeared again with my car.

The library stood a block from downtown in a one-story square brick building with large windows. It appeared to be a quiet oasis among the activity surrounding the festival. I peeked in the window and saw a couple of people browsing the stacks. A young woman sat near the inside entry at a small table. She was high school-aged with lank blonde bangs that fell just above her eyebrows. She stared at me as I passed the table and called out, "You need to sign in."

"Excuse me?"

She pointed to a clipboard. "We have everyone sign in—you know, so no one steals books."

"Um, I don't think that's legal. It's a violation of privacy."

Flustered, she stared at me with her mouth open. "Pru said everyone had to sign in now."

"Is Pru in charge? If so, I'd like to talk with her."

"Ah…"

The poor girl was rescued when Jessica stepped out of the stacks. "Oh, Liza, hello. Surprised to see you here."

I pointed to the girl with the clipboard. "I'm surprised you're asking people to sign in."

Jessica tugged me away from the girl and said in a loud voice, "Oh, it's voluntary. The library board is trying to get a sense of who uses the library. You know, for funding."

She led me back to an office behind the checkout desk. She spoke in a low voice. "Remember, I told you about the monitors, the volunteers who have been installed to observe? Well, this is part of upping the ante. Started yesterday after the funeral. It didn't take Pru long to make changes."

I shuddered thinking about how this represented more erosion of privacy. "So now they will know who uses the library?"

"Worse, they will know who refuses to sign in."

"Scary," I glanced at the few customers. "Seems quiet in here today."

Jessica rubbed her temple, "I think people are afraid to use the library."

"Didn't the Nazis forbid books and destroy libraries?"

Sighing, Jessica motioned for me to sit down. "How can I help you?"

Before I could ask about Mrs. Wilkens, we were interrupted when a tall woman dressed in what I would call country club casual knocked on the door. She wore open-toed sandals, creased capri pants, and a pink silk blouse. I noted immediately that her fingers were as carefully manicured as her toes.

"Hello, Pru. Can I help you?"

Pru stood at the door, looking me over. "Who are you?"

I looked back at her, "You first."

Pru's eyes narrowed. I guessed she wasn't used to being challenged.

Jessica stood, "This is Liza. She came with Ginny Wilkens for the funeral. And Liza, this is Pru Santos, the new chair of our library board."

Before I could say anything, Pru spoke, "Oh, I see. You were a friend of Fannie's?" It sounded more like an accusation.

My lips formed a tight smile. "Remarkable woman. What a loss for the community, don't you think? And the service for her was nice."

When Pru wrinkled her brow, I noted how tight her skin was on her face. She'd had work done, but it didn't make her look younger; it made her look more severe. She hesitated before replying. "I wasn't able to attend."

Probably getting her nails done.

Jessica stepped from behind her desk. "What can I do for you, Pru?"

Pru stood up straighter, "I wanted to give you this. The board is reviewing how the library is being run, and I have a questionnaire I'd like you and the rest of the staff to fill out."

Jessica's cheeks colored as she took the form.

I switched into innocent mode. "I'm impressed that you care so much about the library. I'd heard some bad things—like it might be in legal trouble. You know, like that library where the board got sued for trying to monitor what people checked out. I heard the settlement was huge and it came out of the pockets of the board members."

Pru's jaw dropped. "I haven't heard such a thing."

I smiled sweetly. "You could maybe look it up. I believe the case was called

Johnson versus the Desantis County Library Board."

Cute, but it's time to quit toying with her. Jobs are on the line here.

Of course, Charlee was right.

Pru took out a handkerchief and dabbed at her forehead, "Well, see that it gets filled out." She turned on her expensive sandals and left. She didn't even say goodbye.

"Sorry," I picked up a small paper weight of a chicken from the desk and set it down. "I shouldn't have said that. I know the library is on shaky ground."

"Was there really a legal case like that?"

I shrugged. "I read about a library in a small rural county near Seattle. The extremists were so frustrated about the evil books on the shelves that they decided to pack the board and shut the library down. They lost in court. As for Johnson versus the library board, I kind of made it up."

Jessica laughed, "It'll give Pru and her KGB something to worry about. Meantime, I plan to slow-walk this and perhaps forget to give it to the staff."

"I hope I didn't get you into trouble. I'm only here looking for Mrs. Wilkens. She went a little AWOL this morning."

"Sounds like the Ginny Wilkens I know. She's on a mission, isn't she?"

I nodded. "She thinks Fannie's death wasn't an accident and she's not ready to let that go."

Jessica didn't reply, but I saw her make a fist before she relaxed her hand.

As I was about to leave, a couple of high school students walked in the door. Jessica waved at them. "They're good kids—not the KGB."

Once outside and halfway down the block, my phone rang.

"Liza, I'm at the motel. Where are you?" Mrs. Wilkens sounded out of breath.

"I'm just leaving the library where I was looking for you. What happened?"

"Long story. Wait in front of the library, and I'll pick you up."

I hoped her story wasn't so long that we couldn't get out of town as quickly as possible.

Since we had no motel room where we could talk in private, Mrs. Wilkens drove us back to Swanson Park. On the way, I told her about my conversation with Alex.

"He simply clammed up when I asked if he thought something was odd about Fannie's death. Like the temperature dropped twenty degrees."

She said nothing, staring straight ahead. She drove carefully, even making full stops at stop signs rather than the rolling kind. Something was seriously wrong.

We sat down at the same table. Crumbs from the rolls Alex had bought were still on the table. Once Mrs. Wilkens was settled in across from me, I brushed away the crumbs. "Well? I think you have some explaining to do."

Her eyes filled with tears. Mrs. Wilkens was not the emotional type. When she focused on something, I would describe her as steely. I waited as she dabbed her eyes. When she spoke, her voice trembled.

"The lily and card at our door last night? I knew it meant something important."

I nodded as a crow landed on a wire and cawed at us.

She took a deep breath. "I thought about it all night long. I couldn't sleep, and I couldn't let it go. This morning, I drove to the Santos Farms to talk with her."

"Wait," I raised my hand. "You went where? To talk with who?"

She folded her hands as if in prayer and gazed at them. "Lily. Lily Swanson, although she's Lily Santos now."

"You mean Alex's mother? Your son's former girlfriend?"

On the other side of the park, a dog barked. I glanced in the direction of the bark and saw a man throwing a stick. It wasn't unusual for a park, except the man was Trey—out of uniform. A shiver crawled up my back. Was this a coincidence?

Mrs. Wilkens didn't notice the activity as she continued. "Yes. She's still beautiful like she was when Peter dated her. Except..."

"Except?"

Mrs. Wilkens sighed. "Lily's mother was a peculiar woman. At least when I knew her—forgetful and odd. Turned out she had early-onset Alzheimer's. I could see the same with Lily. It's like sometimes she was talking like old times and then she'd forget what she was saying."

I was slow to put it together. "Wait. Did she send you the card and the lily?"

"Yes. Although when I asked her, she didn't know what I was talking about. She has a caretaker who later took me aside and said she'd sent it."

The dog barked again as Trey threw the ball closer to us. I leaned toward Mrs. Wilkens. "I think we have a spy. Perhaps we should talk about the weather until he goes away."

She glanced over with a surprised expression. "You really think he's trying to listen to us?"

"He suddenly shows up at a deserted park? Like the detectives in those British mysteries always say, 'I don't believe in coincidences.'"

Mrs. Wilkens folded her arms and pursed her lips. "Well, let's get to the bottom of this." She turned to call out to him.

"No," I hissed. "He's dumb enough to think we haven't noticed." In a loud voice, like I was speaking to someone hard of hearing, I said, "Well, it looks like the weather is perfect for our drive back to Minneapolis. We should get going soon." I stood up and whispered, "Let's talk more in the car. I'll drive."

As we pulled out of the parking lot, I noted that Trey suddenly didn't want to play with the dog anymore. He grabbed the dog's collar and shoved him onto the bed of an old pickup truck.

Mrs. Wilkens fidgeted with her purse. "Where should we go?"

"We need to pick up our luggage. Alex has it in his van. Let's go to the clinic and get my cat and our things."

I drove slowly through town, glancing often in the rearview mirror to see if Trey was following. Other than an SUV that turned before we reached the vet clinic, I saw no evidence of him.

When we arrived, the parking area in front of the clinic was empty. Since it had been dark last night when we brought Goldie here, I hadn't gotten a good look at the house on the other side of the clinic. It was a dilapidated old Victorian complete with a cupola and a large front porch. It sat shadowed by several old oak trees. For some reason, gazing at it, a shiver ran down me.

"That's quite a wreck. Wonder if it's haunted." It appeared to be abandoned.

Mrs. Wilkens unlatched her seatbelt. "I think it's a house of sorrow."

Chapter Thirteen: Swanson Acres

"What do you mean, 'a house of sorrow?'"

"The house has been in the Swanson family for generations. Even when I lived here, though, it was rundown and…sad. Peter said Lily wouldn't let him come in, but sometimes when he picked her up, he heard sobbing from upstairs."

"Lily's mom?"

"Probably."

We were interrupted when Alex's white van pulled up next to us. I unlatched the door to step out when Mrs. Wilkens grabbed my arm.

"Wait. I have to tell you this before we talk with Alex. I mean, I know Lily isn't thinking straight, but she was clearly upset when I talked with her."

"About what?"

"At first, when I walked in the room, she recognized me. 'Hello, Mrs. Wilkens, nice to have you visit,' she said. Like it hadn't been forty years since we last saw each other."

She paused to take out a photo. It was a faded photo of a couple dressed for the prom. The girl in it had permed long blonde hair and a dazzling smile. "I showed this to her."

I squinted at it. "She looks just like the woman at the funeral—Annalisa, and he looks a little like Alex. But this is an old photo."

"It's Lily with Peter, my son, at their senior prom just before they broke up."

I stared at Mrs. Wilkens for a moment. "Are you thinking Alex is related in some way to your son?"

"No, although there is a resemblance."

"So, what happened to upset her?" I prompted.

"We chatted for a little bit about Peter and the old days, and suddenly she wrinkled her brow and glared at me. 'I didn't take the car, and I certainly didn't hit a deer. I wish they would all stop asking about it.' I had no idea what she was talking about, but it was clear to me that there was some issue with a car."

I thought about the car that hit Fannie. "She was talking about hitting something?"

Mrs. Wilkens nodded. "And getting quite worked up. Before I could ask her anything more, her caretaker swooped in and took her to her bedroom. Our chat was over."

I pulled the car door shut. "No more about a car?"

"No."

The plot thickens.

Oh, be quiet. At this rate, we won't get home until after the school term starts.

Ha! Stay with it.

We met Alex at the door as he was unlocking the clinic. He smiled, "Oh, the lost roommate."

The unflappable Mrs. Wilkens suddenly looked flapped. She stuttered, "Ah, I had…I had some business."

He beckoned us inside. "I assume you want your luggage and your cat."

It was with great restraint that I didn't blurt out, "Did you know your mother has a thing about cars and accidents?"

Mrs. Wilkens gripped my hand, squeezing so hard I was sure I'd have bruises in the morning.

Our luggage was sitting in the corner of the small waiting room. Alex pointed to the surgery door. "I'll be right back as soon as I check on the patients."

"Say hello to Goldie while you are there."

As soon as he left, Mrs. Wilkens glared at me. "Don't you say a thing. I don't want him to know I was bothering his mother."

We were whispering as she filled me in.

"When we looked at the photo, she said, 'he died, you know, and I couldn't tell anyone about him.'"

"She was talking about your son?"

Mrs. Wilkens picked at a button on her blouse. "I think so. I think she has periods where she's lucid and longer periods when she's not. The sympathy card didn't have anything to do with Fannie. It was about Peter."

"Oh." What else could I say?

Ten minutes later, Alex walked back into the waiting room. He rubbed his brow before speaking, pushing back his hair. I was afraid he had bad news about Goldie.

"I know you want to get on the road, but Goldie is running a bit of a temperature. I'd like to keep her one more night. I'm sure she'll be fine by tomorrow. Tough cat."

I studied him. Yes, he did sort of resemble the boy in the prom photo, but he appeared to be taller, thinner, and with eyes set wider apart.

Alex caught my gaze. "Is everything all right?"

My cheeks warmed with a blush. "Oh, yes. Sure. Just worried about Goldie."

Nice catch.

"I'm glad you found your roommate." He smiled, and the smile was definitely not the same as the boy in the photo.

Mrs. Wilkens stared at the floor, ignoring his comment. Silence surrounded us as if we were a group of awkward teens until Mrs. Wilkens blurted, "I visited your mother today."

A shadow crossed Alex's face. "Oh?"

She held out the card. "She left this for me at the motel."

Alex took it. "That's her drawing all right. She always loved drawing and painting lilies." He handed it back to her.

"She dated my son in high school. I knew her as a little girl and a teenager…" Her voice dropped off.

"Did she know who you were when you visited?"

"Yes. At least some of the time."

"She's got dementia just like my grandma Swanson." His arms fell limply to his sides. "Sometimes she knows me, and sometimes she calls me by another name."

Mrs. Wilkens raised her eyebrows. "She seemed upset about a car."

Alex blinked, opened his mouth, and then closed it quickly. Abruptly, he tapped his watch, "Sorry, I have patients to tend. Let's get your luggage to your car."

I felt dismissed, like he wanted us out of his clinic.

Outside, the air had heated in the cloudless blue sky. In the distance, a small plane descended. Alex glanced at it. "People coming in for the fest. We get visitors from all over the country who enter the barbecuing contest. My dad and my uncle always throw a big party before the opening of the festival."

While he and Mrs. Wilkens were watching the airplane, I studied the old Victorian house set back like a hulking stranger beneath a dying oak tree. It appeared to be a classic from the late 1890s. The architecture reminded me of the courthouse in the town square. The roof needed new shingles, the wide porch sagged, and paint peeled from the wooden siding.

"You're wondering about the sad state of the house, aren't you?" Alex looked at me with a strange glint in his eyes. "It was a beauty in its prime. I have old photos."

Mrs. Wilkens tsked, "I remember it from my time here. It needed work even back then. We used to call it…" she hesitated. "Well, never mind."

Alex nodded. "Right now, it might be a good place to film a horror movie. Except, a film crew would never get insurance to be inside. It's dangerous— rotting floors, mold, and lots of critters. I've been told the best thing I can do with it is have it bulldozed."

I noted the sadness in his voice. "A shame to lose an historic house like that."

"It was in bad shape for years, and then Grandpa let it slide more after Grandma got so bad. Someday I want to fix it up like it used to be. Meanwhile, I live over the clinic. It's handy for taking care of my patients."

I found it odd that his mother was married to an obviously rich man, yet her childhood home had fallen into such disrepair.

Mrs. Wilkens pointed to the land behind the clinic and the house that sloped gently down into a valley. "Didn't the Swansons have a horse farm here at one time? If I recall, they called this part of town the Swanson Acres."

Something seemed to pass over Alex when Mrs. Wilkens spoke. Almost like a shadow. He spoke in a low, harsh tone. "My mother owns all of it now, but Uncle Vince is pressuring her to sell. He wants to put a housing development down by the river." He folded his arms and muttered, "Even my sister agrees with Uncle Vince. She's too young to have spent much time here..." His voice trailed off.

His words put a damper on any further discussion.

We were interrupted by a dark SUV pulling into the parking area. Alex turned to it with a scowl. "Family."

A man with deep brown eyes and dark hair rolled down the window. "Hi, kid. How's it going?"

Alex's shoulders stiffened. "Uncle Vince."

Mrs. Wilkens stepped forward and spoke in a loud voice. "Hello, I'm Ginny Wilkens. I think I remember you from years ago. Didn't you come to the library when you were a teen?"

Uncle Vince grinned. He had a beautiful smile, white teeth and all, but a flatness to his eyes. "Oh yes. I remember you."

His words were not friendly, and I had a visceral reaction to the way he spoke them.

Get off your duff and say something.

As if someone had poked me in the backside, I stood next to Mrs. Wilkens. "Hi, I'm Liza, the driver."

He glanced at my old car with a puzzled expression. "Uber?"

"Neighbor."

This is not a man to be toyed with.

"I came with Mrs. Wilkens to attend the funeral. We were both fond of Fannie."

It was at this point that I noticed a boy in the backseat of the car. He had a long, greasy mop of hair and a bored expression as his fingers flew over his cell phone. I saw the resemblance immediately between Vince and the boy. I wondered if this could be the Josh Santos the girls at the funeral talked about—the one they thought betrayed their banned book club.

Alex scraped his foot back and forth on the gravel. "What brings you here?"

"I was out this way doing business. Annalisa asked me to stop. She's hoping you'll come to the opening fiesta tonight. You know it's good to have the whole family—for the community."

Alex stared at the foot that was scraping the ground. "Not sure I can make it." He gestured to us. "Their cat was poisoned, and I'm keeping an eye on her."

The boy in the back seat turned his head toward us and then quickly looked away.

Vince frowned before answering. "Another damn poisoning. Don't like this. Not good."

I wondered if "not good" meant not good for the image of the community or not good for the owners.

Mrs. Wilkens found her voice. "Alex has been taking great care of Goldie. I appreciate what he's done."

Vince regarded her for a moment. "Perhaps you'd like to come to the fiesta as well. The community is all invited. People will be glad to hear that my nephew is doing good work."

Mrs. Wilkens smiled at him. "Sounds fun. Of course, we'll come."

I opened my mouth to say something when the kid in the backseat of the car called out a four-letter word that was not allowed to be spoken in my classroom even if it was everywhere else in the movies and television.

Vince glanced at the rearview mirror and spoke through clenched teeth. "Joshua, what did I say about swearing? Aren't you in enough trouble?"

Josh glared at him. "Whatever."

Vince turned back to us and shrugged. "Kids these days. What are you going to do?"

Alex pressed his lips together in a pained expression but said nothing.

"We'll see you tonight, then." Vince put the SUV in gear. "My wife Pru will be excited to meet you."

Alex didn't wave as Vince turned around and drove away. "Not my favorite relative."

"He does seem to command authority."

"More like a brutal dictator. My dad could never stand up to him. Sorry you had to witness that."

The urge to flee was so strong I nearly collided with Mrs. Wilkens on my way to the car. "This is not a good place," I hissed under my breath.

Mrs. Wilkens planted her feet and glared at me, arms akimbo, "We still don't know what happened to Fannie. We have more work to do. And…"

"And what?" Now I sounded more like Josh than an adult.

Mrs. Wilkens whispered, "And I need to know if Lily has some information about Fannie."

I sighed, "Great, but meanwhile, where are we going to stay? We've been kicked out of the motel, and I'm guessing every place is booked up."

A slow smile grew on Mrs. Wilkens's face. "Well, as it happens, Lorrie has invited us to his house. He was at the motel when I stopped to get you and heard that we'd checked out. Such a nice boy."

I wanted to cover my ears and jump around and say, "No, no. I want to go home!" But, of course, I didn't, which gave Charlee the opportunity to crawl into my head.

Hey sis, you're being a brat. What's wrong with you? This is important. You need to find out about Fannie.

Not my circus, not my monkeys.

Shame on you! A librarian has been killed, kids are being denied the opportunity to read, and someone is poisoning cats. Really?

Mrs. Wilkens stared at me with a concerned expression. "You look like you just had a seizure. Are you okay?"

Having been thoroughly raked over by a voice in my head, of course, I wasn't okay. Charlee had hit the nail on the head, damn her.

"I'm fine! Let's get on with the snooping."

As we pulled out of the clinic and away from the house of sorrow, I noted a car parked on the side of the road. Looking in my rearview mirror, I saw it start up and follow us. Yes, it was time to buck up and snoop.

Chapter Fourteen: Lorrie and Henry

"First, we need to stop at Lorrie's and drop off the luggage and then…"

I raised my hand. "We're being followed."

Mrs. Wilkens glanced back. "I've seen that car before. It was outside the entrance to the Santos Brothers Estate when I visited Lily."

It appeared to be an old car, and it was too far away to catch the license plate. "I wonder who it is?"

Mrs. Wilkens had her phone out. "I can call 911."

"Not on your life. I don't want to deal with Trey the Stupid again."

She rested the phone on her lap. "Well then, let's see if it follows us to Lorrie's." She directed me across the Rabbit River bridge to a housing development along the river with sixties ranch-style houses. "Lorrie's parents owned the house, and when they died, he moved in. I'm sure it will be okay for one night."

As soon as we turned into the development, the car that was following us drove on. "He's gone. I guess I'm a little paranoid."

Mrs. Wilkens stared out the window but didn't reply.

I pictured Lorrie's house as messy and neglected, like his personal appearance. When she pointed to it, I was surprised to find a white one-story rambler with a blue shingled roof and a neatly trimmed front lawn. Lorrie's Frankenstein's monster car was parked in the driveway. The rest of the neighborhood was quiet.

"Where are all the people?"

"A lot of them commute to Mankato or Marshall now unless they work for the Santos Brothers."

Lorrie greeted us before we could get out of the car. He beamed. "Henry will be so glad to have guests. It's been a long time. Come in. Come in."

When I opened the trunk, he grabbed Mrs. Wilkens's large suitcase and my small bag and led us to the front door. Before going in, he rang the doorbell. "I like to warn Henry that I'm coming."

Would a cat care? I pictured Goldie in my apartment, ignoring the door if someone knocked.

We stepped back into an era before my time. Beyond the little entryway was a living room complete with a green shag carpet. The furniture was covered in faux velvet brown flowered upholstery with white lacy doilies covering the arms of the couch and chairs. Cream colored drapes were pulled tight across a picture window, emphasizing a gloom of days gone by. A thick layer of dust had settled on the coffee table. The stale air still had a whiff of old cigarette smoke.

Lorrie took our bags down the hall and dropped them in a bedroom. "Mrs. Wilkens, I'm giving you the master suite." He called out, "And Liza, if you don't mind, you can have the spare. Mama always had it ready in case people showed up."

I wondered when the last time the sheets had been changed.

Mrs. Wilkens looked around. "Why, Lorrie, this looks just like it did when you were a child."

He grinned. "Mama liked to keep things neat. I try to do the same. Henry agrees."

I looked around for signs of a cat but saw none.

"The upstairs is all yours. I have my place in the basement. Always have, and Henry and I like it down there. You make yourselves at home while I check on him."

He disappeared into the kitchen and down the stairs to the basement. I walked over to a bookshelf and picked up a dusty framed photo. It was of a younger, slimmer Lorrie in uniform with a wide smile. Next to him was a boy about his age, also in uniform."

"My son, Peter. After they finished basic training. It was the last time they were together in the army, despite what the recruiter told them."

I studied Peter. "He does kind of resemble Alex."

"I think Lily was attracted to a certain look—tall and blonde."

"I doubt Heck Santos fits that description based on what his brother Vince looks like."

Mrs. Wilkens held the photo with a distracted expression. "Lily said something about Peter today that made me wonder."

"Yes?"

"I think Lily knew that Peter was gay even though Peter didn't. I think that's why they broke up."

I thought about what it must have been like back then, before the era of LGBTQ and gay pride. "It probably was confusing for her."

She sighed, "And him."

We were silent as she put the photo back.

Lorrie joined us a few minutes later with a worried expression. "Henry doesn't want to come out. He's worried."

"About what?"

"He thinks the poisoning is part of something bigger, and he says he'll stay in my room, thank you very much."

We came because of Fannie and her death. Then we discovered Pru and her book-banning schemes. And in the middle of it, Goldie was poisoned, which led us to Alex. I pictured him and how he spoke to Goldie and felt something I hadn't felt in a long time. A little awakening in my chest. A little wondering about how good his hands might feel touching me.

You need a cold shower, sis, and a stiff drink.

No kidding. Could you get me one?

Hey, I'm a voice in your head, not a servant.

Mrs. Wilkens sat down on the couch and patted the cushion beside her. A cloud of dust motes floated into the air. "Lorrie, sit and tell me what you…uh…or Henry are thinking. I agree something is wrong here."

He plopped down beside her like a little child, leaned back, and clasped his hands together. "So, I hear things at the Nevermore."

"The Nevermore?"

"It's the bar outside of town. I've got some pals there. We play dice and shoot the…uh…shoot the you know."

Clearly, he was respecting Mrs. Wilkens by not using the word that was also banned in my classroom.

"What things do you hear?" I settled in an upholstered chair across from the two of them.

He turned to Mrs. Wilkens, "You remember what a great place this was. Peter and me grew up riding our bikes around, swimming in the river, and all that stuff. Well, kids stay indoors now. And you hardly see people in the park anymore. Like they're afraid to be out."

I held back a sneeze. "Do you know why?"

"I know when. It started with them chickens."

"You mean the Santos Brothers?"

"Sort of. It's when they got bigger and built that processing plant over by the county line. Next thing you knew, we got Pottersville."

Mrs. Wilkens sat up straight. "Pottersville?"

Lorrie pushed a stray hair away from his forehead, "You know, like the movie?"

We all sat in silence for a moment, and then I remembered. "*It's a Wonderful Life*? You mean the Pottersville from there?" Boy, either I was very confused, or Lorrie was off in another land.

Mrs. Wilkens squinted up at the popcorn plaster ceiling. "Wait, I think I understand. You mean, Potters Acres, where we used to dump things?"

Lorrie nodded vigorously. "Yes. Yes. They covered the old dump and turned it into a trailer park."

I ran my hand through my hair, trying to put this all together. "People don't come outside because of the trailer park?"

Lorrie slumped, "Well, that's what I hear at the bar. People don't like who's living there. You know, folks who work in the processing plant."

I saw Mrs. Wilkens's face darken. "Because they're poor and migrants?"

He shrugged. "I guess. I don't mind 'em. They're just trying to make a living, and they don't bother me. Paulie at the motel is one of them—or at least he was." He picked at his thumbnail. "The Santos people don't like anyone to call it Pottersville. The real name is Elm Park. But everyone calls it, you know—Pottersville because it's so raggedy."

Interesting, sis. Didn't I tell you to get off your duff?

Go away!

I must have spoken out loud because when I looked across the room, both Lorrie and Mrs. Wilkens were staring at me.

"Sorry, I was thinking that we should…uh…go away to find some clothes for tonight."

Lorrie gave me a wide smile. "Mama left her clothes. Maybe you could try something of hers."

Mrs. Wilkens patted him on the leg. "Sweet of you, Lorrie, but if you remember, your mother was about five feet tall and rather substantial. I'm afraid they wouldn't fit."

Overhead, we heard another airplane. Lorrie stood up and walked to the door. "Always liked to watch the airplanes. Back then, with Peter, we'd pretend we were chasing them."

We left Lorrie to watch for more airplanes while I drove with Mrs. Wilkens in search of clothes to wear to the fiesta. We were almost to downtown before either of us spoke. I was trying to puzzle out what Lorrie had told us, and I couldn't read Mrs. Wilkens's expression. We found a little consignment store a couple of blocks from where the festival was being set up. It was in an old two-story bungalow with a porch. A rack of clothes sat on display next to an old-fashioned porch swing.

"This used to be the house where Peter's piano teacher lived. The teacher was a soft- spoken German man who lived alone. Rumor had it that he'd escaped from the Nazi's when he was a boy. He was a good teacher." We walked up the steps. "I didn't understand at the time why, when Peter was thirteen, he came home and said he wasn't going back. I think I understand now, and I wish Peter had been able to talk with me about it."

A bell jingled when we opened the front door. A woman came out from the back with a smile. "Welcome. You must be here for the Wing Festival."

"We came for Fannie Porter's funeral and decided to stay for the festival," Mrs. Wilkens put on her chattiest voice. "I'm sure you knew Fannie."

The woman's smile faded. "Yes. Well, she was the librarian. Not that I agreed with the books they kept."

I was tempted to turn around and walk out.

Be nice. She might have information you need.

Mrs. Wilkens had more sense than I did. "I understand there was some controversy."

The woman folded her arms. "Those books were corrupting our youth and turning them into hooligans."

"Lots of crime here?" I made an effort to sound casual as I walked to a rack of clothes that looked like they might fit me.

"Well, I heard they were bringing in drugs. You know to get our children hooked."

I picked out a multi-colored skirt and held it up, and Mrs. Wilkens spoke in a sweet voice. "You mean the library was bringing in drugs? I'm confused."

The woman's voice rose. "No, not that. Fannie was spending time with those Pottersville kids. And you know that place is filled with drugs and crime." She lowered her voice to almost a whisper, "And prostitution."

"Oh?" Mrs. Wilkens kept the sweet tone, but I saw how she tensed her jaw. "Fannie was mixed up with drugs and prostitution. How awful."

"Well, that's what pastor Vogel and Pru Santos said—right in church, so it had to be true."

I wanted to take a giant stride over to the woman and punch her in her self-righteous face. Mrs. Wilkens must have sensed it because she moved between the woman and me. "Oh, how terrible. I didn't know all that. For me, Fannie was the librarian who wanted to make sure that Ravens Valley had the freedom to read and learn. I didn't know she was a drug dealer."

The way she spoke must have gotten through a little to the woman. She seemed to deflate in front of us. "Well, anyway, that's a real nice skirt, and it's on sale."

Much as I hated to give the woman my money, she did have some decent used clothes. I bought the skirt along with a peasant blouse, a couple of t-shirts, and a pair of shorts. Hopefully, we would only be here another day, or I'd have to find clean underwear as well.

Back in the car, Mrs. Wilkens muttered, "Welcome to Ravens Valley, home of the people who elect politicians I despise. Now I remember why Mr. Wilkens and I left when we did."

I only half listened as she rambled on. I was trying to put together the pieces of what I'd heard this afternoon. Ravens Valley had a secret that involved a trailer park that everyone called Pottersville. And Fannie had mentioned *It's a Wonderful Life*. Perhaps she was referring to the trailer park. But why?

I interrupted Mrs. Wilkens as she started to talk about the political corruption. "We need to find out more about this Pottersville. Let's go to the motel and talk with Paulie."

Be careful. The kid is skittish.

I'm always careful.

Remember how someone set your apartment on fire?

You are a pest!

I didn't want to think about a summer ago and the adventure that left me with a cat who was now racking up a huge vet bill. Which reminded me that, besides everything else, someone was poisoning cats. "Aarg..."

"Is that your stomach rumbling?"

"It's my head getting ready to explode."

Mrs. Wilkens patted my thigh. "We'll get to the bottom of this."

Chapter Fifteen: Paulie

The parking lot in front of the Ravens Nest Inn was nearly full when we arrived. Judging by the cars and trucks, the Wing Festival attracted a lot of pickups and older SUVs. This was not the Tesla or Mercedes crowd. I guessed those people were the ones coming by private airplane to the Santos Estate.

Big Mike stood at the registration counter, taking down information from a couple holding a baby. I did not see Paulie. When he had them registered and taken care of, he looked up at Mrs. Wilkens and me and scowled. "We don't have open rooms. Booked up."

I scrambled to come up with a reason to talk with Paulie when Mrs. Wilkens rescued me. "You know that nice young man who was at the desk this morning? We wanted to give him a tip. He was so polite. You are fortunate to have an employee like that."

He softened as she spoke. "He's a good kid."

"I wonder if we could give it to him in person and let him know how much we appreciated his help."

I stood back admiring how easily she was wrapping the gruff guy around her finger. Perhaps she should run for office.

"Uh, he went to see them set up for the festival. He'll be back tomorrow." He tapped the counter, "You could leave it with me."

Mrs. Wilkens smiled, "That's kind, but we'll check back in the morning."

We walked back to the car amid the rumble of the traffic on the highway. "I don't trust that man." Big Mike watched us from the door as if he was guarding his motel.

Mrs. Wilkens slid into the passenger side of the car. "We'll find Paulie in town."

We parked in front of the church where Fannie's funeral had been. I glanced at the closed door of the church and thought about the dismal service. Even though I'd never met Fannie, she deserved a better send-off than what she got. She was clearly a lone crusader for the freedom of speech. I silently wished Jessica good luck against Pru Santos and the mysterious pastor.

The town square and side streets were blocked off for the festival. Weatherwise, a low front had crept in, bringing languid clouds and August humidity. I couldn't wait to get out of my funeral clothes and into the shorts and t-shirt sitting in a bag in the backseat of the car.

First, we had to find Paulie and see if he could tell us anything about Pottersville.

Downtown, the carnival was set up and ready to open this evening. A group of teenage boys and girls hung out by the fence around the Tilt-a-Whirl. Paulie was not with them.

I spotted Jules and Rochelle near the ticket booth for the Ferris wheel. Waving, I joined them while Mrs. Wilkens stopped to talk with someone setting up a food booth.

"Hey, are you waiting for a ride?"

Jules wrinkled her brow. "What?"

I pointed to the Ferris wheel. "Are you waiting for them to open?"

They sent a look to each other that reminded me that I wasn't of their teenage tribe.

"Just hanging," Jules finally replied.

I noted that they weren't with the other crowd of teens. "So those are your classmates?"

"Like, we stay away from most of them. They're Josh's acolytes."

Acolytes? Pretty sophisticated language.

Rochelle noticed my questioning expression. "We call them acolytes because they're—you know—followers."

"And idiots." Jules leaned close to me and spoke in a whisper. "He's the biggest drug dealer in high school."

I pictured the sullen kid in the back of Vince's car, and I could see it.

I whispered back, "I don't suppose his mother knows about it."

They both giggled.

"Listen, I'm trying to find a kid named Paulie. He works at the motel. Walks with a limp? Maybe in your class or a bit younger?"

Again, the glance between the two of them. Jules stiffened a little. "Why do you need to talk with Paulie?" Her tone had taken on a defensive quality.

Tell her the truth.

"I was going to."

The girls stared at me. "What were you going to do?"

When would I ever learn to stop talking to Charlee out loud?

"Sorry, I sometimes talk to myself and forget that other people are around." I twirled my finger by my ear. "Used to drive my mother crazy." Except Mother never noticed I had Charlee inside my head.

Try again, and this time tell them you want to know about Pottersville.

"Okay, here's the truth. Someone told me today about Pottersville and that Paulie lived there, and I thought he could tell me about it."

Rochelle stared down at her shoes and mumbled, "My dad doesn't like it if we talk about that place. We got into some trouble about it when we tried to help Miss Porter."

Jules added, "She was one of the only people around here who cared."

Now I was lost. "Back up just a little. First, tell me about Pottersville. I hear it's a trailer court. The lady at the consignment shop said it was filled with drugs and crime."

Jules made a fist with one hand. "Of course, she'd say it. She's one of *them.*"

"Them?"

"Those book banner people who were harassing Miss Porter."

Both girls kept their voices low as if someone might overhear them. Jules continued, "Miss Porter wanted to raise money for a mobile library for the kids in Pottersville. Many of the people who live there don't have cars, and they haven't been exactly welcome in town."

"After someone heard what she was trying to do, my dad told me to stay away." Rochelle ran her fingers through her hair. "Like we were doing something illegal."

"Yeah, the only person in town who stuck up for her was Dr. Alex, the vet."

Finally, a connection between Alex and Fannie that was more than a running partner.

"Were they seeing each other or anything?"

Jules tapped her foot nervously. "I don't know. He found her, you know."

"Found her?"

"Miss Porter. After she was hit. By the side of the road. I heard he tried to do CPR and everything."

Another little piece of information.

Several crows landed on the top of the ticket booth, cawing and making a racket. At the same time, Rochelle mumbled, "Those guys over there are watching us. We should probably go."

"Wait. I don't want to get you into trouble, but can you tell me anything more about Pottersville and Fannie?"

"Like she wanted to put together a mobile library for them. They're just poor people who came to get away from bad things in their country. Pru and the others don't like them in town."

"Like they have germs or something," Jules added.

The teen boys approached rapidly. Josh was in the lead, walking with a swagger that looked more theatrical than threatening. I turned to the girls. "Why don't you head on your way. I think I'll talk with these kids."

One thing I've learned as a schoolteacher, most teenagers are self-centered and think the whole world is looking at them. They want attention, but they don't trust you because you're not one of them. First rule—don't try to be friends with them. Second rule—if you want information from them, be patient. Third rule—ask them to do you a favor. It's surprising how well the old adage works—if someone helps you, they become your friend.

While Jules and Rochelle inched away, I stood tall with my arms folded. "Hi Josh, good to see you again."

Josh stopped cold. "Uh, hi."

"What can I do for you?"

He looked at his small gang. "We were wondering what you were doing here."

Remember the honesty thing.

I'm not sure about that with these kids.

Best policy if you want information from them.

Okay, you win.

"To be honest, I'm snooping."

Jasper, the boy I'd seen with the Reverend Vogel at the motel, tittered and punched Josh in the arm. "Snooping?"

Josh ignored him. "What?"

I followed Charlee's suggestion. "I came here yesterday for Fannie Porter's funeral. You guys know her, right?"

They shuffled their feet, waiting for Josh to talk. "So?"

"I don't get it. I heard people were nasty to her and slashed her tires and threw manure at her house. But no one is investigating her death."

Again, the boys shuffled their feet. Jasper was the first to speak. "We heard it was a hit and run and they think it was one of the…" he hesitated, "one of those dirtballs from Pottersville. The sheriff will catch him."

"Shut up, Jasper." Josh glared at him before turning to me. "Why do you care?"

I defied Charlee and lied. "She was my cousin. And I'm wondering if she was targeted. You know, like murdered?" Now I had their attention.

Jasper's eyes widened. "I didn't know she had cousins."

Neither did I.

"If I understand it, she was found on County Road 8. Is that by that trailer place?" I took out my phone and did a Google search for a map of the county. The boys gathered around me and showed me where Pottersville was located and where Fannie was found. Pottersville was west of town, and where she was found was east, about two miles.

"Does that make sense?"

Josh scratched his head. "Maybe they were drunk and lost?"

"At six in the morning?"

Josh's body language told me he was growing more uncomfortable with my questions. He seemed to shrink back. I used my Maybe You Can Help Me card.

"Listen, guys. If you hear anything, could you let me know? I'll be at the festival tonight. Come and find me."

Josh said nothing but turned quickly away. "Let's check out the beer garden."

I assumed they would be looking for ways to sneak in.

After they left, I found Mrs. Wilkens near the poster for the Barbecued Wings contest sign-up. She was handing a twenty-dollar bill to Paulie, whose eyes were wide as he took the money. Leave it to Mrs. Wilkens to make a lifelong friend.

I joined her. "Thanks for all your help this morning."

He stared at me. "I didn't do nothing except throw you out of the motel."

The kid had a sense of humor. "Well, maybe you can help us now. I know that Fannie Porter was trying to help the people at Pottersville. I was told you lived there. Do you know anything that might help us understand what happened to her?"

Paulie's eyes opened wide. "I can't...I signed the form, so I can't talk about it."

"What form?"

"They said if I signed it, I could live with Big Mike and maybe go to college someday."

Before I could ask him about the form, Josh and his band came around the corner. Without a word to us, Paulie hurried away, his limp even more exaggerated as he tried to move quickly.

Mrs. Wilkens spoke before the boys reached us. "It appears that something is very rotten in Ravens Valley."

No kidding.

Ditto.

Chapter Sixteen: The Santos Party

After Paulie made his exit, Mrs. Wilkens and I decided it was time to clean up and get ready for the Santos Party. At Lorrie's house, the vinyl shower curtain was so old it crackled when I pulled it closed. The pipes shuddered before spewing out a rust-colored water. I guessed the shower hadn't been used since Lorrie's mother died.

I let the water run until the pipes had cleared out and had a refreshing, hot shower. Dressed in my new used clothes, I joined Mrs. Wilkens, who wore the same shirt waist dress she'd worn for the funeral. Once outside, we were blasted with the hot, sticky August air.

"This humidity is enough to wilt…" I stopped because I couldn't think of what it would wilt.

Mrs. Wilkens helped me. "Mrs. Vlasic's prize pickle."

"Sure."

She was in fine form. Considering all that we had discovered in 24 hours, I had to admire her. She chatted as we drove to the party. "Heck and Vince Santos built their houses right next to each other. When I went to see Lily this morning, I stopped at the wrong house. Hard to tell them apart."

The Santos Brothers Estate was located north of Ravens Valley on a hilltop overlooking the Rabbit River. Cars lined the side of the road by the entrance. We parked behind an old pickup truck and walked through an open wrought iron gate attached to a stone wall surrounding the front of the property. The front yard could have been a golf fairway, it was so green and manicured. Several white canopy tents were set up near the two houses.

I had expected to at least see the Santos Brothers living in mansions.

Instead, both the houses on the grounds were one-story ramblers like Lorrie's, except bigger and done with a brick exterior.

"It doesn't look like they flaunt their wealth."

Mrs. Wilkens stopped and surveyed the area, hands on her hips. "Back when I lived in Ravens Valley, this was the Nelson place—an old farmhouse with a barn in the back and the chicken coop over there. She pointed to a free-standing building. Now they tell me the chicken coop has been replaced by offices and an education center."

I laughed, "You mean they're educating their chickens?"

"More likely they're filling people's heads with Santos Brothers propaganda."

The lawn was crowded with people holding red Solo cups of assorted drinks. In the background, a Mariachi band warmed up. We made our way to the refreshment tent. Pru Santos, in a designer pair of silken pants and a thigh-length short-sleeved jacket, appeared to be in her glory as people lined up to greet her. Reverend Vogel, with his red hair, stood next to her.

I felt heat in my cheeks as I watched them. The minister had a smugness to him that tempted me to pinch his cheeks and tell him to go to hell.

Cool it, Sis. No need to get arrested for assault.

I noted the expression on Mrs. Wilkens's face and realized she was thinking the same thing. I touched her arm to stop her from marching ahead. "Pru and I have met. I'm guessing she isn't interested in chatting with me about the illegal things she's trying to do to the library."

"You stay here. I'll go greet her. Maybe I can charm her out of her book-banning fever."

"Please don't punch her or her clubby minister. I'm going to look for Alex. I have questions for him."

I picked up a plastic cup of white wine and wove through the crowd. People were gathered in clumps, and as I walked by, I caught snatches of conversation.

"They say it was suicide."

"I heard some city people were asking questions..."

"Dora Porter knows something. She isn't as addled as they say. I heard..."

I stopped behind the man who was talking and turned my back to him, so it didn't appear I was eavesdropping. I didn't catch his next words because people applauded as Vince Santos and the man I assumed was his brother, Heck, walked into the crowd shaking hands and looking like local politicians.

Vince and Heck approached, nodding and smiling. Both had beautiful teeth to go with their practiced smiles.

Introduce yourself. Make nice and maybe you'll learn something.

Quit bugging me! I gestured like I was trying to shoo a fly away, and my drink splashed onto a man who was approaching the brothers.

"Oh, I'm sorry." I recognized the man I'd dumped my wine on as the county sheriff. He wore sunglasses like he was on the set of a movie about a stupid sheriff.

"Are you drunk?" His words were not friendly.

"Sorry, I felt a mosquito on the back of my neck. I hope I didn't get you too wet."

Oh, you liar!

Extending my hand to him, I smiled. "I'm Liza—an acquaintance of…" I had to scramble to come up with an appropriate lie. "Dr. Alex. He's caring for my cat."

"I know about you. You're the one who's been asking questions." I sensed a threat in his voice.

Putting on the sweetest smile I could manage, I replied. "I'm sure you are looking into the poisonings. Such a bad thing to happen in such a nice town."

A woman standing next to him, who looked a little tipsy, slurred, "Poison wasn't a problem until that vet came back. Some say he's looking for business. Should have tended the chickens instead."

"Marjorie!" The sheriff took her by the arm. "I think it's time that we find your husband."

To my relief, he led the woman away. I did not want to talk to the sheriff—yet.

Vince approached as Marjorie wobbled away with the sheriff. "Well, it's Liza, isn't it?"

I extended my hand. His handshake was like a vice grip. I held back from yelping. "Thank you for inviting us. This is quite a party."

He introduced me to Heck, who stood slightly shorter than his brother with a radiant smile worthy of any up-and-coming politician. "So glad you could come." He pumped my hand and dropped it quickly as Vince turned to talk with more people.

I wanted to ask him about Lily, but clearly this wasn't the time or place. Over by one of the tents, the Mariachi band started to play. The crowd began migrating in that direction.

I found Alex emerging from the Santos Brothers' office building, talking intently with Annalisa. Much shorter than Alex, Annalisa stood waggling a finger up at him. "You know Dad won't give you the money, so leave it be!"

"Hi," I waved to them.

He looked at me with a red face. It took a moment for him to acknowledge me. "Oh, you."

Not the greeting I had hoped for.

Annalisa's first reaction was annoyance, which changed quickly to formal friendliness. Like her father, she could be a politician.

Alex introduced us, "Liza, this is my sister Annalisa." He turned to his sister. "Liza came for Fannie's funeral, and unfortunately, someone poisoned her cat."

She extended a hand. "Nice to meet you."

I was surprised that she carried herself with such confidence, yet her handshake was worse than holding a limp dishrag. We did the usual chat about the weather and the humidity before Annalisa glanced at the phone she held in her hand. "Oh, sorry, I have to go. Maybe we can talk later?"

To me, the question oozed with insincerity.

At last, I had Alex alone and wasn't sure what to ask him. He helped by commenting, "My dad and sister want me to mingle more. They think it will help my business, but I prefer to schmooze with cats and dogs and cows."

I laughed. "You are an introvert in a family of extraverts."

He motioned to a picnic table under an oak tree. "Would you like to sit?"

Once we'd settled in across from each other, he rested his elbows on the table. "So, why are you really here?"

"You mean at the party? We were invited."

"No, why are you in Ravens Valley? You drove here from Minneapolis to a funeral of someone you hardly knew, and you've been asking a lot of questions."

I could have said a number of things, including my anger over Protect Our Children and how they treated Fannie. I could have said I didn't like the town and wanted to know why. Instead, I leaned forward and told the truth. "Fannie was helping me, and she was in trouble." I stopped when Alex frowned.

"What do you mean, 'in trouble?'"

I shrugged; not sure I should trust Alex. "She told me about the incidents, like her tires being slashed. I think she was afraid."

Alex's eyes narrowed. "Do you know what she was afraid of?"

"No, but Mrs. Wilkens thinks she was deliberately run over."

Alex blinked, and I thought a little color drained from his cheeks. "What makes her think that?"

"She thinks Fannie was targeted and someone ran her down on purpose, and there's a great conspiracy to keep it quiet. Somehow, the Santos family is involved."

Alex sat up straight. I wondered if he was going to stand up and stalk off. He studied me before he spoke. "And what do you think?"

"Something is wrong here, but I don't know what it is." I hesitated. "And I don't know if you are involved with it."

A mosquito landed on my bare arm. I slapped it with too much vigor, leaving a red mark. Alex looked at me with a thoughtful expression. "Fannie was a friend, but something changed with her a couple of weeks ago. We used to run together in the mornings, and suddenly she wasn't where we'd usually meet. And she wasn't responding to my texts." His shoulders tensed. "I think she was into something way over her head, but she didn't tell me about it."

I sensed this wasn't the whole truth. "Do you know what it was about? Something to do with Pottersville, maybe?"

He grew paler. "What makes you ask that?"

Instead of answering his question, I leaned toward him. "Tell me about Pottersville. Why is everyone so hush-hush about it?"

Alex's face was damp with sweat. A little bead rolled down from his temple. He wiped it with his hand. "Here's all I know. It's a trailer court outside of town where a lot of the workers at the processing plant live. It's…well, as my dad says, it's a blight on the landscape."

"Because the people who live there are poor?"

He shrugged. "Places like Pottersville spring up where the food processing plants are. Migrants come, and they don't have a place to live, so they gather in encampments."

"Who owns it?"

He shrugged, but his expression said he knew more. I would have asked him except Annalisa marched over still holding her phone. "There you are! Dad wants a group photo, and they've been looking for you." She glared at me as if I'd spirited him away.

He eased out of the bench. As soon as he was up, she grabbed him by his arm. "They are over by the drinks tent." Ignoring me, she marched him away.

She's something else.

I think he knows more than he's telling me.

Well, get in there and find out what he knows.

You are a damn pest. Maybe I should collect my cat and my neighbor and get out of Dodge.

Sissy!

My conversation with Charlee lasted until I reached the crowd now standing by the stage where the Mariachi band played. Mrs. Wilkens was nowhere in sight.

Behind me, I heard, "Psst!"

I turned to find one of the servers beckoning me. She wore a red apron embroidered with *Santos Brothers* and a happy chicken. "Your friend, the lady. She's at the house and wants you to come." She pointed to Heck and Lily's house.

I found her on an open front porch talking with a woman in a cushioned wicker chair. "Oh, hello, Liza. This is my friend Lily." Mrs. Wilkens spoke loudly as if Lily couldn't hear. Her tone surprised me because she often complained that people assumed because she was old, she was deaf.

I knelt and took Lily's hand. "Nice to meet you." The resemblance to Annalisa was uncanny. They could have been twins or at least twins born thirty years apart, except Annalisa had darker skin and a wider mouth.

She squinted at me. "Are you my nurse? I told Heck I didn't need someone constantly hanging over me."

Mrs. Wilkens answered. "No, Lily. She came with me to Fannie Porter's funeral."

"Oh, yes. Fannie. I heard she died the other day."

Despite Lily's looks and beauty, it was clear her thinking wasn't straight. "It's a loss for the town," I said.

Lily held on to my hand, "You will get me out of here, won't you? I want to go home to Dad. I know I made a mistake. Can you take me?"

Mrs. Wilkens pulled up a wicker chair and sat down next to her. "Lily, what kind of a mistake?"

She let go of my hand. "Oh, nothing. It's all about the chickens, and I'm so tired of them and how they go on and on. So many lies all the time." She dropped her head and started to cry. At first, it was a whimper, but within seconds it turned into sobbing.

Annalisa ran over. "Mama, it's okay." She took her hand as Lily continued to cry. "We need to get her inside. I'm afraid all this activity sets her off."

I helped Annalisa get her up. Lily shuffled toward the door, sniffling. Before she went in she turned to Mrs. Wilkens. "You know, don't you? Haven't you always known about him?"

I beckoned to Mrs. Wilkens. "I think the party is over, and it's time to leave before the sheriff shows up to arrest us."

To the sounds of the Mariachi band playing *Cielito Lindo* we hurried away from the party to the car. When we reached it, a piece of paper held by the windshield wiper riffled in the breeze.

Scrawled in childlike letters was a message: Go home.

Chapter Seventeen: Chicken Wings

Maybe we would have gotten more information if we'd stayed at the party or if we had gone to the opening of the festival, but frankly, both Mrs. Wilkens and I were thoroughly spooked by the note. I drove back to Lorrie's. His mismatched car was not in the driveway, which meant we had the house to ourselves.

The living room was oppressively warm and close. I pointed to the back door. "Let's see if we can sit outside. I need some fresh air."

What I needed and wanted was to grab my cat and head back to Minneapolis like the note told us to do. **Go home.**

Lorrie's back patio had several lawn chairs along with a dusty Weber grill and a battered wooden table. Mrs. Wilkens brought out two glasses of water and set them on the table. "I was afraid to open the refrigerator in case it hadn't been cleaned since Lorrie's mother died."

"Possible mold poisoning," I agreed.

The setting sun cast long shadows on the backyard. I noted the sagging clothesline and a rag that dangled limply from one clothespin. I wondered how many years it had been there.

Mrs. Wilkens squinted at the note on her lap. "It's not exactly a threat. More like a warning."

"Let's go over what we know and maybe something will be clear." I yearned for a flipchart. Instead, I pulled up the notes app on my phone.

Mrs. Wilkens started, "We know someone hit Fannie, and no one has been arrested."

"The high school kids I talked with said it was probably some 'dirtball' from Pottersville."

"Do you believe that?"

Two houses over, smoke arose behind a cedar fence, and the aroma of grilled hamburgers wafted through the air. It reminded me that I hadn't eaten much, and my stomach was now complaining.

"Too many things tell me her death was no accident." Once I said it, a shiver ran up my spine. If someone wanted her out of the way, how much danger were we in?

We continued to list everything we knew from the hit-and-run, the attack on the library, to the hush-hush about Pottersville.

Look for connections.

Charlee, that's exactly what we're trying to do. Why don't you tell me what they are!

Mrs. Wilkens stared at me. "You have the look again."

"What look?"

She shook her head, "Never mind. Don't forget to add Lily and Alex."

As if the goddess of coincidence had swooped down on us, my phone rang. Ravens Valley Vet Clinic popped up. I hit answer immediately, my fingers tensed around the phone.

"Liza, this is Alex—the vet?"

I jumped in before he could say anything more, "Is Goldie alright?"

"Oh, sorry. I didn't mean to scare you. She's fine. Should be able to go home tomorrow."

I let out a huge sigh while Mrs. Wilkens stared at me. "What can I do for you, Alex?" I emphasized his name, so she knew who I was talking to.

"I'm wondering if I could treat you to barbecued chicken at the festival. I have a proposition for you."

I frowned. What was this about?

Go!

He could be a serial killer, you know!

Pshaw!

Don't you pshaw me!

Alex's voice came through. "Are you still there?"

"Sorry, I'm sitting outside and was distracted by—a rag." It was the best I could do.

"What? A rag?"

Rather than explain, I simply said, "Chicken sounds good."

We agreed that I would meet him at the festival in half an hour. He told me that the Baptist Church made the best barbecued chicken at the festival.

"The Baptist Church?"

"It's a big fundraiser for them. They marinate it in the gospel."

"Excuse me?"

He laughed. "I was trying to make a joke."

I promised Mrs. Wilkens I'd bring back dinner for her before I took a quick shower and put on my new shorts and t-shirt. When I stepped outside, Mrs. Wilkens was dozing in the lawn chair. "I think you should go inside before the mosquitoes find you."

She perked up long enough to ask me, "Can you find out what he knows about his biological father? Uh…well, he does look a little like Peter."

"Sure, I'll demand a history—after he pays for the chicken."

The festival was in full swing when I arrived. With the nightfall, the temperature had gone down enough that I didn't feel like everything was sticking to me. Alex waited for me outside the tent of the Baptist Church.

I stopped before stepping inside. "Is this the book-banning church? If so, I don't want to help them raise funds."

"No, these are good old Minnesota—no drinking, swearing, or dancing— Baptists. The church you are talking about used to be filled with Lutherans. Since the new pastor arrived, it's full of people I don't like."

Once we had our paper plates with barbecued chicken wings, potato salad, and coleslaw, we found an unoccupied picnic table. By the looks of it, the Baptist cooks were getting ready to close. I glanced at my watch and saw it was nine. Probably bedtime for the farmers.

The wings were as good as any I'd ever tasted, but the potato salad was amazing. I pointed to it. "What do they put in this?"

"Blessed mustard, I think. Plus, the parishioners grow their own potatoes for it."

I noticed for the first time that his eyes had a playful sparkle to them. This was not the serious doctor who had saved my cat.

Enjoy!

Not sure I need someone who likes cows better than people.

Come on. He's cute. And he knows something. Sparkle back at him.

Alex cleared his throat. "As I was saying…"

I turned my full attention to him. "Yes?"

He lowered his voice to a near whisper. "I've been thinking about what you said at the party, and I don't think Fannie's death was an accident."

Before he could say anything more, a large woman wearing a red apron with the Santos Brothers logo on it lumbered over with a gray bussing tray. "Sorry, we're closing. You can put your dishes in here."

Kicked out by the Baptists.

The festival was going strong as we emerged from the tent. I wanted to find a quiet place to hear more. Alex must have read my mind. He pointed to the Ferris wheel. "No one will eavesdrop if we take a few turns on the wheel."

I felt people staring as we made our way to the ticket booth. Alex greeted a few of them. While we waited in line, an older man wearing a John Deere baseball cap approached us.

"Hey, doc, I hear another cat has been poisoned. Any idea what that's all about?"

"I don't, Maynard. I'm checking with the University to see if they can isolate the poison."

"Well, when you find out who's doing it, let me know so I can shoot 'em." Maynard grinned.

Alex laughed. "In that case, my lips will be sealed."

"Don't forget, we have that other matter to talk about."

Alex nodded, "Gotcha."

After he'd walked away, Alex explained. "Maynard is one of the good guys around here. First organic farmer in the area. Got a lot of flak over it, but he's doing well."

We settled into the swaying Ferris wheel seat. My stomach lurched as we were swept up and around. I hoped the blessed mustard in the potato salad would save me from getting sick. Few people know this, but I have acrophobia. I hadn't realized it until I took a high school trip to New York City. We went to the top of the Empire State Building, and while all my classmates went to the edge, awed by the vista over Manhattan, I had to cling to the inner wall, suddenly dizzy and sick to my stomach.

Why did you agree to the Ferris wheel?

"I forgot how much I hate this."

"What do you hate?"

"Oh, sorry." We stopped suddenly halfway up, and without thinking, I grabbed Alex's hand with a gasp.

He turned to me. "Are you afraid?"

I clenched my teeth. "I…uh…yes."

"Well, hang on. The ride won't last long, judging by the line of people waiting."

I held his hand until we finally reached the landing, and the attendant let us off. I walked carefully down the ramp, clutching the handrail as my heart pounded like a bass drum.

"Listen, maybe we can talk somewhere else. I guess the Ferris wheel wasn't the place for a serious conversation," he peered at me.

I wiped my forehead that had broken out in a cold sweat. "I'm just glad you didn't suggest the Tilt-a-Whirl. I might have lost all the wonderful Baptist food."

We walked away from the festival and, within a couple of blocks, found ourselves on a quiet residential street. By then, my breathing was back to normal, and I was no longer shaking. "So sorry to be such a wimp. I have no excuse."

He put a hand gently on my shoulder. "No worries."

We strolled down the darkened street with the calliope music in the background. I turned to him, "Tell me what you're thinking about Fannie's death."

"I hadn't seen much of her this summer. I was busy with my practice, and she was busy fending off the book banners. Or so I thought."

"What do you mean?"

We reached a little park at the end of the street with a newly painted wooden bench under the streetlight. He motioned for us to sit. "I sensed something else was going on. Maybe it was the threats and the cow dung and slashed tires, but Fannie didn't strike me as someone who was easily scared off."

I thought about the frightened librarians in some of the ultraconservative states. "Maybe she was threatened with more than vandalism or worse."

Alex grimaced, "I don't know. But over the last couple of weeks, I thought she was getting paranoid. In my last conversation with her, she said to me, 'I have to stop talking to you. You might be part of it.' I asked her 'part of what?' and she walked away. I'm sorry I didn't try harder to find out what she was talking about."

"You mean this might be something more than the book banning?"

He wrinkled his brow, "I don't know."

"What about Pottersville?"

"Again, I don't know."

I wasn't sure I believed him. We might have had more conversation except a police car pulled up to us. And yes, Trey stepped out.

"Hell," Alex said under his breath.

"Alex, your family is looking for you. Don't you have your phone?"

Alex took it out of his pocket. "I must have turned it off. Is this an emergency?"

"Don't know. Sheriff just said to look for you." He stared at me as if he wanted to say something. I stared back.

"Thanks, Trey. I'll call them. You'd better get back to the festival. I'm sure you'll be busy when the beer garden closes."

As if he needed the last word, he huffed, "Well, check in with them." He pointed to me, "And you should be moving on, don't you think?" His words weren't kind.

I said a word or two under my breath that I wouldn't allow in the classroom.

Alex stood and walked away from me with his phone. Trey eyed him for a few moments before lumbering back to his car.

Did they make him up from a B-grade movie?

Don't kid yourself. He can be dangerous.

"Thanks! I'm well aware of that."

Alex joined me on the bench again. "Who were you thanking?"

Damn it, I had to learn to not talk out loud. "I'm thanking my mother for not bringing me up in this town. Is everything okay with your family?"

He took a deep breath. "It's Mother. Something at the party upset her, and she wants to talk to me. They can't get her settled, so I'll have to go."

"Do you know what upset her?"

"She keeps talking about Peter. She must be stuck in the past."

"You should go. Mrs. Wilkens and I are going home tomorrow once I pick up Goldie. I'm sorry we didn't find out what might have happened to Fannie."

We walked back to my car in silence. For a crazy moment, I felt like a teenager and wished he would take my hand.

He's gotten to you.

Nonsense, and quit reading my mind.

When we reached the car, I dug into my bag to get my keys. He watched me with a little gleam in his eyes. "Ah, women and their bags. My wife used to have one that would have been too big to carry onto an airplane."

"Oh?"

Maybe he read my thoughts because his eyes lost that gleam. "I wanted to bury the bag with her."

"Excuse me?"

"Long story. After she died, I moved back here."

"Oh, Alex. I'm sorry. I didn't know you had lost your wife." Hadn't someone said he was divorced?

He smiled in a sad kind of way. "Those last years with her were difficult, and we were headed for divorce. Still, it was a loss."

I waited a moment before holding out my hand to shake his. "I guess on that note, I'll see you tomorrow to pick up Goldie. I hope your mom is okay."

I watched him walk away, his back straight and a nice runner's swing to his hips. I was so pleased Charlee had no comment.

Chapter Eighteen: Lorrie

A subdued light was on behind the drapes in the living room of Lorrie's house. It wasn't until I let myself in that I remembered I'd promised to bring Mrs. Wilkens something to eat. Great, while I was out whirling around on the Ferris wheel and supporting the Baptists, she was probably starving.

The aroma of barbecue greeted me when I walked in the door. Mrs. Wilkens sat on the couch happily finishing off a chicken wing.

"Oh, those Baptists. They know how to cook." She licked her fingers. "They used to have a booth at the county fair. Their booth and the 4-H exhibits were the only reason anyone went to the fair in those days."

Lorrie sat in a wingback chair sipping a beer. "Now the Chicken Wing Festival has lots of people. We even have a Chicken Wing queen."

Why not, I thought.

"How was your date?" Mrs. Wilkens wiped her mouth with a paper napkin.

I decided to play it straight. "Well, Alex treated me to supper and a ride on the Ferris wheel. Then we walked to the river, where Trey, the deputy, found us."

Lorrie's eyes widened. He probably thought we'd gotten caught making out. "Did you get in trouble?"

Now it was Mrs. Wilkens's turn to stare at me.

"No. Trey was looking for Alex. The family needed him because they couldn't get Lily to settle down. She was apparently very upset about something." I left out the part about Peter.

Lorrie slowly shook his head with a sad expression. "Poor Lily, getting that Alzheimer's like her mother. I remember her mother, Pauline, sat in that wicker rocking chair on the porch and rocked and rocked."

Mrs. Wilkens folded her hands. "I knew Pauline a little before she got so sick. I thought she was depressed. In fact, about the time Lily was dating Peter, I remember they took her to a doctor in the cities. He diagnosed her with depression and gave her shock treatments. It confused her even more."

"Those shocks, they ain't good for everyone."

I watched Lorrie as he spoke and wondered if he'd had treatments, too.

Lorrie continued, "Poor Lily. The wife of one of the guys at the Nevermore works for Heck, taking care of her sometimes. Says she can be fine and then confused, like she doesn't know where she is. He said the wife told him sometimes she gets away."

"You mean like wanders?" One of the tenants in my apartment building wandered away from her husband a few times before they had to put her in a memory care unit. The last time before they moved her, they found her at least a mile from home.

He set his beer down on the coffee table. "Worse, she gets in the car and drives. She once got all the way to Mankato before they found her."

Interesting considering her statement at the party about wanting to go home. Funny what goes on in a shrinking brain.

"So sad to see it." Mrs. Wilkens looked up at the ceiling. "Before they knew what was wrong with Lily's mother, I remember that she drove their car into a tree. After that, they had to hide the keys." Mrs. Wilkens yawned and stretched. "I think I need to go to bed. Probably will have nightmares after filling myself with all those chicken wings, but I can't keep my eyes open."

I reminded her, "We're picking up Goldie at ten. I want to get on the road before we hit the Twin Cities in the middle of rush hour."

"Henry thinks that's a good idea," Lorrie pointed to the bedroom. "Sheets are clean."

I wondered if the sheets were clean back when Mama died and hadn't been changed since.

After Mrs. Wilkens retired, Lorrie offered me a beer. I decided I'd earned it. Through the open front door, the music from the carnival wafted over the river.

Ask him about Alex.

I want to relax. My brain is too full.

You know you're dying to know about him. I can tell.

Hush.

You giggled when he said goodbye.

"Did not!"

Lorrie looked at me with a startled expression. "What?"

"Just talking to myself. It's a bad habit."

Ask him.

I sighed, "Lorrie, what do you know about Alex? I mean, other than he seems to be a nice guy."

Lorrie picked up his beer and settled back in the chair. "Came back here a couple of years ago. They say it was a sad story."

"You mean that his wife died?"

"They say he met her in veterinary school. She was a lab assistant or something. When he graduated, Heck planned on him coming back and taking over the vet duties for the farm—you know, the chickens and such."

I'd never thought much about whether chickens needed a veterinarian, but I guessed they could get sick like any other creature.

"Did they come back here?"

"Nah, she wanted to stay in the Cities. They started a clinic in one of the suburbs. Can't remember which one. They say he didn't really want to take care of pets, but that's what she wanted."

He fell silent with his brow furrowed as if he was trying to retrieve information from his brain. I waited long enough so that I wondered if he'd forgotten he was talking to me.

"What happened?" I asked.

Lorrie scratched his head. "That's the thing. I can't quite remember what they said. Something about her having a drug addiction and taking money and drugs from the clinic. Turned into a big scandal, I think."

I set the empty beer can down, sorry I'd finished it. I was full and uncomfortable, and even Lorrie's dusty sheets looked good to me. I fought back a yawn because I wanted to know the whole story. "Did he lose the clinic?"

"That's what they say. The clinic went bankrupt, and she took off with someone she'd met at the casino."

"Alex told me he was a widower."

"They say she died before he could divorce her, but I never heard anything more except that's when Alex came back here and started up his grandpa's practice again."

I took a deep breath and let it out slowly. "Wow. That's a sad story."

"Yup. And the town hasn't been real nice to him,"

"What do you mean?"

"Oh, some talk at the bar. Heck doesn't want his vet clinic to do well because he wants Alex in the family business. Or at least that's what I've heard. And if Heck doesn't like something, the town doesn't like it either."

I wasn't surprised to hear this. When you have a company town, you want to keep the company happy. "I heard that Fannie wasn't popular either."

"The guys said she was a 'troublemaker.' I guess because they didn't like how she was fighting those book-banning people. Especially since Pru Santos is one of them."

I fought back a little shiver. Would I be brave enough to go up against a whole town?

Yes, you would, sis. That's why you're here.

Nope. I will be happy to get out of this place, even though the Baptists know how to make potato salad.

Lorrie stood, "I guess it's time for me to turn in. Henry doesn't like it when I leave him too long."

Outside, we heard a boom followed by a popping sound.

Lorrie flinched and spoke in a tight voice. "Fireworks for the festival. The Santos Brothers pay for it every year. Gotta go keep Henry company. He doesn't like the noise."

"Can we see them from here?"

Lorrie pointed to the back door. "Pretty good view from the patio." He moved quickly to the basement door, calling, "Henry, it's okay. I'm coming."

I stood outside in the humid warmth of the night and watched across the river as fireworks lit up the sky. As a kid, I loved fireworks. Mother took me to the State Fair every year, where they ended the night with fireworks. One of my ex-boyfriends made fun of me when I told him how much I liked the splashes of colors and the booming that went with the display.

"Noise pollution. Air pollution. Should be banned." We broke up the next week.

Another one of my failed relationships. As I mused about him, my thoughts turned to Alex. Had I felt a spark with him? Was he to be trusted? I recalled how he'd reacted when I asked him about Pottersville. Yet, he also told me he was suspicious about Fannie's death.

Time to leave Ravens Valley and all its secrets to the people of Ravens Valley.

Don't give up, sis.

I'm tired of the intrigue.

It's a lovely night. Take a walk.

"For once, you have a good idea."

As the fireworks reached their crescendo, I walked down Lorrie's street past the two blocks of ranch-style houses. The neighborhood was quiet. Either everyone was asleep or at the festival. At the end of the second block, the road turned into a gravel driveway. In the dark, I could make out a small house at the end of the drive. Like the rest of the houses, its windows were dark.

A small sign by the mailbox said, "Private Drive." Another loud boom came from the fireworks on the other side of the river. I looked up to see a spray of lightning in red, white, and blue. In the distance, I heard a band playing a faint Star-Spangled Banner.

Closer to me, I heard a different sound. It was the sound of breaking glass, like someone had smashed into a window. It came from the house at the end of the drive. Peering through the darkness, I caught a glimpse of a figure running in front of the house and the sputter as someone started a motorcycle.

At the same time as the motorcycle came to life, I heard an explosion coming from the house. For a moment, I stood frozen, staring as yellow flames lit up the front window of the house. The motorcycle revved.

Hide!

It was careening toward me, skidding on the loose gravel. I don't know if the driver saw me or not. I threw myself into the ditch just beyond the mailbox and flattened out as much as I could. The motorcycle roared by. I looked up long enough to see that it carried two people. One of them, the passenger, had long blonde hair streaming out from under a helmet. The driver's face was covered by a helmet and face shield.

I counted to twenty as the sound of the motorcycle faded. The fireworks were over, and the house at the end of the drive was engulfed in flames. When I stood on shaky legs, I read the name of the mailbox. Porter

Someone had torched Fannie Porter's house.

Chapter Nineteen: Ruston County Sheriff

The next few minutes were like a dream nightmare. I took out my phone to call 911 and immediately dropped it into the weeds by the side of the road. A car drove slowly down the road, its lights blinding me as I dug through the weeds for my phone.

The car pulled into the driveway. I glanced over to see a man getting out of the driver's seat. I yelled at him, "Fire!" Pointing down the gravel drive.

As I scrabbled on the ground to find my phone, he must have made the emergency call. By the time I found my phone and hit the emergency button, he was running toward me. I thought he was coming to help. Instead, when he reached me, he grabbed my arm and screamed, "What did you do?"

Startled, I tried to pull away from him. "Did you call 911? Is anyone home there?!"

He gripped me so tight I'm sure he bruised my arm. "What are you doing here? Did you start that fire?"

I gaped at him before I jerked away. "We have to find out if anyone is inside." I turned to the house, but before I could move, he had me in a bear hug. "You aren't going anywhere." Next thing I knew, I was on the ground face down. I had visions of George Floyd as he pushed his knee into my back. I might have been stuck there except Lorrie came lumbering down the road.

"Hal, what the hell are you doing?"

"I caught this one. Probably set the fire."

"Geez, you dumbass, she's my guest."

"Huh?"

Before this conversation could continue, the firetruck arrived at the same time people started coming out of their houses in the neighborhood. Hal helped me up with a mumbled, "Sorry."

I was brushing myself off when Trey arrived. All his equipment jiggled as he made his way through the crowd to where I stood.

"What are you doing here?" He demanded, his eyes narrowed. "You seem to show up a lot around here."

"I didn't start the fire, if that's what you mean."

Don't rile him.

I want to punch him in his fat face.

Be nice.

I took a deep breath, rubbing my hands together to get some of the dirt and dust off them. "I was out walking to see the fireworks when I saw two people..."

Trey interrupted. "Why weren't you at the park like everyone else to watch them?"

His voice had an accusatory tone to it, like it was illegal to watch fireworks anywhere but the park. "Excuse me? What kind of question is that?"

"Missy, I don't like your attitude."

Even Hal, who had tackled me, wrinkled his brow in confusion. "Trey, what are you saying?"

"I'm saying none of this adds up."

As if Trey was capable of adding.

I might have parried with Trey all night except his boss, the sheriff, arrived. He marched toward us with a puzzled expression. "You set that fire?"

Really? Was I in the middle of a very badly written Hollywood script? I raised my voice, "As I was saying before, Trey interrupted me. I was out walking when I heard glass breaking. Then two people on a motorcycle sped by from the house. One of them..."

I was interrupted again by Trey. "You say you were out for a walk? In the dark?"

Lorrie saved me from turning and stomping away. "Hey Wayne, she's visiting me, and she went outside to watch the fireworks. She didn't start a fire."

Mrs. Wilkens arrived, breathless, wearing a robe and slippers. "Oh, Liza, are you alright?"

Other than the fact that my new t-shirt was covered in dust from being tackled, I was fine. "Yup, just dandy."

All around us were shouts as the firemen worked to put out the flames. It looked like the fire had blown a hole in the roof, but the building wasn't completely demolished. One of the firemen beckoned to Trey and Sheriff Wayne.

I leaned over and whispered to Mrs. Wilkens, "Let's get out of here before I end up in jail for arson."

We turned to go back to Lorrie's when Wayne yelled, "Wait, I need to talk with you!"

Not tonight, he didn't. "I'm going to bed. If you still need to talk with me, call me in the morning. Trey has my phone number."

On the way back to Lorrie's, I muttered, "They didn't even want to know about the people I saw before the fire. What's wrong with them?"

"Ravens Valley is what's wrong with them," Mrs. Wilkens gripped my arm. "This is a bad place."

"Thank God we're going home tomorrow."

Optimistic, aren't we?

I didn't bother to reply or even think of a reply.

It turned out that the sheets on the guest bed at Lorrie's were freshly laundered and smelled vaguely of lilac. I hardly cared, I was so tired. I fell asleep thinking lovingly about my apartment and how Goldie would appreciate settling down with my smelly old slipper once we got home.

I was awakened at 7:00 a.m. by my phone. Caller ID said Ruston County. My guard went up immediately as I answered, "Yes?"

I recognized Trey's voice. Had he been up all night? Did he ever get time off? "Need you to come in and make a statement. Be here at 8:00."

I ended the call without replying. If I could get my statement done, maybe we could still pick up Goldie by ten and be on the road.

Oh, silly me.

Remember to be nice.

You are a pain, and this whole place is a pain.

Except maybe Alex?

"Shut up!"

Mrs. Wilkens's voice rose from down the hall. "Liza, are you alright?"

I would be once I was back in my apartment. "Fine."

She already had the coffee perking when I walked into the little kitchen in my now dirty shorts. I wasn't having a good time with my clothes this trip. One pair muddied from jumping in the ditch to avoid Alex's van, and now this pair, from being tackled by a vigilante neighbor.

Mrs. Wilkens and I went over the events of last night before going to see the sheriff. She insisted on accompanying me. I wasn't sure if she would make things better or worse.

The streets around the festival were quiet with the rides asleep and the tents closed up for the night. Activities would begin again around ten. By then, I hoped to be picking up my cat and heading back home. The sheriff's office was in a one-story new building that held most of the county offices and was located a couple of blocks from where the festival was being held.

When we walked in, a deputy in a short-sleeved khaki shirt looked up from the desk. He picked up the phone before we could tell him who we were. We sat in yellow plastic chairs in the drab waiting area. Amazing how they could take a new building and make it so dull. No wall decorations, no hint of humanity.

Fifteen minutes later, Sheriff Wayne walked out with his lips pressed together in a grim line. He motioned us to follow him. I wondered if we would be taken to an interrogation room like in the movies—one with a one-way mirror. Instead, he led us into his office. Compared to the waiting area, his office appeared lavish with a heavy oaken desk and bookshelves. The shelves contained copies of some of the typical books on banned book lists.

Had he pulled them from the library for some nefarious reason? My hands started to sweat. This wasn't going to be a good interview.

We sat on cushioned straight-back chairs as he eased himself behind his desk. The desk was clear except for a folder in front of him and a closed laptop computer. He rested his clasped hands on the desk. "Now, tell me about last night."

I couldn't read his expression as I went over being outside for the fireworks and walking down the road. I told him how I heard glass breaking just after the band had played the Star-Spangled Banner.

He leaned forward, "Are you sure of the time?"

"Yes."

"Okay, go on."

I wondered what he was after. I described the motorcycle roaring out of the driveway and how I got a glimpse of the passenger's blonde hair.

"That's all? Can you describe the driver?"

I shook my head. "He wore a helmet with a dark visor."

Sheriff Wayne closed his eyes for a moment and muttered, "Wish you had a better description."

Mrs. Wilkens, who had been silent, sputtered, "Well, it was dark, you know." Then she surprised me by adding, "It took me a while to place you, but now I remember. You must have been about six when you used to come into the library. Loved to read anything about science. Am I right?"

The sheriff's face changed from grim to surprised, "You remember me?"

"We librarians are a treasure trove of information."

The surprised look changed to a smile. "Did you know I stole a book or two back in those days?"

Mrs. Wilkens's eyes twinkled. "Of course, I knew. I figured you'd put them to good use."

I stared at her and then back at the sheriff. This wasn't the interchange I expected. I had him pegged as a bigoted small-town sheriff.

He leaned back, "My mother found those books back when she moved to the senior buildings. Made me take them to the library and confess."

"Ah, your mother was always a treat. How is she?"

"Died last year."

I felt antsy listening to them chat. I raised my hand, "Excuse me, are you going to need me to write anything, sign anything?"

"Ah, no. We'll consider this a preliminary investigation."

"You'll be looking for those two on the motorcycle?"

Any amusement washed out of his expression. "As I said, this is preliminary. You are free to go. Best for you to get back to your lives in the Cities."

This interview went so quickly that I forgot to ask about the banned books on his shelves.

Outside his door, we nearly bumped into Trey. I wondered if he had been listening in at the door.

"Excuse me," I brushed by him.

His face flushed, "Listen to the sheriff then and be on your way."

Thinking about all that had occurred since we'd arrived in Ravens Valley, I found I was furious. Poisoned cat, pathetic funeral, Trey everywhere, and a burned down house, I turned to face him, ready to say something as my mother used to say, "loaded for bear."

Choose your battles, sis.

Humph, I don't even know what loaded for bear means.

On the way to the car, Mrs. Wilkens commented, "Something is really off-kilter here."

"No kidding."

"He wasn't interviewing you as much as giving you a warning. I'm sure of it."

"Do you know anything about him?"

She slipped into the passenger seat and clicked on the seatbelt. "His father was the sheriff when I lived here. He was just a kid who liked to read."

It was time to pick up Goldie. I wondered what Alex would say when we met with him. Nothing in this town was predictable.

Chapter Twenty: The Barn

It was only 9:00 a.m., and already the air felt heavy. As we drove to the clinic, I was reminded of a scene from a movie where people sat on a wide porch fanning themselves and talking in a deep southern drawl. Pulling into the parking area by the clinic, I glanced at the old house with its sagging porch and imagined the cast of that movie sitting around with mint juleps, saying things like, "I declare it's going to be another hot day."

Mrs. Wilkens interrupted my thoughts. "I know a good restaurant in Mankato. Let's stop there for lunch on our way home." Clearly, she wanted out of Ravens Valley as much as I did.

Alex's van was parked near the door, but the clinic was locked. I checked my watch to see we were almost an hour early.

I rang the buzzer anyway, but no one answered. Shading my eyes, I looked up to the second floor where Alex had his apartment. The shade was pulled. "He might still be in bed. We were supposed to meet at ten."

Mrs. Wilkens tapped her watch. "Still, doesn't he have animals to tend to?"

I rang the bell again. After a few minutes of standing waiting in the early morning heat, I noticed that Mrs. Wilkens appeared to be wilting. I gave the car keys to her. "Why don't you go get us something cold to drink. I'll stay here and wait."

In truth, I wanted a few minutes alone with Alex and planned to call him as soon as she left.

Mrs. Wilkens brightened. "I'll get caramel rolls from the diner." She lowered her voice to a grumble, "Other than the Baptists' chicken wings, they're about the only good thing in this town."

As soon as she backed out of the driveway, I called Alex. It went immediately to voicemail. I left a message to call me back and walked over to the house. Despite its dilapidated state, it had good bones. The porch might be sagging, but the rest of the house appeared to be solid.

Stepping onto the porch, I peeked in the window. White sheets covered the living room furniture. Everything looked faded, including the flowered wallpaper. I had the sense that it had stopped somewhere in time. I wondered if it was when Lily was in high school, and her mother had become so demented.

I circled around to the back, which looked over a large rolling meadow. Beyond the meadow, water from the river sparkled in the sun. I imagined horses grazing in the grass. To the right of the house stood an old barn. It was the kind with a large front door to allow the tractor and other equipment in, and a hip roof that allowed for a loft to store hay. The white paint on the barn had peeled in many places, exposing bare wood.

I'd read that this kind of old-fashioned barn was growing scarce as they were torn down and pole buildings used instead. It had the flavor of an era gone by, much like the house.

Curious, I walked down the driveway, hoping Alex would call me back. The weedy gravel drive indicated not much activity had occurred at the barn lately. Except, I noted what appeared to be fresh car tracks. Maybe Alex stored his car in the barn. The barn door was a sliding door, and it was not locked. I tugged, opening it up enough to slip inside. I half expected Charlee to chide me about trespassing, but she remained quiet.

The main part of the barn was lighted by dusty, grimy side windows. It appeared the barn was used now mainly for storage. I saw no evidence of farm equipment, but did observe several old metal filing cabinets along the wall and a number of cardboard and packing boxes scattered around the floor. I also saw the tire tracks in the dust and dirt of the concrete floor. I followed them to a car parked close to the other end of the barn. It was covered in a canvas sheet.

"Curious." I'm not sure what I thought I would find, but the lone car in the murky old barn intrigued me.

Remember the hit-and-run.

At last, Charlee was back. It occurred to me that if someone hit Fannie, their car would be damaged, and the damage might be significant. I remembered a friend who hit a deer that jumped out at the car one night in Northern Minnesota. The deer died, and the car was totaled.

I found I was tiptoeing. What if I lifted the canvas and found a damaged car? What if Alex was somehow implicated in Fannie's death?

As I neared the car, it felt like the barn was closing in on me. I was never good in dark places, and something about this building felt sinister. Suddenly, I wanted to cover my ears and run out of the barn.

You need to look.

No. I need to get back to the evil big city.

I inched forward as if a force was pushing me back. The other voice in my head, the one that was me, whispered to me, "Leave."

You know you need to look.

I reached the car, took a deep breath, and lifted the cover from the hood. "Oh God, no!" It was a bright red SUV. The left front bumper was smashed in, and the windshield was shattered. Taking out my phone, I used its flashlight to survey the damage. I wasn't sure, but I thought I detected dried blood on the hood.

When my phone rang. I was so startled, I dropped it on the hood of the car. With shaking hands, I grabbed it. The call was from Alex.

Willing the tremble out of my voice, I answered, "Hello?" How do you sound normal when you've just discovered a murder weapon?

"Liza? You sound faint. Are you okay?"

"Sorry." My hand still shook.

"I'm out running. I should be back in about ten minutes."

"Um…Good. I'll be here."

Before putting the canvas back on, I snapped several photos, including one of the license plate. Sunlight poured in through the opening of the door. I hurried out and pulled the door shut. By the time I reached the clinic, I was drenched in sweat and so preoccupied with the car in the barn that I didn't see that a car had pulled up by Alex's van. It wasn't Mrs. Wilkens.

Annalisa stepped out of the white Lexus and peered at me. "Can I help you?"

I must have had a derelict look to me—disheveled with dirty shorts and a stained t-shirt. It took me a moment to find my voice. "I'm waiting for Alex. He has my cat. She was poisoned, you see, and Alex saved her life."

I might have continued to babble, but Annalisa interrupted me. I guessed she wasn't used to listening to people who appeared so bedraggled. "Where is Alex? He said he'd be back by now."

"He should be here in ten minutes."

"Oh." Without saying anything more to me, she walked away, phone to her ear.

I didn't care if she was impolite. I cared that Alex had a car stashed in his barn that might have killed Fannie. I cared that I liked Alex. Did I have the guts to confront him?

Yes, you do.

Leaning up against the door of the clinic, I worked to calm my breathing. Annalisa was halfway down the driveway to the road, speaking on the phone, when Alex came jogging towards her. He stopped, and it appeared they had an intense exchange. She had her back to me, but I saw how her arms flew as she gestured to him. At one point, she turned to look at me, and I read either anger or anguish on her face.

Amid this exchange, Mrs. Wilkens pulled into the driveway. She braked immediately so hard the car screeched. I started down the drive when Alex and Annalisa moved over to let Mrs. Wilkens by. When she parked, I hurried to her.

Through the open driver's side window, I hissed, "He has a car parked in his barn!"

She wrinkled her brow, "What?"

"Car in the barn."

Before I could explain, Alex and Annalisa joined us. Annalisa held out her hand to me and apologized. "I'm sorry I was so rude. I remember meeting you at the party last night."

I took her hand, surprised at how she had changed from suspicious to gracious. I looked down at my dirty clothes. "I'm sure you thought I was a vagrant. Can't wait to get home and into clean clothes." And away from here.

Alex punched the code and let us into the waiting area of the clinic. "Have a seat, and I'll be right with you."

He and Annalisa walked down the driveway again, resuming their animated discussion. Meanwhile, I sat on the plastic chair and motioned for Mrs. Wilkens to also sit. "I found a car," I repeated, nearly choking on the words.

"So, you said. What are you talking about?"

In a whisper, as if the clinic waiting area was bugged, I showed her the photos on my phone and told her about going into the barn and finding a car with a canvas cover. "I think it's the car that killed Fannie."

Mrs. Wilkens's eyes widened. "Well, that's a stinking kettle of fish."

"We have to ask him about it. I can't leave knowing it's there. Maybe he has an explanation."

Alex returned, and through the window I saw Annalisa drive away.

"Do you mind if I run upstairs and take a quick shower. Then I can give Goldie the once over and hopefully send her home with you."

I nodded. "Sure." I was tempted at that point to break into the surgery of the clinic, grab my cat, and run. Mrs. Wilkens, for once, calmed me down.

"When he comes back, we'll ask him. It's that simple. If he can't explain the car, we'll turn it over to Wayne."

"But what if he's a serial killer or something?"

"The doctor who saved the life of your cat? Psychopaths kill cats, not save them."

I didn't find this reassuring.

Twenty minutes later, Alex emerged from the surgery with Goldie. She appeared content in his arms and no worse for the poisoning. He handed her to me along with a small pill bottle. "These are antibiotics for the next five days. One pill a day mixed in with her food, and she should be good to go."

How could he be giving me instructions for my cat when he had a murder weapon in the barn? Mrs. Wilkens nudged me. "Don't you have something to ask Alex?"

Oh shoot.

"Um…while I was waiting for you, I…um wandered around and sort of stepped into the barn?" I sounded like a junior high kid trying to explain why the homework hadn't been done.

Mrs. Wilkens rescued me. "What Liza is trying to ask is why you have that car hidden in the barn? Did you hit Fannie?"

Boy, nothing like going for the throat.

Chapter Twenty-One: The Car

The color drained from Alex's face as he stared at Mrs. Wilkens. She stood with her arms folded like a principal waiting for an explanation.

I hoped he had a good story that had nothing to do with a hit-and-run.

Alex motioned to the plastic chairs. "Please sit down, and I will tell you what I know."

The waiting room felt cold and sterile as I sat next to Mrs. Wilkens, stroking Goldie. She purred, clearly not understanding that we were about to hear the confession of a murderer.

Alex pulled a chair over and sat facing us. "The car…um…it belongs to my mother."

"Lily?" Mrs. Wilkens looked confused. "Your mother drives? In her condition?"

Alex pressed his lips together in a grim line. "We thought we'd hidden the keys."

I wasn't interested in hidden keys and keeping a car from a person with advanced dementia. I glared at him. "Did you hit Fannie with your mother's car?"

Alex's eyes widened. "What? No! Fannie was one of my only friends here."

"What's it doing in your barn?" I felt my cheeks flush either with anger or disappointment or something else.

Alex stared at his hands. "Dad brought it over. He found it parked a mile from home with my mom in it. He thinks she hit a deer, but she didn't remember where she'd been." He took a deep breath. "I asked him when he found it, and he told me a couple of days before Fannie was hit. Mom didn't do it."

Mrs. Wilkens frowned, "Then why are you hiding it?"

Alex rubbed his temples. "I wish I could give you a straight answer. Dad didn't want to report it to insurance because Mom isn't supposed to drive. The only way he could put in a claim is if he first reported it stolen. He didn't want to go down that road. And after what happened to Fannie, he didn't want it around the house and grounds because people might…"

"Jump to conclusions?" I stroked Goldie, who was getting restless.

He nodded. "I don't like having it here, but Dad doesn't want to get it fixed until they've found the car that hit Fannie."

Right, worried about the Santos's reputation.

I took out my phone and showed him the photos. "It looks like dried blood to me. Are you sure it was a deer?"

Before he could answer, a truck with a broken muffler roared up to the clinic. A door slammed, and Maynard, the farmer Alex had introduced me to at the festival, lumbered in.

He tipped his John Deere cap to us. "Morning. Looks like you're having one of those patient care conferences. I could come back."

Alex was quick to reply, "No, we're done here." He pointed to Goldie, "She was one of the poisoned cats, but she's doing fine now."

Maynard looked at me. "You're lucky Alex was the vet. He knows what he's doing."

Like running over librarians?

Turning to Alex, Maynard took out his wallet. "I'm wondering if I could get more of that special feed while I'm in town."

I thought I caught a hint of a wink from him as Alex stood up. It struck me that they were talking in some kind of code—yet another secret in this town?

Goldie stretched on my lap and tried to jump to the floor. The door was partially open. I grabbed her mid-leap. "Ah, no, you don't."

"I'm sorry for all you've gone through here. Goldie is going to be okay." Alex motioned for Maynard to take a seat. "I'll be right with you."

Without further discussion about the car, I settled up with my credit card, and we were on the road ten minutes later with Goldie safely in her carrier.

Mrs. Wilkens spoke in a thoughtful voice, "He didn't have very good answers for our questions, did he?"

I sensed her disappointment. "No, he didn't."

Behind me, I saw in the rearview mirror that a white sheriff's SUV followed. I glanced over my shoulder. "I think we are getting an escort out of town."

Mrs. Wilkens scowled. "Humph."

The sheriff's car turned off when we reached the sign for the city limits. "Farewell, Trey and this shadowed place."

As if to answer, a Santos Brothers truck pulled onto the highway just ahead of me. I glimpsed the side of the truck with the smiling girl and her basket of eggs. A definite contrast from the darkness that emanated from the town.

Once Ravens Valley was behind us, Mrs. Wilkens spoke.

"I think Alex is lying."

Sadly, I had to agree with her. "Something is way off."

We were both lost in our own thoughts until we reached Mankato. Mrs. Wilkens directed us to a little restaurant off a side street near the University. "It's a cat café, so you can bring Goldie inside. But I think you should keep her in her carrier."

I had no intention of letting my cat out—possibly ever.

The restaurant turned out to be a throwback from my mother's sixties era, complete with psychedelic posters on the wall and a menu filled with dishes only an old hippie could love. Sitar music played softly in the background, and the server had a snake tattoo encircling her arm.

Mrs. Wilkens beamed at the menu while I held back a French fry lover's groan. I ordered the daily soup special only because it didn't have kale in it. Over cups of chai, we discussed the past couple of days.

"Here are my questions," I sipped the chai and discovered it wasn't too bad. "First, who hit Fannie, and was it intentional or an accident? All we know at this point is that no one has been found. And second, what about the car in Alex's barn?" I felt a momentary wave of sadness, wondering if Alex was involved.

Mrs. Wilkens frowned. "I hope he's not part of this. I'm also wondering what it was that scared Fannie. Was it threats from the book-banning group or something else."

I remembered Fannie's comment about "it's a wonderful life" and wondered if it had to do with Pottersville.

The server brought the food, including a steaming bowl of soup with black-eyed peas and unknown green things in it. At first, it tasted bland, but quickly the spices came out. "Not bad." However, I wasn't about to ask for the recipe.

Goldie meowed weakly in the carrier next to my chair. I bent down and saw that she was talking in her sleep.

"Well, and someone burned down Fannie's house. Was it dumb vandalism or were they trying to destroy something?" Mrs. Wilkens gazed at me as if I had the answer. "And what about this Pottersville and everything else that's wrong with the town?"

I shrugged. "Really, too many threads on this. Let's go home."

Good idea.

Maybe you could stay in Ravens Valley, solve the mystery, and leave me alone.

Hah! You'd miss me.

Mrs. Wilkens wrinkled her brow. "Really, Liza, you do flake out sometimes."

On the drive back, I reviewed everything I knew about the last couple of days. Fannie was under attack from Pru Santos and the Protect Our Children zealots. Fannie knew something and was afraid, but we didn't know what it was. The name Pottersville came up, but again, we didn't know what it meant. Two people on a motorcycle tried to burn down Fannie's house. On top of that, someone was poisoning cats.

And then there was Alex. Possibly Mrs. Wilkens's grandson, but possibly not. I glanced at her. She snored softly; her head tilted back against the seat. Did I detect a hint of Alex in her profile? A wave of something swept through me as I thought about him with his dark hair and runner's physique.

Sorry, sis, about the vet. But don't jump to conclusions.

"It hardly matters. I doubt I'll be exploring Ravens Valley again. At least I hope I won't."

Except you'd like to see him, wouldn't you?

"You know my history with relationships. He's probably a cat poisoner and serial killer."

Doubtful!

Mrs. Wilkens opened her eyes. "Did you say something?"

"Just thinking out loud."

"We didn't accomplish much on this trip, did we?"

I reached over and patted her on her thigh. "Maybe not, but we certainly raised a lot of questions."

"Yes." Mrs. Wilkens dug in her purse for her phone and busied herself reading emails.

Up ahead on the two-lane highway was a slow-moving combine. I pulled into the next lane to make sure no cars were coming before I passed the combine. It occurred to me how easily a situation like this could result in a head-on crash. Is that what happened to Fannie? Maybe she was in the wrong place at the wrong time. Just a stupid accident, and no one was coming forward to confess. As Charlee would say, doubtful.

As I was musing, Mrs. Wilkens muttered, "We missed something. I know we did."

"Excuse me?"

"I was scrolling through old emails and reread the last one I got from Fannie. Remember, she said, 'It's a wonderful life around here.'"

"And?" I slowed as we approached the little town with the big sign about Guns, God, and Country.

"I think she was referring to Pottersville. I think there's more to that place than a trailer court."

A banged-up pickup truck pulled onto the highway ahead of me, and I had to brake. Thankfully, I didn't hit him.

"Let's table Pottersville and everything else until we get home. I'm guessing the traffic is going to get bad as soon as we hit the suburbs. I need to concentrate."

Something told me I'd be back on this road heading for Ravens Valley again.

Chapter Twenty-Two: Rosie's Revelation

When I let myself into my apartment that evening, the first thing I noticed was that I'd forgotten to take out the garbage before our trip to Ravens Valley. It struck me as an appropriate ending for the trip. Both my apartment and Ravens Valley reeked.

"Phew, I might need to get the place fumigated."

Goldie didn't care. The first thing she did was walk delicately to her kitty litter box. When she was finished, she stood by her empty dish with an accusing expression.

"Listen, cat, I just spent every penny I was saving for school supplies to save you from a cat poisoner. Don't look at me like that."

Of course, that didn't change her attitude at all.

The next day, I stared at a blank page, trying to muster up the energy to write a college-level paper on the attitudes that lead to book banning. I hadn't gotten much insight into Ravens Valley other than a sense of fear among those who were opposed to what was happening in the library. I should have asked Pru when I met her, but I knew I wouldn't have been an objective interviewer.

I searched the internet and found quotes from parents worried that books on race, gender, and sexuality might sway their children. I thought about my fifth graders, so eager and curious. If they didn't get information from books, where would they get it—or not get it?

I was pondering this when Mrs. Wilkens let herself in. She looked rested and had that gleam in her eyes that said I was about to get into something I didn't want to get into.

"I found out a few things this morning."

"Oh?"

Listen to her.

She's about to ruin my day.

You've already ruined your day by not getting this paper written.

I wanted to slap my head to make Charlee go away, but it didn't seem like a good idea with someone watching me.

Mrs. Wilkens pointed to her phone. "Rosie told me that Dora knows something about Fannie, and it's big."

I blinked in confusion. "Who is Rosie?"

"You remember. Rosie, the aide from the assisted living place. She was with Fannie's mother at the funeral. Really nice person with a long braid."

"If you recall, I was with Jules and Rochelle after the funeral. I didn't meet Rosie."

Mrs. Wilkens ignored my remark. "She told me that Fannie was afraid of something."

"We already know that."

Again, she ignored me. "I called Rosie this morning. Her mother used to volunteer at the library. The nicest woman, except she had terrible breath. I had to keep her in the stacks away from the other patrons. I found out later that she had terrible gum disease."

I motioned to Mrs. Wilkens to sit down before I had to hear the whole dental history of Rosie's mother. "What did you find out?"

"Well, first of all, they arrested someone for the hit-and-run. She said he was a Guatemalan refugee applying for asylum."

A wave of relief coursed through me. Alex wasn't a murderer—even if I never saw him again, at least I knew that.

"That will certainly feed into the anti-immigration people."

"But there's more. Rosie said they didn't find the car. They picked him up after someone called in an anonymous tip."

"Sounds kind of shaky."

"Worse, they're also accusing him of arson, burning down Fannie's house, too."

"Wait a minute? A man trying to get asylum hits and kills Fannie and then burns her house down? Does that make sense? Why would he do that?"

Goldie jumped onto Mrs. Wilkens's lap and settled in. "No, it doesn't make sense. I think it's a set-up and we should go back and figure it out."

See Charlee? Now she wants to go back!

Listen to her!

Although seeing Alex again had some appeal, I wasn't willing to return to Ravens Valley and be followed by Trey the Stupid. I held up my hand. "Wait. Let's think about this. What would we find out that the sheriff doesn't already know?"

Mrs. Wilkens pressed her lips together in a stubborn expression. "Rosie didn't exactly say it, but she implied that Sheriff Wayne isn't—well, isn't totally engaged in investigating."

None of this added up. "Why do they suspect this guy burned down Fannie's house?"

"She said the tipster told them he was angry with the United States for how he was treated at the border."

I rubbed my temples. "Still doesn't add up. In fact, it sounds to me like the anonymous tipster was framing the Guatemalan man. But if somebody had a grudge against border agents, why would he target a librarian?"

Goldie purred so loudly she sounded like she was revving a jet engine. Mrs. Wilkens stroked her for a few moments before speaking again. "Good questions. When we go back, we can ask them, except we need to wait until next week because I've got a big rally this weekend."

"And I have a paper due."

She set Goldie down. "Good. That's settled. We'll go back next week."

At least I had a short reprieve. "I still wonder what Fannie was afraid of. It had to be more than Pru threatening her job. Don't you think?"

"Rosie did mention one more thing. When they told Fannie's mother, Dora, about the house, she said, 'Fannie told me they would be looking for it.'"

"Any idea what 'it' was?"

"Rosie didn't know, but she said yesterday on her day off, someone visited

Dora in the nursing home. After they left, she was so upset they had to sedate her."

"Did Rosie know who came?"

"She thought it was that smarmy minister who has Pru wrapped around his clerical collar."

I couldn't picture wrapping anyone around a clerical collar. I let it go. "Does this go back to 'Protect Our Children'?"

Mrs. Wilkens's phone rang before she could answer me. "Oh, it's my co-chair of the Garden Tools event. I'd better see to it."

With that, she swept out, and I sat wondering what, if anything, to do next. I needed Charlee to guide me, but as usual, she'd disappeared. I looked at Goldie. "What do you think? Should I let this go?"

Goldie stared at me as if to say, "Coward," and walked slowly to the kitchen to carry on a vigil by her empty cat dish.

After Mrs. Wilkens left, I made progress on the paper. The people who wanted to ban the books were not only afraid of their children being swayed and led astray but also afraid the books might incite questions they couldn't answer. I thought about Jules and Rochelle, who were probably trying to sort out their own sexuality and feelings, and how important the books were to help them feel normal. They were seeking normalcy from the books because they couldn't get it from their parents, their peers, or their church.

After staring at the computer for another thirty minutes, my head was spinning. It was time to make a trip to see Ed, my retired janitor friend. He used to be our elementary school janitor. I discovered he had a learning disability and struggled with reading. I also discovered that he was a bit of a savant. Ed is one of the few people in this world who knows about Charlee. Moreover, he likes her.

See. Someone believes in me.

Go back to bed or wherever it is you go!

I tugged on my bicycle shorts, ready to retort if Charlee showed up. She must have listened to me because she stayed quiet. I rode my bicycle to Ed's little Craftsman-style house about two miles from my apartment in South Minneapolis. He met me at the gate to his yard.

"Thought you might be coming."

I'd long ago given up asking him how he knew these things. He was a stocky little man with close-cut white hair, glasses, and hearing aids. When he retired, I'd helped him get through the maze of Social Security and Medicare. We walked around his house to the backyard, where he'd already set out lawn chairs and a plate of Oreos.

During our visit, we'd usually chat for a short while and then get down to business, reading books about baseball. Last summer, we'd finished W.P. Kinsella's *The Iowa Baseball Confederacy*. This year, we were reading Chad Harbach's *The Art of Fielding*.

As soon as we settled on the plastic lawn chairs, he peered at me. "You been up to something. I can tell."

Ed could read me.

"I've been to a funeral in a town that has a group who want to ban books from the library. And a town that owes its current existence to organic chickens."

"Hmmm." He took another cookie as I told him about Fannie and Ravens Valley and Protect Our Children.

He pondered what I'd said for a few moments while he finished eating his Oreo. "I think you need to go back. Those people aren't getting justice for that librarian."

With that, he opened his book and slowly read the next ten pages of *The Art of Fielding*. We always stopped after ten pages. He looked at his watch. "Twins have a late afternoon game. Got to listen on the radio. They're trying out that new catcher." He quoted me statistics on the new player and a history of his successes in the minor leagues. It was time for me to go.

A crow landed on the roof of his house and cawed at him. It reminded me of being in the park at Ravens Valley. I looked up at it and had a sinking feeling that my story with that town wasn't over.

As if to make it worse, as I unlocked my bicycle, Ed commented, "Maybe them chickens aren't organic."

"Excuse me?"

"You get justice for that librarian." He turned and walked to his front door.

What did he mean, the chickens weren't organic? The crow cawed again and flew away.

132

Chapter Twenty-Three: The Fire

All the way home, I pondered Ed's words. The town of Ravens Valley was dependent on Santos Brothers and their organic chicken brand. What if Fannie uncovered something about the chickens? What if she discovered they weren't organic at all? I could see the danger in being a whistleblower.

It's an interesting thought, sis.

Charlee's voice in my head startled me, and I nearly ran into a parked car. "See what you almost made me do!"

Tut. I thought you could think and ride at the same time.

"What if Ed's right?"

You have to go back to Ravens Valley.

A car honked at me when I rode through an intersection without paying attention to the light. "Go away, Charlee, before I kill myself!"

She must have heard me because my head was silent the rest of the way home.

The first thing I did after feeding Goldie and watching her walk to the bedroom to settle down with my old slipper was Google organic chickens. For the next hour, I was transported into the world of licensing and regulation. You couldn't simply declare your chickens were organic. They had to be certified. I tried to read through the information on certification and eventually closed the lid on the laptop. The complexity included assuring that the chickens received certified organic feed and were raised without antibiotics or other chemicals.

I could understand why these chickens were more expensive. They were raised in a more humane environment that involved giving them more space to be considered cage-free.

Who knew? I thought back to the party at the Santos estate and the education building. Perhaps I could set up a meeting with Annalisa to talk about how they raise their chickens.

My phone rang while I was musing about chickens. I didn't recognize the caller ID, but noted the number was the southern Minnesota area code.

"Hello?"

The female voice on the other line was muffled. "It's on fire, and we can't get out!"

In the background, I heard crackling noises followed by coughing. "Can you speak up? I can hardly hear you."

"Please help!"

I recognized the voice. "Jules? Is that you?"

"The library. It's on fire! I tried calling my mom, and she didn't believe me. Rochelle is with me. Please help!"

I strained to hear her. "The library is on fire?"

More coughing and gasping. "Can't get out."

I pictured the building with all its books. "My God. Are you inside?"

"Can't get out and can't breathe."

I went into fifth-grade teacher emergency mode. We had annual fire training, and one of the things they emphasized was to stay low to avoid as much smoke as possible. "Okay, I'm going to help you. Stay on the line and get down on the floor and keep as low as possible."

Jules coughed. "Trying to."

"Good, now try to remember where the exit door is. Can you do that?"

For a millisecond, I wondered if I was being pranked, but the intuitive part of my brain told me the girls were in big trouble. "Jules, look for the exit sign. I'm going to call 911."

She sobbed, "Tried 911. Hung up on me."

"That's okay. I'll call them from here. You stay low and get to the exit." I put her on hold and called 911. A Minneapolis operator answered, and I told her the fire was at the Ravens Valley library and could she get us through to their emergency services. When the call was transferred, I worked to stay calm. "I just got a call from a friend who's in the Ravens Valley library. She says she's trapped and the building is on fire."

For a moment, I wondered if the operator thought this was a prank call. I nearly shouted this time. "Someone is trapped in the library. You need to get there!"

"Sending a firetruck. Please stay on the line." The call cut out.

Quickly, I switched back to Jules. "Are you still there?"

"Help, can't breathe."

"It's okay. The firetrucks are on their way. Can you see an exit sign?"

A voice in the background mumbled something.

"I think I see it."

"Stay low and crawl toward it. Now." Above the roar of the fire, I heard a faint siren. "They're coming. Try to get to the exit."

"Can't breathe. Can't find Rochelle."

I pictured them in the smoke-filled building with the flames eating up the library books. I'd once been in a situation like that, and I still had nightmares about it. I kept coaching. "Go to the exit, Jules!" I felt so helpless trying to guide her from a distance, having no idea where she was in the building. Was I sending her toward more danger?

Stay calm for her. You are doing your best.

I took a deep breath. "Jules, are you there?"

No answer.

On the line, I heard a crashing sound like something had fallen. I imagined a bookshelf tipping over, trapping the girls. It was followed by a muffled cry.

The sirens were close, and at last I heard shouts in the background.

"Jules, help is here. Yell out and tell them where you are."

A hoarse voice just above a whisper. "Here. We're here."

I raised my voice. "Jules, can you shout? Shout like you are angry. Someone set the library on fire. Shout!"

She raised her voice, "Help!"

The line went dead. I stared at my phone, feeling sick. Goldie wrapped her body around my ankles as if to give me comfort. I tried calling the number back, but got a "call failed" message.

"What do I do?" I'd been in a few emergencies with students, but nothing like this.

Call Alex.

Good idea.

When I called, it rang almost eight times before he answered. "Liza?"

The words tumbled out, "The library. Two girls are trapped. Can you check it?"

"What?"

I took a deep, calming breath, "I just got a call from one of the high school girls I met at the funeral. She said she was trapped in the library, and it was on fire."

"What? I'm in the surgery, let me step outside."

While I waited, I again had that sinking feeling that maybe I'd been pranked.

Alex came back on the line. "I hear sirens."

"Can you find out if everything is all right?"

He muttered something I couldn't quite make out before he replied. "I'm on my way. I'll call you when I know something."

I paced the living room with the phone in my hand, waiting for him to call back. Goldie sat on the couch watching me. When he hadn't called after fifteen minutes, I decided it was time for a gin and tonic.

An hour later, while I sipped the drink, staring at the phone, it rang. "Thank God he's calling back." Except the caller ID said Ruston County Sheriff's office. I took a large swallow of the drink, noting that I'd put way too little gin in it. If it was Trey, I'd hang up.

"Is this Liza Johnson?"

I recognized Sheriff Wayne's voice. "Yes?"

He paused, "Ah, we understand the girls called you."

Was he going to tell me it was all a hoax, and I was in trouble for calling 911? I answered carefully, "Yes, they did. Are they alright?"

"Um...they're being treated at the hospital."

"And the library?"

"Severely damaged."

Fannie dead, and the library burned down. None of this would end up on the Ravens Valley webpage.

Sheriff Wayne continued. "I'm wondering why they called you. Are you in town?"

Let's see. I'd been in town for two days, and Fannie's house had gone up in flames. Now the library. I guess I could be considered a suspect.

"Sheriff, I'm at home in Minneapolis. I don't know why they called me, except Jules said she tried her mother, who hung up on her, and 911 hung up on her. I'm guessing she called at random, hoping to find help."

"We've had some...ah...glitches with the 911 system."

I wondered why the library didn't have a fire alarm system, but decided this wasn't the time to ask.

"I'm sorry I couldn't have been closer to help them."

"Ah, yes. Well, I might have more questions later. Have a nice day." He ended the call.

I stared at the phone. "Have a nice day?"

Two minutes later, Alex called. "Liza, sorry it took so long. It was a mess—even worse because of all the people from the festival. Yes, the library burned, and there were two students inside working after hours. The assistant librarian, Jessica, was there but stepped out to get something to eat. That's when the fire started."

I took it all in. The mother and the 911 system failing them. The only adult in the building leaving. The two girls left inside. "Alex, your town is cursed."

The line was silent for a moment. When he spoke, he sounded tentative. "I know this is a lot to ask, but would you be willing to come this weekend? I need to talk with you."

This was not a heart going pitter-pat moment, but I did feel a little flush in my cheeks. "Let me think about it."

We left it that I'd let him know this evening.

Chapter Twenty-Four: What Alex Knows

I was about to mix a second gin and tonic when Mrs. Wilkens walked in. She exuded energy pacing between the kitchen and the living room. "It's going to be quite an affair. We've already got fifty people signed up to bring their guns in. Imagine getting fifty guns off the street!"

I didn't tell her that fifty guns was just a drop in the bucket compared to the arsenals that were out there. At least she was trying to do something positive about gun safety. Better than the second amendment dopes who wanted to arm the teachers and turn schools into fortresses.

She pointed at the glass I held in my hand, "Is that a gin and tonic?"

"Want one?"

"You sit. I'll fix another for you." A testament to our friendship, she knew where I kept all the ingredients. She also knew that I was too stingy with the gin.

Once she was back with the drinks, she studied my face. "Something is wrong, isn't it?"

"Ravens Valley and everything about it is wrong." I told her about the girls, and the library, and Alex's call. "I need to decide whether to drive there tomorrow. Alex wants to see me, but I have mixed feelings."

Unmix those feelings, sis. You need to see this through.

Easy for you to say. You're just a voice in my head. You don't have to do the driving.

Mrs. Wilkens stared at me for a moment while I was having this argument with my non-existent twin. She set her drink on the coffee table. "Nonsense. Of course, you should go. I'll make sure Goldie is fed." Goldie took the opportunity to gaze up at her with adoring eyes.

I took a big swallow of the drink. "Goldie will probably be grateful to have quality time with you."

"We all know Goldie adores you."

"More like ignores me."

I told her what I knew about the library fire. "I'm sure the fire was arson. Someone was watching, and when Jessica left, they assumed the library was empty."

Mrs. Wilkens gazed at her drink with a puzzled expression. "I've seen a lot in my years, but I thought we'd gotten beyond the days of censorship. Who would want to burn down the library?"

"Good question. If you know that, we might find out who hit Fannie with their car." I shivered thinking about Alex and the car stashed in his barn.

My phone pinged with a text from Alex. **Can you come?**

Of course you can.

Don't push me!

"What?" Mrs. Wilkens looked at me.

Instead of telling her I was being annoyed by Charlee, I told her about Sheriff Wayne. "The sheriff called me. He wondered where I was when Jules called. When I told him I was home in Minneapolis, he seemed confused. I wondered if he thought I'd started the fire."

"Well, that's a load of dirty laundry."

"You know what he said at the end of the call? 'Have a nice day.' The library burns down, the librarian has been killed, and her house set on fire, and the best he can do is 'Have a nice day?'"

Mrs. Wilkens stirred her drink. "I didn't know Wayne other than how much he loved to read. His father was the sheriff when I lived there. A big blowhard. Of course, we didn't have much crime other than break-ins and vandalism. Never understood why the boy followed in his father's footsteps."

I thought about it for a moment. "Maybe he's scared now. I wonder how much control he has over his deputy."

With that comment, we must have both silently agreed to change the subject.

Mrs. Wilkens told me about the Guns to Garden Tools project while I let the gin go to my head. In the brief alcohol euphoria that comes after the first gin and tonic, I imagined what it would be like to kiss Alex. Would it be a soft, gentle kiss or a hard, passionate one?

"Liza?" Mrs. Wilkens pulled me out of my reverie.

I blinked the thoughts away, "I guess I'll drive to Ravens Valley. Do you think Lorrie would put me up for another night?"

Mrs. Wilkens took out her phone and called him. He answered right away. They talked for a bit about the library while I strained to figure out what he was saying. Mrs. Wilkens side of the conversation had a lot of "Oh nos," and "Oh mys," in it. I drifted off to the kitchen to mix another gin and tonic. She found me staring at an empty bottle of gin.

"Oh yes, I forgot to tell you, you're out."

"Probably just as well. I don't need a hangover pounding my head if I'm driving to Ravens Valley tomorrow." I put the bottle in the bin for glass recycling. "What did Lorrie say?"

"You can stay with him anytime. He said to make yourself comfortable. The door is always open, and Henry loves the company." I couldn't imagine not locking up—especially in Ravens Valley, where things seemed to burn down easily.

"Anything else?"

"The talk in town is that some of the kids from Pottersville who were at the festival started the fire."

I sighed. Blame it on the outsiders. "Why?"

"According to Lorrie, that's what Trey said. He thought it was a conspiracy to let the drug cartels in."

"Well, at least he didn't claim I did it magically from my apartment in Minneapolis."

Did I really want to go back to that place?

I texted Alex back. **Coming. Be there late morning.**

***

Saturday dawned bright and sunny. A sprinkling of rain in the night left a sheen of dew on the grass. I stood in the parking lot of my apartment building, taking in the freshness of the day. Perhaps this was a sign. Perhaps Alex would have a more reasonable explanation for the car in his barn. Perhaps the fire in the library and Fannie's house were unrelated. Perhaps Fannie's death was an accident. Perhaps pigs really could fly.

A crow perched on a wire connected to the apartment building and cawed. It was soon joined by three other crows, making a cacophony of sound as a hawk landed in the large pine tree next door. I tried not to take this as an omen.

I drove away from the comfort of my little apartment filled with both excitement and dread. Charlee stayed away. The drive through southern Minnesota was uneventful and peaceful on this cloudless day. When I reached Ravens Valley, the traffic picked up as people gathered for the Chicken Wing Festival parade. Since I wasn't meeting Alex until noon, I found a parking place and walked to the parade route. Sure enough, they had a float for the Chicken Wing Festival Queen. Fortunately, she wore an off-the-shoulder pink formal and not a chicken costume. On the float were three little girls also in formals, holding baskets with candy. When they passed by, they tossed brightly wrapped candy. Next to me, two little boys with Hispanic features gathered candy.

Almost immediately, a couple of older boys, including Jasper, the minister's son, swooped in and grabbed the candy away from the little ones. The little boys' eyes grew big as the older boys shoved them away from the candy on the ground.

It didn't appear that anyone in the crowd near me was paying attention, or if they were, they'd decided to stay out of it. I stepped forward and spoke in a loud, firm teacher's voice. "The candy belongs to them. Please hand it back."

A woman, who was probably the mother of the little boys, scrambled out of the crowd. "No trouble. No trouble."

For a moment, Jasper stared at me with an expression that was both defiant and embarrassed before he dropped the candy onto the street. "Didn't want it anyway after they touched it."

I grabbed his arm when he used a derogatory term I would never allow in my classroom. "You need to apologize." I tugged him closer while his friends took off into the crowd.

An older man with white hair wearing a clerical collar found his way through the crowd. "Jasper? What have you been up to?"

The boy stared at his shoes for a few moments before looking at the older minister. "My dad said they fired you! He said you were a bad influence."

I stared at the two of them. What was this all about?

The old minister shook his head with a sad expression. "Apologize and leave the little kids alone. I'm sure you don't want me to talk with your dad."

Jasper's cheeks blazed pink. He muttered, "Sorry."

As he left, he said a few words under his breath that disparaged anyone whose color wasn't white. He then took off so fast that I hardly saw him leave.

The minister studied me for a moment as he stretched out his hand in greeting. "I've heard about you—asking questions around town. So glad to meet you. I'm Walter Christianson, former minister of the church on the hill."

"Nice to meet you. Sounds like you've had other dealings with young Jasper."

He smiled, and his white hair gleamed in the sunshine. "Let's just say 'like father, like son.'"

I wasn't sure how to respond when a woman walked up to him and said, "Reverend, we sure do miss you." I took it as a cue to move on.

I left the parade as the high school band marched by playing a somewhat discordant version of "Seventy-Six Trombones." Walking away, I wondered if Reverend Myron Vogel, the co-chair of Protect Our Children, only wanted to protect nice white middle-class children.

The parking area in front of the veterinarian clinic was empty, and the clinic door locked. I rang the bell several times before texting Alex. After he didn't respond to the texts, I called him. It went directly to voicemail.

"Where are you?"

In the distance, soft sounds from the carnival and the marching band created a backdrop for the peacefulness of the clinic and the old house. I was tempted to go back to the barn to look at the car, but my feet wouldn't take me there. I didn't want to believe that Alex was involved in Fannie's death.

"Liza, are you kidding yourself because you're attracted to him?" I waited for Charlee to reply, but she stayed hidden somewhere in my brain.

Even though it was still summer, I noted a hint of fall. Maybe it was the humidity that always crept up on me at State Fair time as the end of summer approached. Usually, I felt the change with excitement because it meant the new school year was coming. Right then, though, I had a lingering sense of dread. Was it this town, or was it my life and my lack of male companionship? I remembered what Charlee had said, *You scare them away.*

As if to answer, Alex's van pulled up the driveway. He stepped out with his hair a little askew and a grim expression. Maybe I did scare them away.

"Hey." He walked to me, holding a cardboard carrier with coffee cups. "Sorry to be late. Had a bit of drama at the parade."

Had Jasper told his dad about the mean woman who took his candy away?

He pointed to the old house. "Let's sit in the back and talk. I need the coffee and fresh air."

We sat on plastic lawn chairs looking out over the pasture below. The coffee was hot and strong—just what I needed right now.

"Tell me about the drama."

Alex scratched his head before pushing a lock of hair away from his forehead. Boy, did he have a beautiful head of hair. No thinning, no male pattern baldness. I nearly pinched myself to send away the thoughts that were going through my head.

"It's Mother. Every year, Heck, Vince, Pru, and Mother ride in the parade. Heck has a vintage Ford pickup, and they sit on hay bales in the bed of the truck. It was Annalisa's idea to give the message that the Santos Brothers were like anyone else in the community."

"Except, they're rich. Right?"

Alex took a piece of the caramel roll and lobbed it out for a squirrel in the weedy yard. The squirrel ignored it. "Yup."

"What happened this morning?"

"Mom wouldn't get out of the car. They called me because I can sometimes talk her into things." He turned to me, and the distress was obvious in the downturn of his lips. "Today, more than ever, she reminded me of my grandmother just before Grandpa had to put her in a nursing home. Those eyes, so bright and so confused."

I wanted to reach over and touch him, but I held back. "I'm sorry."

"It's worse, though. As I was trying to coax her out of the car, she whispered to me, 'Peter, I'm sorry, I didn't mean for it to happen.'"

"That's odd."

"Ever since your friend Ginny Wilkens talked with her, she's been fixated on Peter. I know he was her boyfriend."

We were interrupted when a car roared up the driveway with its horn honking. Someone shouted, "Alex, dammit! Where are you and why aren't you answering your phone?"

Stick to him like glue, sis.

I hurried around the house with Alex to find Annalisa standing by the car with her arms akimbo and her eyes slits. "Mom has gone bonkers. You need to do something."

Much as you irritate me, Charlee, I think you're right. Where do I get the Superglue?

Chapter Twenty-Five: Lily Santos

Annalisa looked at me like I was an insect buzzing around her head as I hurried to keep up with Alex. She called out in an irritated tone, "Come to the house, Alex. Maybe you can settle her down."

Alex said a few words under his breath that I was glad I didn't catch. I stopped while he dug through his pocket for the van fob. What should I do?

Go with him!

He didn't invite me.

Since when did that stop you?

I slipped into the passenger side of the van without asking permission. He glanced at me before following his sister. His jaw tensed, "I think Heck lied to me about the car, and I apologize for passing what he said on to you."

At least he wasn't planning to throw me out of the van, "That's what you wanted to talk with me about?"

He stared straight ahead. "Some other things have come up as well. Let's see if we can get Mom straightened out, and I'll tell you what I'm thinking." A car pulled out in front of him. He slammed on the brakes. "Sometimes I hate this damn place! And sometimes I think I'll never leave it."

The Santos estate was quiet. The tents and canopies had been taken down, and the lawn was country club green and carefully groomed.

Annalisa parked her Lexus in front of the Heck Santos house and stood by the doorway talking on her phone. Alex brushed by her, worry lines etched around his mouth. I followed, pretending I had a part in this play. Annalisa gave me what one of my mother's friends used to call the stink eye, but kept the phone glued to her ear.

I wasn't warming up to Alex's half-sister.

While the outside of the Heck Santos house appeared modest, the inside radiated a subdued luxury. The floor was tiled in an intricate mosaic pattern, and the walls were painted in creamy pastels. The house had a peacefulness to it that spoke of artistry in the décor. I wondered how much Lily had contributed to the ambiance.

While the outward appearance of the house was a typical three-bedroom ranch, it had an addition in the back that included a sunroom overlooking a pond in the backyard. In the sunroom, Lily paced back and forth, mumbling to herself and waving her arms. She reminded me of the unhoused man near my apartment who used to wander up and down Lake Street, always talking, always moving.

"Mom." Alex approached her.

She noticed him and immediately stopped pacing. "Peter. You've come."

I stood in the doorway watching mother and son, not sure where I should plant myself.

She took his hand, "I'm so glad you're here. I have things to tell you."

"Mom, it's me, Alex."

She continued to look at him as if he hadn't spoken. "I've kept your secret all these years. I'm so sorry."

Annalisa stood beside me and whispered. "If your old lady friend hadn't shown up, she'd be okay. I don't know why Mom got so crazy about her." I felt like she was accusing me of a great sin.

I turned to her, gearing up to retort.

Show some empathy, sis.

I wanted to bark back at the voice in my head. Looking at Annalisa, though, I saw the pain on her face. "I'm sorry you are going through this."

She appeared startled, and her tone softened. "I could never smooth things with her like Alex. I guess because he was the first-born. Sometimes she hardly remembers me."

I didn't know what to say, so I kept quiet while Alex guided his mother to a white wicker chair. "Mother, the doctor wants you to take your pills and rest. It's been a long day."

She sat down. "Oh, yes. You're Alex. But you look just like him. Tell him I'm sorry. He should have known."

I leaned toward Annalisa, "Do you know what she's talking about?"

She took a deep breath and let it out. "She rambles sometimes. I think the disease chips away at her brain, and she goes deeper into her past."

Alex squatted down in front of her, holding both her hands. She gazed at him with a tender smile. The moment was broken when an aide in white pants and a flowered top came in from a side door. "Mrs. Santos, I have your pills now."

She glared at the aide. "Are you trying to poison me?"

Annalisa tensed, "Here we go again."

Alex took the glass of water and the pills and handed them to Lily. "Here, Mom. It's best if you take these." He hesitated, "Peter would want you to rest."

Lily took the pills and waved him away. "You can go now. I have work to do." She pointed to the easel and paints set up in the corner of the room. "The light is just right."

Alex guided me with a light touch as we walked down the tiled hallway to the front. Behind us, Annalisa was back on the phone.

Once outside, he took a deep breath and let it out slowly, "Let's get something to eat away from town and chicken wings."

The August heat was refreshing after the brittle coolness of the house.

Alex drove west on the highway until we came to a small town no bigger than two blocks long. "They might not have anything else here in Nelsburg, but the diner has decent food. It's run by a Vietnamese family. They do the standard burgers and also great Pho."

"Pho and fries?"

For the first time since we'd left the Santos estate, he smiled.

The restaurant was nearly empty. We took a booth by the window. Alex was right about the menu. I ordered the Pho, and Alex ordered a Banh Mi sandwich. As if to ward off the discussion we needed to have, he told me about the Vietnamese migration to Southern Minnesota.

"Believe it or not, it was because of Little House on the Prairie."

"Really?"

"I guess one of the families loved the show and decided they wanted to live in Walnut Grove. Others followed. At first, it was a culture shock for everyone, but things have settled down."

The server brought us coffee. Sadly, it was Minnesota coffee—watery and in need of lots of cream and sugar.

You need to tell him.

I wanted to whine a little and tell her it wasn't my place to share Mrs. Wilkens's conjectures.

Coward.

But Charlee was right. The fact that Lily was getting Alex and someone named Peter mixed up was a huge clue. I stirred a packet of sugar into the coffee. "Alex, I need to tell you something."

He leaned on his elbows. "And I need to tell you something."

If this had been a romance, maybe we would be reaching the point of "I have this thing for you." However, I hardly knew the man, even if he did have nice legs and a nice way with cats.

"Let me go first, Alex. I overheard your mother calling you Peter."

He raised his eyebrows, "She's done that off and on for years."

Quit dancing around.

"Can't you leave?"

Alex's mouth dropped open. "What?"

I shook my head. "Sorry, sometimes things slip out that don't mean anything."

"And what did you want to say?"

"I'm going to be straight with you, and if I need to hitchhike back to my car—so be it."

He didn't react.

"Mrs. Wilkens, my friend? I think she's your grandmother."

If I expected either a "you're kidding or get your thumb out," it didn't happen. Instead, he nodded with a thoughtful expression. "As soon as I saw her, I had an odd feeling. In fact, I've wondered for years, particularly lately, with Mom's dementia. She's more apt to call me Peter than Alex."

"Did you ever ask her?"

"Oh yes. When I was about ten, I asked about my 'real' dad. She cut me off so fast we never talked about it again."

The server brought a basket of fries that were hot and crisp. I grabbed one, savoring the fact that Mrs. Wilkens wasn't here to "tut, tut," me about poor eating habits. "Mrs. Wilkens didn't know about you. If you'd seen the look on her face when we brought Goldie to the clinic…" I let the words fade.

Alex stared at the fries but didn't take any. "My birth certificate has Heck as my father. I long ago decided to leave it at that. Why stir things up?"

With all the DNA testing, maybe Alex's lineage would find its way out eventually. I felt the same way about leaving things the way they were. My father drowned when I was four, shortly after Charlee died, and that's all I wanted to know about the Johnson side of the family.

Alex continued, "Then, yesterday, Lorrie came by the clinic. He brought the yearbook from when he was in high school and showed me the photo of Peter Wilkens."

I took a deep breath. "Mrs. Wilkens showed me an old photo of her son and compared it to the one you have on the wall of the clinic. It's telling."

He stared at the coffee cup in front of him. "It wasn't hard to do the math. Mom must have been pregnant when she went off to college. She never talked about her first husband—my supposed dad. And after that one time with her, I didn't ask. Besides, Heck has been my dad since I can remember."

The food arrived, and the Pho was better than the little Vietnamese take-out place down the street from my apartment. Pho and fries, great combination.

"Uh, can I tell Mrs. Wilkens that you know?"

Alex put his hand up. "What do the kids say now? TMI. I'm still digesting it as a possibility. It could be that it's a fluke that I look like Peter Wilkens."

We ate in silence. I was preoccupied with how to keep my mouth shut around Mrs. Wilkens and imagining her questioning me when I got back to Minneapolis.

It will work out, sis.

Easy for you to say.

I was so busy talking to myself that I almost didn't hear what Alex said next.

"…something not right about the car in my barn."

"Excuse me?" I blushed. I didn't want to explain that I'd been distracted by the voice of my dead twin.

"Heck said he found the car two days before Fannie was killed."

I nodded.

"But I looked at my calendar. Sometimes I drive Mom to her doctor's appointments in Mankato. I use her car because all I have is the van and a motorcycle. I drove her car to Mankato that day."

I felt something drop in my stomach. "He lied?"

Alex rubbed his forehead. "The day after Fannie was killed, Annalisa called me. She said Mom had wandered the day before and they found her car keys in her pocket."

"Are you telling me you think your mother might have hit Fannie?"

Alex looked away and said nothing.

Before we could continue, we were interrupted by Alex's phone. He looked at the caller ID and excused himself. I watched through the diner window as he talked, his head down, kicking a piece of gravel. I drank my over-sugared coffee, feeling like I'd just been blasted with a lot of pieces of information and not much of a picture of what was happening.

Alex, the probable grandson of Mrs. Wilkens. Lily, the driver of a hit-and-run car. And the arson at the library. Time to bid farewell to Ravens Valley, go home, write my paper, and prepare for another year of fifth graders.

You know you can't leave yet.

Oh, go away! Please?

Alex returned, slipping his phone back in his pocket. "Sorry. A problem with a newborn calf. I share on-call with a vet over by Worthington. He's out of town, and I need to take care of this."

I was afraid for a moment that he was going to tell me I'd have to go with him. One thing I am not is a farm person. I don't even like to go to the State Fair to see the animals. I tend to stay near the midway where it smells like deep-fried cheese curds and not manure.

"Can I drop you back at your car?"

"Yes. I'm going to check up on Jules and Rochelle."

Alex frowned. "How bad are things when someone decides to burn down the library—with people inside?"

I wanted to say, "It's your town. Fix it." But I knew Alex had enough to deal with.

Chapter Twenty-Six: Library Arson

Alex gave me directions to the Ravens Valley Hospital. It was a new one-story building with a parking lot on one side and a cornfield on the other. Large pots of flowers welcomed visitors to the lobby.

Inside, when I asked for Jules' room, the receptionist asked who I was. I told her my name, thinking she'd call back to make sure I could go in. Instead, she grinned at me. "I know who you are. You saved those two girls. It's all over town!"

I felt like shoving my hands in my pockets and saying, "Aw shucks." I refrained and smiled back at her. "Glad everyone was okay."

Don't get a big head, sis.

Never.

Hah!

When I walked into Jules' room, she was sitting up in bed sipping on a milkshake. Her face lit up. "Liza! You came!"

An overweight woman sat on a chair next to the bed. She had a rounded face, but I saw the similarity with Jules.

"Mom, this is Liza, the person who called 911 for me."

She hoisted herself up and extended her hand. "Lorraine." Looking down at her shoes, she added, "I'm sorry I didn't listen to Jules. I should have."

I had no response to her except, "Nice to meet you."

Jules set down her milkshake. "I hear that scumbag 911 operator is going to get fired for hanging up on me. They say that 911 had gotten so many 'swatting' calls about the library that he figured mine was fake."

I thought about the girls stuck in the burning building and shook my head.

"I'm so sorry for what you had to go through."

Jules sat up a little straighter. "Well, this town should be sorry for all the stupid things they've been saying about the library and books! Like that Reverend Vogel and Pru Santos!"

Jules's mother visibly winced at her words. "Now, honey, you shouldn't be saying those things."

Yes. She should.

I couldn't argue with Charlee on that one.

"Do they know who set the fire?"

Jules folded her arms. "I doubt they'll even look. I think whoever did it saw Jessica leave and decided it would be a good time to burn the place down! Maybe Vogel did it himself to save us from evil."

"Now, Jules," her mother nearly squeaked. "We should be quiet."

Ask her why.

Charlee had a good point. "Why should you be quiet?" I peered at her.

She appeared startled by the question.

"Tell her, Mom." Jules raised her voice. "Tell her why everyone is afraid."

Lorraine cleared her throat and looked at the doorway as if someone might be listening. "Ah, well. It started a couple of years ago. Santos Brothers was smaller then. My husband worked for them—doing the books and handling business. Then…" She hesitated.

"Then what?"

"I guess things changed when Annalisa came back after getting her MBA. She thought they needed to hire a business manager and…"

Jules broke in, "and they fired my dad. Just like that. Said they were laying off people, except he was the only one they laid off."

I was puzzled. What did this have to do with book banning?

"Well, they brought in this new manager—Elvis Gates. It seemed like Vogel came with him."

"You mean the management of Santos Brothers changed at the same time the church got a new minister?"

Lorraine bit her lip. "Sort of. The church was dying, and Pru Santos was the one who convinced them to bring him in. He'd had a church down in Texas, and she thought he could help save the one here. I heard Elvis recommended him because he knew him from Texas."

Jules coughed a deep, painful hack before grabbing the inhaler by her bed and taking a puff. "But, when he came and started talking about the evil books, a couple of us did a Google search on him. He was kicked out of his last church, although we couldn't find out why."

I was having a hard time following. "Okay, so Santos Brothers brought in a new manager, and the minister came around that time. I still don't understand why people are afraid."

Lorraine picked at her blouse but didn't say anything.

Jules rolled her eyes at her mother. "Oh, Mom, you know why everyone is afraid. If you say anything around here about the church or Pru Santos, bad things happen."

"Bad things?"

Lorraine took a deep breath before she spoke. "Well, Jules told me about the minister, and I told a few other people, and all of a sudden, we started getting…ah…nasty calls. Whispered voices saying terrible things." She shook her head. "It's better not to say anything."

Jules folded her arms. "Sure, and let the library burn down and let someone murder our librarian."

"You think Protect Our Children is behind this?" These sounded like extremist right-wing tactics of intimidation.

Lorraine's hand flew to her mouth before she exclaimed, "Jules! Please don't cause any trouble."

At that moment, Rochelle walked in. A man behind her stopped at the door. She was in a hospital gown and a robe. She rushed to Jules and gave her a big hug. We adults stood back and watched as Rochelle burst into tears. "I was so afraid you were dying." She wiped her eyes and looked at us. "Jules was so brave. She got me to the door even though I was being so stupid."

The man with Rochelle stepped forward with his hands in the pockets of his jeans. "I'm Rochelle's father, Marlon."

I introduced myself. "I'm Liza. The girls called me when the 911 operator hung up on them."

Marlon was shorter than me and had the body of a wrestler gone to seed. He scowled at me. "I don't get why they called you—a stranger."

"Dad, I already explained. Her number was in Jules' phone. Remember?"

He scratched his head. "Still doesn't make sense. You aren't one of them environmental people are you?"

I was taken by surprise at the hostility in his voice.

Stay calm. He might be an idiot, but you don't want him as an enemy.

I'm always calm.

I tried my benign smile that I used with upset parents at teacher conferences. "I came for the funeral. Fannie Porter was…ah…a cousin and also helping me with a project." I decided not to mention that Jules and Rochelle were also at the funeral. The worried expression on Rochelle's face told me it was a good move.

"Oh."

No words of thank you for saving his daughter. Marlon continued to scrutinize me as he rubbed his eye in a nervous gesture. "I heard it was one of them, you know, illegals from Pottersville who ran down that librarian. Nasty characters out there. Lots of crime. They don't care who they run over as long as they get their drugs in."

Rochelle turned to me with a stricken expression. "Dad…"

I worked to keep a neutral expression on my face. "You're saying Ravens Valley has a big drug problem?" I pictured the Chamber of Commerce website. "I'll bet the Santos Brothers aren't happy about that. Not good for the reputation."

Suddenly, we had gone from arson and the death of the librarian to illegal immigration. Marlon looked down at his shoes. He wore workman's boots. "Well, they're a bad element. They should go back where they came from. Taking jobs from folks around here."

Jules looked daggers at him. "And you want to pluck chickens?"

Rochelle pleaded. "Dad, please."

It was time for me to leave. I gestured to my wristwatch. "Sorry, I need to be on my way. I hope your library will get rebuilt quickly. I'm sure Fannie would have wanted that. A town without books is just a sad little backwater. I can't imagine the Santos Brothers would like that." I smiled at Marlon. "Right?"

That's telling 'em.

Hush. I really wanted to strangle him.

Best not to commit homicide in front of witnesses.

"Good point." I brushed by Marlon as I made my way out the door.

"Excuse me?" I didn't realize Lorraine had followed me.

"Sorry, I have a bad habit of talking to myself."

"I wanted to apologize for Marlon. Not everyone in town feels the way he does. And I wanted to thank you again for helping Jules. I guess I need to be braver and speak up. I don't like the book banning either. It's wrong!"

Her vehemence surprised me. "Your daughter is special. You are lucky. Maybe you can find more of the people in town who support the library and create a 'Friends' group."

"Ah, that's an interesting idea." Judging from the expression on her face, she wouldn't be taking the lead.

When we reached the lobby, I turned to her. "What is all the talk about the people in Pottersville? I know Fannie wanted to set up a mobile library there."

Lorraine glanced around the empty room and lowered her voice. "Those workers that the Santos Brothers brought in to process the chickens? They're mostly foreign. You know? Like from Mexico? The town wasn't exactly excited to have them live here, so they set up trailers closer to the processing plant. The locals call it Pottersville, but it's just a trailer court."

"Is Marlon right that they're taking jobs from the locals?"

An expression of anger crossed her face. "No one wants to pluck chickens and gut them and do the dirty work. He's just a blowhard." She stopped talking abruptly as Marlon walked into the lobby.

Here's your chance. Ask him to coffee and find out about the underbelly of this town.

Do I have to?

Remember, you have a paper to write. Aren't you supposed to interview people on both sides of the issue?

I sighed heavily enough that Lorraine wrinkled her brow and asked, "Are you alright?"

I would be if I didn't have this damned voice in my head.

"Sure, I'm fine. Just need some coffee." I watched her walk out the door before I approached Marlon, who had been standing behind me with an uncertain look. I wondered if he wanted to say something.

"Marlon, I'm so glad Rochelle and Jules are okay. Just wondering if I could buy you a cup of coffee?"

His jaw dropped. "What?"

"Remember I said Fannie was helping me with a project? Well, it's a paper for a college class I'm taking, and I need to interview a few people about their thoughts on books. I wondered if you could help me."

Once again, I used the old adage if you want a friend for life, let them do you a favor. I certainly didn't want Marlon as a friend for life, but I thought he might give me more information about why the town was so hostile to the library and to the workers at the processing plant.

I didn't give him time to think up an excuse to say no. "Thank you so much. Should we meet at the diner on the highway? My treat."

I was just out the door when Trey came striding up. "I heard you were here."

"Not to overuse the old cliché, but news certainly travels fast in Ravens Valley."

"Uh, well, I wanted to ask you some questions."

I waved him away. "No need. I'm meeting with the sheriff later this afternoon."

Trey wrinkled his brow. "But I can talk to you now."

"Sorry, I have a date."

Quit playing with him.

Can't stand the guy.

"A date?" He stood up straighter. "You mean with that veterinarian?"

Boy, no secrets here. I glanced at Marlon and shook my head. "No. I have a date with a cup of coffee and my thoughts. I'll see the sheriff later."

Trey appeared to be flummoxed by my answer until he spied Marlon. "Well, then I'll talk with your daughter."

To my surprise, Marlon uttered an emphatic, "No! She needs her rest."

I took this as my cue to leave, hoping Marlon and Trey didn't get into a physical fight. I sensed no love lost between them.

Well, that's interesting.

No kidding. Marlon wasn't quite fitting into my stereotype. I wondered what he would have to say about banned books. If he showed up at the diner, that is.

Chapter Twenty-Seven: Marlon's Story

For mid-afternoon, the diner was busy. Fortunately, it had one booth open. I slid into it, hoping Marlon would show up. Not only was I interested in his thoughts about book banning, but he might reveal a little more about the fear in this town.

I ordered coffee and a piece of apple pie à la mode at the recommendation of the server. I was halfway through it when Marlon walked in. Several people greeted him as he approached me.

"Hey, Marlon, I heard about your girl. Is she okay?"

"That 911 dispatcher should be fired. I heard he's from out of town."

The diners sounded concerned and kind. I wondered if they would have shown the same concern if they'd been talking to the mother of one of the Pottersville kids.

Marlon scowled as he sat across from me. "I don't understand why they keep Trey on the payroll. He's a royal…"

We were interrupted by the server who took his order for coffee and pie.

"I don't get the sense you like him."

He dumped a couple of packets of sugar in his coffee and stirred it with more vigor than necessary. "Him and me go way back. He was a bully in high school, and he's a bully now." He lowered his voice, "Used to hang around with the Blackmers. Bunch of mean losers."

"I think I saw a couple of them at the festival. Tattoos and motorcycles?" Alex had pointed them out and said something about how every small town had a family like the Blackmers. Trouble from birth.

"Muscle boys. Or more like muscle heads."

Once again, Marlon, who thought immigrants were bringing in drugs, surprised me.

The server, a woman in her early thirties with short frizzy hair, brought the apple pie. When she set it down, she gave Marlon a dazzling smile. "Hope you like it, hon."

Marlon dug into his pie with the same vigor he'd stirred his coffee. When he came up for air, he finally spoke. "What is it you wanted to ask me? If you're going to lecture me on the free speech and all that crap, I'm out of here."

Be gentle. I think he has some interesting things to say.

Gentle is my middle name.

Hah! You can't fool me, it's Catherine.

Marlon looked at me with a puzzled expression. "Seems like you just disappeared."

"Sorry. Sometimes I get distracted." A blush crept up my neck. Charlee needed to go back deep inside my brain. "And, no, I'm not here to lecture. I teach fifth grade, and I want to know how I can talk with parents who are worried about what their children might be reading. Do you mind answering a few questions?"

He wiped his mouth with a paper napkin. "Nope. As long as you make it snappy. Gotta go soon."

"Do you worry about what Rochelle is reading?"

He shrugged. "Guess I never thought about it much until this whole Protect Our Children thing started. They said the library was filled with pornography that could harm the kids."

"Do you know what they meant by pornography?"

He tensed before clearing his throat. "Well, I guess it was stuff about sex."

"Are you concerned that Rochelle might be reading books that have sex in them?"

He wiped his brow. "Um, only when it's unnatural. You know, like…um… homosexual stuff." He nearly whispered the word "homosexual."

I nodded. "Why does it worry you?"

His eyes widened. "You're not one of those lesbian people, are you?"

I laughed. "I'm just an elementary school teacher. No agenda other than to get this paper written. I'm still wondering why it worries you."

Again, he cleared his throat and lowered his voice. "Well, in case you didn't know, I'm a single dad. Shelly's mom, well, she had problems, and she took off when Shelly was just a little girl. I...um...I don't know how to explain things to her. What if she reads one of them books and asks me questions?"

I held back the urge to laugh. Rochelle was seventeen and probably better able to explain things to her dad than he could explain to her. I kept my voice sympathetic, "Do you want those books taken out of the library?"

He shrugged. "Geeze, I don't know. That Vogel and his crew seem to think the books are sinful. I tried to read one once and found it boring with all the slang and stuff."

The server came by with a carafe of coffee. "Refill?" Again, she had a large smile for Marlon and a brisk, "You, too?" for me.

As she walked away, I commented, "She seems to like you."

Marlon blushed but didn't say anything.

Ask him about Fannie.

"I will."

"Excuse me? Did you say something?"

I stirred my coffee, ignoring his question. After taking a sip and enjoying the taste, I asked, "Do you think Fannie Porter's death was an accident?"

For a moment, Marlon's jaw went slack. He blinked before he spoke. "Ah, well...there was talk."

I leaned closer to him. "What do you mean?"

"Like she was being stalked or something. Shelly told me she was worried that someone might hurt her."

"Because of the books?"

He shifted in the booth. "Someone at the Nevermore said he'd heard she knew something about them people at Pottersville, and they didn't want her to talk."

"I've heard a couple of people mention the Nevermore. Is that a place to gather gossip?" I immediately felt a blush rise up my neck. Had I just insulted him by using the word "gossip"?

He waved his hand like it was no big deal. "It's just a bar outside of town. I guess it was named after a poem or whatever. The Blackmers hang out there sometimes." He shook his head. "I don't go there much. Need to be around for Shelly."

Perhaps I was finally getting somewhere with Fannie's death.

"You mean maybe someone deliberately ran her down?"

"I heard they arrested one of them…ah…illegals. Drunk or high or whatever." He pushed himself back as he made motions to stand up. "I gotta run. They're letting Shelly go, and I gotta get back there in case."

"In case?"

"That Trey shows up and tries to ask her questions. I told her not to talk to him."

I nodded, "I don't blame you. He doesn't seem like the brightest law officer."

Marlon snorted, "Lucky he knows how to sign his name."

I raised my hand. "One more quick question that has nothing to do with books or Fannie Porter. I'm curious about the drug problem here."

He stared at me before looking around the diner to see if anyone was listening. While we had been eating and talking, most of the afternoon coffee-drinkers had left. Two men sat at the counter near the door, but the rest of the tables were empty. Still, he kept his voice low.

"I heard they're brought into Pottersville from Mexico. Cartels and stuff. If you ask the Santos people, they'll tell you it's all bullshit. But I think them Pottersville people are drug mules."

"Do you have a big drug problem in Ravens Valley?"

"Someone posted on X about all the drug overdoses here that are being kept quiet. Someone even said that the librarian died of an overdose, not a car accident. I hear there's a lot of that Fentanyl coming in. But no one is talking. And I don't want Shelly to get hooked." His voice rose.

"Wow, that's awful. Is that why everyone seems to be so scared around here?"

I sensed that Marlon realized he'd said too much. Without answering, he crumpled the napkin and left it on his pie plate. "Really, I gotta go, but I can tell you, those Mexicans or whoever they are have come in and taken jobs away from the folks around here."

"Oh?"

"I used to work for Vince Santos doing upkeep on the farm buildings, but when that Elvis guy showed up, a bunch of us were let go because he was going to make the operation, as he said, 'lean.' Lean, my foot, he just got those drug dealers to work cheaper. And if you say anything in town, the Blackmers are suddenly following you around." He stood up abruptly. "Forget I said that."

I stared as he hurried out the door. Blackmers? Another thread?

I paid the bill and stepped out into the afternoon heat. His words had chilled me—both because of the anger at the immigrants and the ignorance about the content of the books. I wondered if Pru and her minister had even read the books she wanted taken out of the library. And what about all the conspiracy crap Marlon had heard about drugs and drug overdoses? I was so engaged in my own thoughts that I was startled to see the piece of paper stuck under the windshield wiper of my car. It was handwritten in block letters similar to the threat Mrs. Wilkens and I had gotten last week.

Get out of town, or you will find yourself in a ditch like that library bitch.

At least the threatener knew how to rhyme.

Chapter Twenty-Eight: Reverend Walter

I surveyed the parking lot, looking for anyone suspiciously leaving threats on cars. Other than my car, a couple of SUVs, and a dusty pickup, the lot was empty. I took a photo of the note and then swiped through my photos to find the other threat. The lettering appeared to be about the same.

Someone doesn't like us.

No kidding.

As I turned onto the highway to go to the sheriff's office, I checked my rearview mirror several times. It didn't appear like I was being followed. Out of the corner of my eye I thought I saw the sun reflecting off something metal that was moving. But when I blinked, it was gone. Perhaps a bicycle, or perhaps my imagination.

All was quiet at the Ruston County Building. The sheriff was in and beckoned me back to his office. I noticed that he walked like his back hurt him. Once he settled behind his desk, he studied the note with a puzzled expression. "You say this was on your windshield? Are you sure it wasn't a prank?"

"If it's a prank, someone has a very poor sense of humor. This is not Minnesota Nice."

After setting the paper down, he pushed his hand through his sparse hair. "I don't think it's anything to worry about."

I felt the heat rise into my cheeks.

Keep calm.

He's an idiot.

No, if you look at him carefully, you will see that he's worried and a little scared.

Charlee was right. What I'd assumed was indifference was something else. His forehead had a sheen of sweat on it despite the coldness of the air-conditioned room. He wouldn't meet my eyes as he mumbled, "Well, I guess we can fill out a report and look into it."

"Sheriff, I think my friend and I have poked the hornet's nest. I don't believe the burning of the library was an accident caused by bad wiring. And I know someone set Fannie Porter's house on fire. Are you looking at the people in 'Protect Our Children'?" I refrained from mentioning Fannie's hit-and-run because I hoped Alex would be investigating with his family.

The sheriff looked away as if someone had slapped him. What I saw in that moment was an aging man with health problems who was hoping to quietly sit out the rest of his term before retiring. I wanted to be angry with him, but instead I felt sorry for him.

Don't let him off the hook, sis. This is his job.

He reached into his desk and took out a bottle of antacid tablets, popping one in his mouth. "Well, then. We'll be sure to take care of it." I noted the way his hand shook.

Leaning toward him, I took the chance. "You're scared, too. Aren't you?"

His eyes opened wide. "What?"

"A darkness has taken control of this town, hasn't it?" And suddenly I had a thought—perhaps a puzzle piece. "Fannie found something out, hadn't she? Did she come to you?"

He stared at me, the color draining from his face. Clearing his throat, he pushed papers around until he found what he was looking for. He handed me a form. "Go ahead and fill this out and we'll look into the note. I'm sure it's a prank. They like to play pranks on out-of-town folks."

I could have demanded to know "who liked to play pranks," but I realized it was futile. On my way out of his office, I brushed past Trey. His expression was as close to a sneer as he could get without actually sneering. He must have been listening in. It was clear to me that the law would not be protecting this out-of-towner.

I sat in the car with the windows down, wishing Mrs. Wilkens were with me. She would have reamed the sheriff out so thoroughly he wouldn't have known what happened. After wishing her here, I wished Alex wasn't dealing with a sick farm animal somewhere in the barns of southern Minnesota. At the thought of him, a little warmth spread through my chest. Maybe something good would come of this mess.

As if to answer, Trey lumbered over to my car and leaned into the open window. "I hear you got some threats." A little breeze wafted in, bringing the odor of sweat and aftershave. Trey must have used it to wash his hair.

I sneezed. "Excuse me." After digging through my bag for a tissue and wiping my nose, I looked at him. "You seem to be able to keep good track of me. I guess if I'm threatened, you'll take care of it."

He grunted, still leaning against the door of the car. "It'd be better if you went back to your big city. Don't say I didn't warn you."

I should have left well enough alone, but that piece of me that even Charlee couldn't control crept out. I was tired of this town and whatever secrets it held, but I was also angry about Fannie, my cat, and the attack on the library. I used the honeyed voice I sometimes used on people who irritated me, "I heard you like to hang around with the Blackmers. Are they as tough as everyone says?"

His cheeks flushed. "I think you need to go back to the big city and deal with all them black folks rioting and burning things down."

It was out before I could stop myself, "It seems the folks here like to burn things down, too."

Trey's face suffused with red, and for a moment, it appeared that both his eyes might pop out. It even looked like he was reaching for his gun.

Geeze Liza, what are you stirring up?

Oops. Guess I went too far.

I toned down my voice and kept it coated with honey. "Sorry. I didn't mean to insult you. I know you and the sheriff are working hard to solve the arsons."

Trey grunted in reply.

I smiled at him, willing my teeth to ungrit, "As long as I have you here, can you tell me how to find Reverend Vogel?"

"Watcha need him for?" Trey squinted at me, his face still red.

"Research."

Someone called to him from the doorway. "I gotta go. Find him yourself." He walked away. It's always good to make friends with your local law enforcement.

Good job. How many traffic tickets before you get out of town?

Go away.

Vogel said he was the minister for the church on the hill. Since Ravens Valley only had one hill with a church on it, I didn't have trouble finding the building. It was an old dark brick church with a spire and stained-glass windows. The sign in the front announced times of the service and featured Reverend Norman Vogel, pastor.

When I walked up to the wooden front doors, I found they were locked. A man mowing his lawn across the street turned off his mower and shouted, "It's locked. You need to go around back to the office."

I waved to him and followed the sidewalk around to the back. The church had an old-world look to it. I suspected it had been built in the 1920s, and sure enough, 1923 was carved into a cornerstone block. The grounds were watered and neatly mowed with flowers planted alongside the sidewalk.

I found a side door and knocked on it. After a few moments, I heard the sound of shuffling feet. Walter Christianson, the minister from the parade, answered, squinting at me.

"Oh, hello. We meet again."

"I'm looking for Reverend Vogel."

"Oh." He sounded disappointed. "Everyone is looking for him all the time. Come on in. I'm sure he'll be here directly if you have an appointment."

I followed him into a crowded office in the back of the church. "He's out doing whatever it is that he does. Can I help you?"

"I was hoping to talk with him about the book banning."

He studied me as a small smile crept onto his lips, "Ah, yes, you're the one who took on his son at the parade. Nice work. By the way, people call me Reverend Walter and sometimes worse. Not that anybody seems to care around here anymore." He extended his hand, like he had at the parade.

"Liza Johnson. I don't have an appointment. I was hoping to catch Reverend Vogel to ask a few questions about the book concerns." I explained my project paper. "Fannie Porter was advising me, and she suggested I talk with some of the people who are pushing the ban."

Reverend Walter nodded. "She was a good woman. Stubborn as hell—but good."

The Reverend and his irreverent attitude surprised me. "Uh, I didn't know her well, but I'm a great supporter of libraries and librarians, and they seem to be under siege these days."

He reached into his desk and took out a flask. "Would you like a shot?"

"Why not?"

He poured some of the brown liquid into a shot glass and handed it to me. I'm not much of a whiskey drinker, but this was definitely smooth. It felt warm going down and brought an immediate warmth to my chest.

He raised the flask and took a swig. "Now, tell me the truth. What are you after?"

His directness surprised me. "I really am working on a paper about communication and censorship. But I'm also concerned that no one cares what happened to Fannie, and no one is doing much about the library. And, of course, someone poisoned my cat."

Reverend Walter sat back with a slight smile. "Right you are. There's a pall over Ravens Valley. I've been here for thirty years, and I have to say the last five have been…ah…interesting."

"Why?"

"My congregation was getting older, and the kids weren't interested." He chuckled. "Not that kids are ever interested in church. Still, Ravens Valley has been stagnant for a long time. Like the rest of rural America, we've lost population. Youth escape to the city, and we have fewer sources of income."

"What happened in the last five years?"

He took another swig from his flask. "Chickens."

"You mean Santos Brothers?"

With the second swig from his flask, Reverend Walter's cheeks turned rosy. "Yes, that and the community turned into a bunch of chickens. Scared of their shadows."

"I've sensed the fear. In fact, I've gotten two notes threatening me. But what is the fear?"

"Did you see the sign in front of the church with the announcement about services?"

"Yes."

The Reverend snorted. "Back about five years ago, Vince and Heck Santos opened up that chicken processing plant out on County Road 14. Brought in Heck's daughter Annalisa, and she hired a guy named Elvis." He paused with a twinkle in his eyes. "Imagine. An Elvis right here in southern Minnesota. Slick as the real one, but claimed he couldn't sing." He laughed to himself.

"And?" I prompted him.

"The plant brought in immigrants and guest workers. Good for the community and good for the schools—except some of the folks around here weren't happy. You know, 'Make America for Americans?'"

I sighed. I was so tired of that line when I knew how much the new blood made our country great.

"Well, I welcomed them into the church. Caused a hell of a ruckus when I suggested we do a service in Spanish. After I said it, the sign was vandalized along with my car. Smeared it with pig's blood and accused me of…well, let's say the same things priests have been accused of."

The Minnesotan came out in me. "Uff dah. Not good."

"Members of the board who supported me also got vandalized, and, suddenly, I was told to drop the idea. Instead, they brought in that Vogel character. Really, I doubt he went to divinity school. I think he bought his degree from an outfit located in a strip mall in Texas. He's been happily indoctrinating the populace since."

I took a deep breath and let it out slowly. "Who's behind the threats?"

"I have my suspicions."

He didn't finish because Norman Vogel walked in the door looking angry. "Walter, what are you doing here? I thought we talked about it. You don't have to keep hours at the church anymore."

Reverend Walter tapped his head. "Oops. Sorry. You know the aging brain. Must have forgotten."

Vogel clenched his jaw and his eyes narrowed.

Before he could speak, I jumped in. "Hello. He was just giving me some history of the church. Actually, I came to see you."

I held out my hand, and he looked like I'd just offered him a dead fish. "What do you want?"

I want to smash you in the mouth. "Just have some questions for a paper I'm working on."

"I heard. Best ask them quick."

Where were the welcoming arms of the church?

Chapter Twenty-Nine: Protect Our Children

Vogel stood in the doorway, glaring at me. "I have a meeting in fifteen minutes. What do you need?"

I noted how he spoke with a nasally twang.

Tell him to go to hell!

Charlee? Sweet Charlee? What's gotten into you?

He's evil.

"I know."

Vogel frowned. "What do you know?"

Speaking out loud again. "Um…I know you are concerned about the books in the library. I'm wondering if you can share your concerns?" After I spoke, I realized I sounded like a school counselor talking with a parent.

Vogel didn't move, and Reverend Walter sat back with an amused expression like he was about to watch a boxing match.

"It's simple. The books are pornographic, use offensive language, and are unsuitable for the children of Ravens Valley."

"Can you tell me more?" I reached in my bag for a notebook even though I had no intention of writing things down.

"The Bible says…"

Reverend Walter guffawed. "When have you ever read the Bible?"

Vogel's face glowed pink. "I *am* a minister of the Word."

I raised my hand to stop the reverends from escalating. "Excuse me." Walter opened his mouth to speak, but closed it as I frowned at him.

"Reverend Vogel, when I have a parent who doesn't want her child to read *To Kill a Mockingbird*, what should I tell her—at least from your perspective?"

Vogel blinked. "It's on the list. That's what you tell that mother who truly cares about her child."

"I'm not here to argue with you—I simply need advice and information for my paper. When you say it's on the list, do you mean the book is pornographic? Or does it have bad words? What should I say?"

Reverent Walter interjected, "Have you ever read it? You know it's about racial injustice?"

Vogel sputtered, "If it's on the list, the book has been carefully studied."

"What's wrong with it?" Walter leaned forward. "I don't recall any pornography. Maybe just the N-word. Norman, have you ever read any of these books you want taken out of the library?"

He responded immediately, "They're filled with pornography and filth."

"You didn't answer the question." Walter's voice rose.

This was going nowhere fast, but I was learning a couple of things. First, like I suspected, Norman Vogel was a one-dimensional bigot, and second, he didn't wield a great deal of power. Pru Santos must have been the steel behind Protect Our Children.

Vogel took a step into the small office, both his hands clenched. Before he could physically attack the old minister, I stopped him with my honeyed smile. "I think you've answered my question for the time being. I can see your concern is for the children."

"Bah! Your concern is for the collection plate from the sheep who follow you." Walter glowered at him.

I walked to the door and took Vogel by the arm. "Let's talk outside for a moment." I really liked Walter and didn't want him to end up with a black eye or worse. Before I left, I winked at Reverend Walter, and he winked back.

I guided Vogel out into the late afternoon sunshine. "I can see you have a difficult position here. Sorry I stirred things up. Perhaps we can talk another time. I want to take note that you are passionate about your work."

He stared at me in confusion. "Well, yes, of course."

As we stood by the church, a couple of crows landed on the electrical wire and cawed as if they were scolding us. I wondered if they were trying to tell us something, and it reminded me of the Poe poem. I pointed to the birds and quoted, "'Tis some visitor, tapping at my chamber door—only this and nothing more.'"

Vogel stared at me, mouth slack. "What?"

"Don't you recognize it? It's from Poe's famous 'The Raven.'"

I think he was about to ask me who this Poe might be, but we were interrupted by Pru Santos striding towards us. She stopped, looking at me with disdain. "I heard you were back."

"Nice to see you again, Pru. I guess you don't have to worry about those forms being filled out at the library now that it's burned down." I smiled in a most insincere way. My fifth graders would have been proud of me.

She licked her lips, reminding me of a cat about to pounce. "Such a tragedy."

"Those poor girls who were trying to help out. I hope the library board plans to offer them counseling."

Pru ignored my remark and spoke to Vogel. "We need to have a meeting tonight. Some of the parents have called me and are upset."

I wondered if they were upset that someone set the library on fire and two girls almost got killed.

Vogel straightened his clerical collar. "Ah, yes. We should meet."

"Oh, good," I interrupted. "Maybe I could attend and get more information for my project."

As the saying went, if looks could kill. Pru spoke in a tight voice. "This is a private meeting."

"But isn't the library board a public service and subject to the open meeting law?"

"Protect Our Children is not a public organization."

"But I checked your website, and it says you are a tax-exempt organization. I'm sure the law applies to you. Plus, don't you want to reach out to as many people as possible?" I used my honeyed smile. If I "honeyed" anymore, someone was liable to spray me with insecticide.

You tell 'em, sis.

I had no idea whether the open meeting law covered private charities, but I decided they probably didn't know either.

Pru clutched her bag a little tighter. "Or perhaps tonight isn't a good night for you, Norman?"

He shuffled his feet, and when he spoke, his Southern twang was more noticeable. "Gosh, I forgot I have other plans."

"Do they involve matches and accelerant?" The words slipped out of my mouth before I could stop them.

Both stared at me. Again, if looks could kill, I'd be six feet under on Boot Hill. Or worse, ashes in a cardboard box in some distant relative's garage.

"Sorry, I didn't mean to imply you were involved. It's just that, as I've researched book censorship for my paper, I've found that the rhetoric of some of the organizations has resulted in threats and violence. I'm sure that's not what you wanted, but someone did set the library on fire."

I watched the flush rise on Pru's carefully made-up face. "It wasn't arson. They said it was old wiring."

Ah, the old "fake news."

Go ahead and slap her across the mouth!

Charlee, what's gotten into you?

It was time for me to leave.

Before I turned to leave, I added, "You must be feeling sorry that your work with Protect Our Children has resulted in the arson at the library and the sad way Fannie Porter was treated in this town. She was a good woman, and I'm sure you're good Christians." With that, I walked away feeling totally unfulfilled and wishing they could experience the wrath of Mrs. Wilkens.

Charlee must have read my mind. Or let's say, my mind spoke to me.

You need to get Mrs. Wilkens back here. You're no good on your own.

Easy for you to say.

As if she had extrasensory perception, Mrs. Wilkens texted as I slid behind the driver's seat.

How's it going?

I replied. **Nearly got an aging minister beat up. Girls are okay. Got another threatening note.**

She replied. **I'm coming tomorrow!!!**

The thought of Mrs. Wilkens barreling down a two-lane highway was almost as frightening as the note telling me to get out of town. **I'll come home tonight. We can drive back tomorrow.**

Nonsense. You stay and investigate more. I'll drive and bring Goldie so Alex can check her out.

I had to give Mrs. Wilkens credit; she sure could tap out a text quickly. Including proper capitalization and punctuation.

Time to take a deep breath, gather my thoughts, and check in with Lorrie.

Chapter Thirty: Lorrie and the Vans

When I arrived at Lorrie's, it was almost supper time. I thought I'd take him out to dinner and get more of the history on how things had changed in Ravens Valley over the last five years. His Frankenstein car was parked askew in the driveway, partway onto the lawn. I wondered if he'd spent the afternoon in a bar.

At the front door, I called out, "Lorrie, I'm here. Can I come in?"

No answer. He must have been in his room in the basement. I let myself in and called again. "Anyone home?"

"On the patio. Grab a beer for me, will you?" His voice sounded off like he was having a hard time getting the words out. Maybe he was drunk.

I took two cans of beer from the near-empty refrigerator and brought them to the backyard. Lorrie sat with his back to me, staring up at the sky. Without turning, he spoke, "Another one of those private planes."

I looked up and saw only wispy clouds and heard no airplane noise. When I approached him, I stopped and suppressed a gasp. His right eye was swollen and black and blue, his lip was split and swollen, and he had blood crusted under his nose. "My God, Lorrie, what happened?"

He shrugged. "I guess I stepped in it at the Nevermore this afternoon."

"What do you mean you 'stepped in it?'" I squatted down in front of him to get a better look at his injuries. I'm used to the scrapes and bruises of kids when they come in from the playground, but not this. Lorrie's eye was swollen almost shut, and he made a little whistling sound when he breathed.

"Guess I said some things I shouldn't have. Just mentioned about those white vans that go to Pottersville every night. Said I'd heard they were bringing people in from the Texas border to work for Santos. Wondered if it was true."

"Who were you talking to?"

"Just the guys at the bar. Except a Blackmer walked in while I was talking. Must have heard me. You don't say anything about Santos in front of the Blackmers unless you want your arms broken."

I quickly scanned Lorrie's arms, but they appeared to be intact.

"One of them was waiting for me outside and popped me." He pointed to his eye. "I'm getting slow. Didn't get a shot in. Those guys are pretty quick."

"Lorrie, we need to get you to the clinic."

"Aw, it's nothing." Except as he said it, I noticed how his speech slurred.

"We're going to the hospital. Now! Can you walk?"

"A little wobbly."

He tried to stand and crumpled to the ground, clutching his chest. "Think they got the ribs, too."

I pulled out my phone to call 911.

Lorrie reached over. "No. I don't trust the ambulance guys! Santos owns them, too."

I quickly found Alex's number and called. He answered right away. "Hey, I'm back in town."

"Alex, I'm at Lorrie's. Someone beat him up, and he needs to go to the hospital, but he won't let me call 911. Can you come?"

"On my way."

While I waited for Alex, I ran in the house and grabbed a throw pillow from the sofa and a bag of frozen peas from the freezer. I placed the pillow under Lorrie's head and held the peas to his swollen eye. I wanted to keep him talking. "Lorrie, tell me exactly what happened."

Lorrie's eyelids drooped, and he slurred more. "Dunno. Jus yakking with the boys. They said some trash about one of the guys I know from Pottersville. I told them Santos was a slumlord."

Pottersville was coming up way too often. I wanted to ask more, but Lorrie was drifting off. As I repositioned the frozen peas, his eyes opened. "Gotta take care of Henry. Henry shouldn't see me like this!"

I held his hand. "We'll take care of Henry. He'll be okay." It seemed like it took Alex forever to get here.

"Doesn't like it when I get in fights. Told me to stay out of the Nevermore." He tried to smile. "Henry said to me, 'Nevermore the Nevermore.'" He closed his eyes once again.

I heard Alex's van door shut. "Hello?" He called out.

"We're in the back!"

He came around the corner holding a leather medical bag. "Lorrie, my God, you look like you got into a fight with a linebacker."

Lorrie tried to lift his head. "Don't feel too bad."

Alex took a penlight out of his bag. Squatting, he checked Lorrie's eyes. "Well, you look awful. Can you follow my finger?"

Lorrie's eyes drifted shut.

Alex grabbed a stethoscope from the bag and listened to Lorrie's chest. Without a word, he pulled out his phone and called 911. I stayed quiet even though Lorrie had told me he didn't want the ambulance. After he filled the operator in on what he was seeing, he spoke to Lorrie. "Listen, friend, it looks like you might have a concussion and a punctured lung. We're going to take you directly to the ER in Mankato."

He whispered to me, "The Ravens Valley hospital doesn't have a full-time doctor. If we took him there, we'd have to wait for the doctor to come over from the clinic. And all they would do is package him up and send him to Mankato. I'm eliminating the middleman."

"I can ride with him if they'll let me."

Lorrie groaned. "No, stay here. Something bad at Pottersville. Fix it and take care of Henry."

I squeezed his hand. "Not to worry. We'll figure it out."

Lorrie's hand relaxed, and he smiled. "Talk to Henry. He knows all about it."

When the ambulance arrived, I recognized one of the EMTs as the minister at Fannie's funeral. She was gentle with him as they lifted him onto a stretcher. While her partner checked vital signs and consulted with Alex, I took her aside.

"Lorrie said he was afraid of the ambulance drivers. Do you know what he meant?"

She frowned, and her lips formed a thin line. "We're an all-volunteer ambulance crew, and some of the volunteers aren't the greatest. Lorrie will be safe with us. Poor guy. Do you know what happened?"

"He said he got jumped outside the Nevermore. He thought it was because he said something about Santos Brothers and Pottersville."

She gritted her teeth. "I feel like we're in the village of the damned. It's time to fix it."

Her partner consulted the Mankato ER doctor and got the okay for them to transport. Before they left, I took his hand and assured him Henry would be safe with me.

You have a thing about collecting cats, don't you?

Who says Henry is a cat? Could be a gerbil.

I called Mrs. Wilkens as soon as they were gone and filled her in on Lorrie. "They're taking him to Mayo in Mankato."

"Are you going there?"

"He wants me to stay here and find out about Pottersville. He says Henry knows all about it."

"You mean the cat? No one should be alone in an emergency room. They ignore patients if no one is with them. I should get in the car right now."

"No." I used my firm teacher voice. "You shouldn't be on the road after dark. Alex and I will go and make sure he's cared for."

After the call ended, I sank into the lawn chair. I told Alex what Lorrie had said about the altercation at the Nevermore. "Do you know anything about white vans at Pottersville?"

A pained look crossed Alex's face. "I asked my dad about Pottersville, and he said Santos Brothers had nothing to do with it other than employing some of the residents."

"Lorrie told the guys at the bar that Santos Brothers were slumlords. Your father could be mixed up in something bad."

Alex groaned. "I've heard rumblings, but Dad denies it."

"If they employ people from Pottersville, he must be involved."

He gestured in surrender, "I don't know. He's always been the face of Santos Brothers. He can pour on the charm and likes to be the center of attention. He's even talked about running for Congress. But I don't think he's ever been much of a businessman. Uncle Vince is the brains behind the operation." He paused. "At least until Annalisa came back. I think she's taken over more and more of it."

I checked my watch. "Should we get on the road?"

"Let's check on Henry first."

We let ourselves in. The basement stairs were opposite the back door. When I hit the switch, a feeble 40-watt bulb emitted a dim light. Alex shook his head, "Probably the same light his dad put in thirty years ago."

I wasn't sure what to expect, but the basement was clean and orderly with a walled-off bedroom to the right of the staircase. The door was shut. I pointed to it. "I suppose Henry would be hiding in there." Alex opened the door slowly. I hoped a cat wouldn't leap out.

No movement, no sound other than the hum of a dehumidifier.

"Henry?" Alex flipped on the switch by the door, and two lamps on either side of a single bed came on. The bed was made up like a military cot with an army green blanket tucked tightly under the mattress. You probably could have bounced a quarter off it.

"Wow," I looked around the room and felt like I'd been transported back to the early 1980s. At least in the 1980s, I knew from television and movies. Several posters were tacked to the fake wood paneling, including one for the movie *ET* and another for *Raiders of the Lost Ark*. He also had an athletic shirt from the high school football team, The Purple Hawks.

More important, though, I saw no evidence of a cat. Nor did I smell evidence of a kitty box or food dishes.

"Henry?" I called out while Alex checked in the closet and under the bed. Alex stood up, hands on his hips. "I don't think we're looking for a cat."

"What are we looking for?"

He pointed to a four-drawer dresser, the top covered with framed photos. The photos had been dusted and carefully arranged around a small wooden box with a gold plaque on it. I squinted in the dim light to read "Henry,

1986-2000."

"You mean Henry is a ghost? Sort of?"

"I've wondered over the last few years when Lorrie has helped me out. I told him any veterinary care would be free if he wanted to bring Henry in. But I never saw the cat. Possibly my grandpa did, although by then he was hardly practicing."

Considering that I lived with the voice of my dead sister, I was hardly one to say anything about Lorrie and his cat.

Smart choice. Or else Alex might think you're crazy.

Oh, be quiet.

I studied the other framed photos. Several were of Lorrie with his parents, including one wearing his high school graduation gown. The picture that caught my eye, however, was Lorrie embracing his best pal and grinning for the camera. "You look so much like this photo."

Alex scratched his head. "Lorrie must have known all along that Peter Wilkens was possibly my father. I wonder why he didn't say anything?"

"Maybe Henry told him not to." I meant the comment to be funny, but neither of us laughed.

I was about to suggest that we take my car to Mankato to the hospital when Alex's phone rang. I followed him up the stairs as he took the call.

"Not again!" he exclaimed as he walked outside.

I waited while he talked, wondering if this was about his mother. When he finished the call, he looked at me with a troubled expression. "I need to get back to the clinic. Another cat has been poisoned. This one belongs to Reverend Walter. What the hell is wrong with this town?"

Good question.

Chapter Thirty-One: Lucy

I sat with Reverend Walter while Alex examined the cat in the surgery. "Alex is good. He saved my cat last week."

Reverend Walter gave me a pained look, "Lucy is an old cat. I don't know. She really belonged to my wife, but after she died, Lucy and I—well, we bonded."

"I'm so sorry." I didn't tell him that Goldie and I had bonded, sort of. We regarded each other as necessities.

Reverend Walter peered at me. "What do you hope to accomplish here? Some of my old parishioners are wondering if you're from the government to 'clean things up.'"

Maybe they think you're a narc.

Hardly.

I decided to be honest with him. "Fannie Porter was a friend. Or not exactly a friend, but she was helping me with this book banning project. I only met her a couple of times, and they were over Zoom. But my neighbor Mrs. Wilkens knew her. That's how I got hooked up with her. The last meeting we had, she seemed stressed and worried. Just before the Zoom ended, she said, 'They know that I know.' I assumed it had something to do with Protect Our Children." I paused. "Mrs. Wilkens told me she also used the words, 'it's a wonderful life'. Does that mean anything to you?"

Reverend Walter tilted his head to the side. "Strange. You mean like the movie? Was she onto something?"

I shrugged. "When we found out she been killed by a hit and run, we decided to investigate."

"Who's we? Mrs. Wilkens? Is she your grandmother?"

Who would call their grandmother "Mrs"?

Despite the seriousness of our conversation, the thought of Mrs. Wilkens as my grandmother brought a smile to my lips. "No, she's my neighbor."

And possibly Alex's grandmother.

"Shush!"

The reverend wrinkled his brow. "Excuse me?"

"Holding back a sneeze."

Charlee, be quiet. Please?

I leaned toward the old minister, "What is going on in this town? What was Fannie into? There must be rumors."

"I think we're in a battle between the old establishment and a new kind of disrupter."

"Disrupter?"

"Ever since the Santos Brothers organic chickens took flight—pardon the pun—we've been living with an 'us and them.'"

A helicopter roared in the rhythm of its rotors overhead. We both looked up as if we could see it from the waiting room of the clinic. "I've got the sense that people are afraid, but I'm not sure what they are afraid of or why—except the contents of books."

He pointed out the window. "You heard that helicopter. No doubt they're bringing in investors for an expansion of the farm. Santos Brothers want to portray the image of wholesome food raised in a wholesome community. But what they have is a factory—no better than some of the big corporate poultry operations except they claim the chickens are organic."

"They're not?"

He shrugged. "Some of my old parishioners used to farm or work for Heck and Vince. They say what used to be traditional is no more."

I remembered what he'd said about things changing five years ago. "Do your parishioners think it's because Heck's daughter came back and is part of the operation?" I thought about Annalisa with her business degree and the phone stuck to her ear.

"I don't know. I remember her as a little girl in confirmation. Quiet and intense. But…"

Reverend Walter didn't get a chance to finish because Alex emerged from the surgery with a pained expression. This would not be good news. I felt the reverend tense as he watched Alex approach.

He sat down in a chair beside Reverend Walter. "I'm so sorry, Reverend. Lucy was too old to fight off the poison." He took his hand and waited a few moments for the news to sink in. "Would you like to see her?"

Walter nodded. Alex guided him slowly back to the surgery door. I watched, admiring how gentle Alex was with him. He seemed to know to stay quiet.

At the door, the reverend stopped. "I…I hope she wasn't in too much pain."

Alex patted his hand. "I made sure she was comfortable."

As I watched, I thought about death and giving bad news. I'd once sat with a fellow teacher while a police chaplain told her that her husband had been killed in a freak car accident. It wasn't his words that struck me, but his ability to be silent as she absorbed the news.

I felt like weeping for the old man. He'd lost his cat, and he'd lost his parish to a twangy interloper. I thought about how this could have been me if Goldie hadn't pulled through.

They were gone a long time. When they emerged, the reverend spoke with a determined look. "We need to find out who is poisoning the cats and who is poisoning this town. I'm going to the Nevermore. Those poor sinners know more of the gossip than anyone else."

Stop him, sis.

Right!

I held up my hand. "Maybe you should wait. We've already sent one person to the hospital. I'd hate to have you be the second. You might be a man of God, but I'm not sure the subhumans who beat up Lorrie would care much."

Alex joined me in trying to calm the minister down. "Maybe you could help me trace the poison instead. I think your wife and Lucy would approve."

Sighing, Reverend Walter sat back down while Alex explained his theory of where the poison was coming from. "This is farm country, and there are a lot of rodenticides out there. Many have been taken off the market, but I've been in barns where they've been stored for decades. I'm guessing someone found a poison that has thallium in it. It's been banned as a rat poison here since 1975, but who knows how much of it is in those old storage sheds."

"Who would know about the poison?" Reverend Walter scratched his head.

"Just about anyone who has access to the internet and wanted to find out how to kill pets."

When Goldie was poisoned, I'd assumed it was a random budding psychopath who'd done it. But what if it wasn't random? "Is it possible the cat poisoning is part of the same intimidation that Fannie experienced? People who didn't like the books? Or the arson at the library?"

Reverend Walter's eyes brightened. "Maybe there's a pattern."

"Let me get my records," Alex headed to the surgery.

While we waited, Walter told me about how he became a retired pastor. "Basically, the church board fired me. They did it in a 'nice' way by suggesting it was time to retire and maybe I could stay on as pastor emeritus."

"Did you know it was coming?"

"I didn't see it exactly until I suggested we do a weekly service for the migrant workers in Spanish. I was hoping to rebuild the congregation. Our numbers were dropping as younger people left the community. I thought we could hire someone who was fluent in Spanish. That's when things really blew up."

"Your congregation was against it? Why?"

Reverend Walter sighed a bit, "Oh, well, yes, they came up with dozens of reasons. How much is it going to cost to bring in this person? When are you going to hold this Spanish service? Is it going to interfere with our service? I like my service at 10:00 am—are you going to change its time? How would coffee hour be affected? Are we going to have two coffee hours, one in Spanish? Will we need to have Mexican food at coffee hour? We would need Spanish hymnals—how much do they cost? Would there be Spanish hymnals in the pews alongside the ones we already have? Wouldn't that be confusing? It was death by a thousand cuts, and it only went downhill from there. There was a church meeting where someone suggested that if we did services in Spanish, next thing you know, 'those people' would take over the church and turn it into an illegal sanctuary."

It sounded to me like the hateful rhetoric at the Southern border that accused those seeking asylum of being criminals and animals.

"Behind my back, they found this Vogel character, and that was it. Except I still have some loyal parishioners, and because of them, I'm allowed to do one service a month."

"Who was behind this?"

He shrugged. "I'm not sure, but I think Pru Santos had a hand in it. And maybe that Elvis guy."

Alex returned carrying his laptop. "I have records of all the poisoned animals I've treated in the past few months. I know this is a break in confidentiality, but if you want to go through them, maybe you can see a pattern."

Walter stared at the laptop. "I'm afraid I'm an old Luddite. Haven't learned to use one of those machines, and I've decided I'm too old to start now. Do you have anything on paper?"

It occurred to me that Reverend Walter and Mrs. Wilkens would make a good pair to go through the records. "I have an idea. Mrs. Wilkens is coming tomorrow. How about if the two of you work on it? She's up on her tech skills." I didn't mention that I'd had to have Mrs. Wilkens help me with my laptop a couple of times. Embarrassing for a thirty-something schoolteacher.

Alex smiled at the two of us. "Sounds like a plan. Meanwhile, Liza and I are driving to Mankato to check on Lorrie."

"I'll pray for him."

We walked out of the clinic together to the sun setting over the river. It was a brilliant orange and yellow, and for a moment, I felt like all would be well.

Then several motorcycles roared by, tossing firecrackers at us. Over the din, I was sure I heard someone shouting, "Get out of town or else." The same warning I'd gotten earlier.

Chapter Thirty-Two: The Emergency Room

We were a few blocks away from the clinic before we spoke. Alex, who insisted on driving my car, stared straight ahead with his shoulders tensed and his jaw clenched.

"Has it been like this since you came back?" I ventured.

"It's gotten worse in the last year. The poisoning, the book banning, and the anger over the migrant workers. It's been simmering for a while, but I think this summer has really brought it to a boiling point."

"Do you have any idea what it was that Fannie was working on? To me, it had to be more than Protect Our Children. Pottersville and the poultry workers are somehow tied into this."

Alex was quiet as he pulled out onto the highway. I looked back and saw that a police cruiser followed us.

"Looks like we have an escort."

"I'm guessing they are escorting you out of town, not me."

"Oh. They are assuming because it's my car."

"Yup."

Alex glanced in the rearview mirror and sighed. "I'm so tired of this. All I want is to continue the veterinary practice my grandfather had. Fannie and I were friends and running partners, and she used to chide me for not being more active in the community. I simply wanted to deal with the animals."

My stomach rumbled, and I realized I hadn't eaten since the wonderful Pho and fries for lunch. "Is there somewhere we can stop and eat. I'm afraid

"

if we get to the hospital, I might be stuck with vending machine potato chips."

He laughed. "There's a drive-in about ten miles from here. We can stop for a burger." He turned to me, "Glad you're not a vegan."

"Well, I am losing my appetite for chicken."

We stopped at a drive-in that had old-fashioned servers who brought the food to the car. While we waited for our burger and fries, I thought about Reverend Walter and the loss of his cat.

"Why would someone pick on a sweet old man?"

"Could be random."

I shook my head. "I don't think so."

Our food came, and the server attached the tray to the car window, smiling with a mouth full of braces. Oh, to be a teenager again! Then I pictured Josh and Jasper and the gang of teens from the Chicken Wing festival. I sensed something malevolent about them.

"What do you think about your cousin Josh? Could he be mixed up in this?"

"You mean like poisoning cats?"

I shrugged, biting into a burger that was mainly bun and ketchup. I didn't care, though, because I was hungry.

"Josh is spoiled and defiant, but I can't see him hurting cats. Still…His mother is Pru, and she's certainly got a mean streak in her."

"What do you know about Pru?"

"She's Vic's second wife. His first wife—well, the family doesn't talk much about her. She liked to play around. I was too young to understand what was going on. Her name was Delia, and I thought she was a lot of fun. I guess so did some of the farmhands. She ran off with one, and I've heard she now lives in California."

"And Pru?"

He looked up at the roof of the car. "Oh, Pru. Poor Vince. Bad choices. She's a product of one of those fundamentalist colleges, you know, like Oral Roberts University or someplace like that. Worked in the Santos Brothers' front office until she married Vince. Since Josh was born, it's been her mission to turn Ravens Valley into her view of Christianity."

"Poor Josh. No wonder he's a mess."

As I finished the last of my root beer, my phone rang, and Mrs. Wilkens popped up on the screen. I told her we were on our way to see Lorrie and that we'd have a project for her tomorrow. "Reverend Walter, the retired minister from the church on the hill, just lost his cat to the poisoner. He's willing to help you sift through medical records to see if there's a pattern."

Although I couldn't see her face, I heard the excitement in her voice. "Well, isn't that another kettle of dead fish. I'll stop to check on Lorrie on my way to Ravens Valley."

"Drive carefully."

She lowered her voice on the phone. "Did you find out anything more about Alex. You know what I'm talking about?"

In all the excitement, I'd totally forgotten to tell her that Alex was probably her grandson. Here in my Toyota that smelled of greasy fries, it didn't seem appropriate. I fudged a little. "I'll have more information for you tomorrow."

Alex watched me with an amused glint in his eyes. "Does she know that I know?"

I smiled and said nothing.

Shame on you. Liking the intrigue and all.

Oh, be quiet.

* * *

The emergency room was filled with people ranging from those coughing and looking miserable to a grade school boy holding an ice pack on his arm. The harried admissions clerk was less than helpful until Alex told her he was the doctor at the scene and wanted to check on his patient.

I blinked, wondering if she'd call security. What doctor goes to the emergency room to check on a patient? She must have been exhausted, because she nodded and motioned us through the door to the emergency rooms.

Lorrie was dozing on a gurney with an IV running. His face looked even worse than when I'd found him. I took his hand and squeezed it, but he had no reaction. Alex kept his gaze on the monitor and finally commented, "His heartbeat looks good." We stood at the bedside until a person in a white coat came in. She wore a lanyard with her identification as Dr. Sharma.

"Are you family?"

I fumbled for words until Alex rescued me. "He's my adoptive uncle."

Nice, reasonable lie.

She accepted what he said and spoke in very clinical terms about his injuries. I didn't catch much of it other than that they'd done a CT scan and he had a concussion. "I will have to report this to the police because it looks like he was assaulted."

"Good luck with that," I muttered under my breath.

"We'll admit to ICU to monitor the head injury."

A nurse beckoned the doctor. After she was gone, a clerk came in to get insurance information. Fortunately, Lorrie had his cards in his wallet. Alex put his name and phone number down as next-of-kin when he saw that Lorrie had listed Henry at his address as the person to contact. He looked at the clerk, "Ah, Henry isn't available right now."

I took Lorrie's hand again, "Mrs. Wilkens will be stopping to see you tomorrow. They'll take good care of you here." At least I hoped so.

He opened his eyes and whispered, "It's all about Pottersville. Check with Henry." His eyes drifted shut, and he began to snore.

I drove back to Ravens Valley while Alex used his phone to make calls, checking up on his patients. As the light from the day faded and the fields whipped by, it occurred to me that Pottersville triggered something ugly in the Ravens Valley populace. It was time to visit the place. I remembered Lorrie had talked about white vans. Was someone bringing in undocumented workers, and that was the issue? Or was it really an illegal drug operation?

As I overheard the bits and pieces of Alex's phone conversation with the farmer who owned the calf he'd treated today, I was impressed with how carefully he explained things to him. It was clear that when it came to veterinary medicine, he was in the right place.

It was nearly midnight by the time we pulled up to the clinic. An outdoor light over the clinic door cast a weak glow over the parking area. Alex's van stood parked where he had left it, and the area appeared to be quiet.

Except.

"My God! What is that?" I exclaimed.

Something hung from the doorknob of the clinic. Alex was out of the car and rushing to the door before I could wrap my head around what I was seeing. It appeared to be a cat with a noose around its neck.

With my heart pounding so loud it hurt my ears, I approached the door. Alex stared at it with his jaw slack. When he looked at me, it was with an expression of defeat.

I reached the door in time to see him grab the cat and wrench it off the doorknob.

"This isn't funny." He tossed the poor cat onto the driveway.

I braced myself as I stooped down to look at the strangled cat. One of the buttons for its eyes was missing, and the fur on its tail was worn off like a child had rubbed it too many times.

"It's a stuffed cat," I gasped.

"My stuffed cat." He picked the toy up. "Meet Felix."

More ugliness in this town. "Who would do this?"

"Or the bigger question, how did they find Felix in the first place? I'm sure I boxed him up when I went off to college."

My homing instinct kicked in with a powerful punch. I was tempted to turn on my heel, make a run for the car, and get the hell out of town.

You can't abandon them now.

"I know. I know."

"Know what?" Alex peered at me, still holding the worn-out toy with a noose around its neck.

I quickly recovered. "I know we have to get to the bottom of this." Meanwhile, the old saying was circulating in my head, not my circus, not my monkeys.

Alex looked at his watch. "It's late. I guess I'll have to pursue the stuffed cat killer tomorrow."

"And I need to check on Henry." A piece of me still wondered if there was another Henry, a live one hiding in the house.

I stood four feet from Alex, not sure how to end the night. Would he invite me up? Would he walk away?

Come on! What are you, a woman of the 19th century? At least give him a hug!

The 19th century part got to me. I stepped over to Alex and hugged him. At first, he stiffened, then I felt his body relax as he hugged me back. "Take care," I murmured, wanting to stay in the embrace.

And maybe something would have happened except a motorcycle roared past the clinic, breaking the silence of the neighborhood.

Chapter Thirty-Three: Cat Poisoning

I drove to Lorrie's, constantly checking the rearview mirror to see if anyone was following. Ravens Valley appeared to be asleep to the world. Other than the motorcycle roaring by the clinic, nothing moved.

When I stepped out of the car, I gripped my phone as if it could protect me from getting jumped. The cool night air held the fragrance of newly mown grass and a hint of the river below. It was hard, in the moment, to think that this place roiled with ill will. I was reminded of it, though, as soon as I saw how Lorrie's car was parked. How he made it home after being beaten so badly was a small miracle.

I looked up at the starry sky and said a silent prayer for him.

I was exhausted and bone-tired but determined to find Henry, if Henry existed, before I crawled into bed. In the kitchen, I scanned the counter and checked under the sink for evidence of cat food. What I did find under the sink was a baited mousetrap. I thought part of the reason to have cats was to keep the mice away.

Next to it was an old box of rat poison. Alex had said this type of rat poison was banned by the EPA at least ten years ago. Gingerly, I picked it up. The box had not been opened. Two things struck me. First, if Henry existed, he wasn't much for catching rodents, and second, Lorrie had access to rat poison.

With a shudder, I put it back and took one more look in Lorrie's room. Nothing had changed except without light coming through the basement window, the room was even dimmer. I studied the box with Henry's label, and the words, "It's with Henry," circulated in my head.

"What's with Henry?"

Keep looking.

"I'm tired, and I can find no evidence of a cat, let alone one that would tell me what's going on here. Please let me go to bed."

Maybe it's a note or a diary or something.

"You're welcome to stay and look, I'm going to bed." I snapped off the light and headed upstairs.

That night in my dreams, I saw a cat-ghost floating over something. But when I tried to look closer, the room darkened, and the cat faded. I woke up to sunlight splashing through the dusty curtains of the bedroom. As I showered behind the cracked vinyl shower curtain, little bits and pieces of the dream came back to me. A cat on top of something important. Charlee's words came back to me.

Maybe it's a note or a diary.

Once dressed and feeling somewhat refreshed, I ventured back into the basement. In the daylight, it had a different feel. The cement floor and walls were surprisingly dry for the humid summer. Outside the bedroom, the rest of the basement was nearly bare except for a washer, dryer, and a wash tub in the corner opposite Lorrie's room. A row of shelves held several boxes along with household tools.

Again, I saw no evidence of either a cat or mouse droppings. In Lorrie's room, I looked through his closet and found only neatly folded clothes and a couple of pairs of worn boots. His dresser drawers were the same— neatly folded underwear, t-shirts, and socks. In the little bathroom off the bedroom, all was in order. I noted that Lorrie had several bottles of cologne that probably dated back to the 1980s.

No diaries, journals, or evidence that Lorrie wrote anything down. Also, no books in his bookshelf, only photos and memorabilia from the 1980s, including a model of a Star Wars starship. Once again, I had the sense that time had stopped for Lorrie as a teenager.

I was about to leave when Charlee spoke to me. This time, it almost felt like she was shouting.

Check out Henry again!

"Charlee, there is no Henry." I wanted to punch her, except of course I'd be punching myself. Never a good move, especially if you're trying to convince people you are sane.

A voice came from upstairs. "Liza, is that you?"

Mrs. Wilkens had arrived. I looked at my watch. It was after ten in the morning.

"Down here in Lorrie's room. I'm still looking for Henry."

Mrs. Wilkens joined me. She was wearing her usual neon orange shoes and a pair of cargo shorts. Her t-shirt was emblazoned with the words, "Read Banned Books. Democracy Depends on It." She carried Goldie in her arms.

Goldie gazed at me and yawned. So much for a joyous reunion.

Mrs. Wilkens pointed around the room. "Oh my, this is not what I expected. I've known some bachelors in my life who lived like Mama never taught them to pick up after themselves. I seem to recall that Lorrie was always neat and well-groomed, even though Peter was a bit of a slob."

As we surveyed the neatness that put me to shame, she told me she'd stopped in Mankato, and Lorrie was sedated, but they thought he'd be okay. "I had to tell them he was my nephew before they'd let me see him."

"Was he able to talk to you?"

She wrinkled her brow. "He was quite groggy, but he told me Henry had the information."

"Maybe we're going about this wrong. Maybe Lorrie has a friend named Henry, and we've assumed it was his cat." Or gerbil or hamster.

I pointed out the box on top of the dresser with what looked like the remains of Henry the cat. As Mrs. Wilkens walked nearer to me, Goldie meowed and leapt out of her arms and onto the dresser.

We both stared at her as she explored the top of the dresser and then sat next to the box that held what we thought were Henry's ashes.

Mrs. Wilkens walked over to it and peered at the inscription. When she reached up to lift the box to look at it more closely, Goldie meowed again.

"What's wrong with my cat?"

"Maybe she senses cat ashes."

I was afraid Goldie might suddenly jump down and upend the little box. As I grabbed her, I noticed that she had settled on top of a magazine. I took the magazine in one hand and Goldie in the other. Goldie wriggled in my arm and projected herself onto Lorrie's neatly made bed. Without asking permission, she curled up on his pillow.

I brought the magazine to the bedside lamp. Mrs. Wilkens followed me. Opening it, I paged through it until I came to a particular article.

Charlee, you were right!

Hah! You doubted me?

"Look, Mrs. Wilkens. I think this is what Lorrie was talking about."

It was a *New York Times Magazine* article about undocumented children being used to work in meat processing plants. Unaccompanied minors were allowed into the United States if they had a relative they could be placed with. The article had uncovered companies that were exploiting those children and placing them in hazardous jobs. No one was speaking out because the kids were making money to send back home.

Her eyes widened. "Do you think that's what the Pottersville secret is?"

"This might be the Santos connection."

"But what does this have to do with Fannie? Or the poisoned cats?"

Up until this point, I'd been "investigating" a wrong—Fannie's death and the book banning, but not feeling totally engaged in it. Now the anger surged in me. When it came to hurting or exploiting children, I was all in on finding out who was doing this and stopping it. I wondered if that's what Fannie was talking about in that last Zoom when she said she'd discovered something and was worried."

"We have to figure this out!" I was halfway up the stairs when Mrs. Wilkens called me back.

"I want to know more about this as much as you do. Fannie was my friend, but we can't go off half-cocked. We need more information." This from the woman who had dragged me here in the first place.

Ah, the voice of reason.

Quiet!

Standing in front of the dresser with Henry's ashes and Goldie snuggled on Lorrie's pillow, we made a plan. First, Mrs. Wilkens would meet with Reverend Walter to go over the poisonings. Maybe the two of them could find a connection between Pottersville and the cats.

I would go to the Santos Farms and ask questions about the poultry processing and get a sense of their hiring practices. Alex would…well, we weren't sure about his role yet. Could he really be trusted if this involved his mother, sister, or father?

As we conspired, it occurred to me that Mrs. Wilkens still hadn't been told that Alex suspected he was her grandson. Perhaps that was the first order of business.

"Let's go to the clinic and see what Reverend Walter and Alex think of our theory and plan."

"Oh yes." Mrs. Wilkens nodded. "Maybe I can ask Alex about his biological father."

I smiled to myself. "Perhaps you should approach it carefully."

We left Goldie to snooze on Lorrie's pillow. Mrs. Wilkens brought in the litterbox and food. We set it upstairs in the kitchen. If another Henry existed, maybe he'd show up, too.

Even though I knew I was taking my life in my hands, I let Mrs. Wilkens drive because I was sure Trey or one of his cohorts recognized my car. On the other hand, her ancient Geo Prizm was a definite oddity around Ravens Valley. She drove surprisingly sedately until we passed the burned-out library. With a screech, she hit the brake.

"Oh, my God! Who would do such a thing?"

The building had a hole in the roof that had a tarp over it and boarded-up windows.

"No one can save the books. They'll be so damaged by smoke and water." Her eyes filled with tears. "It breaks my heart."

When we reached the clinic, Reverend Walter was waiting inside along with a woman who had just brought her dog in for a checkup. She watched us with a curious expression.

"You're not from around here, are you?"

Noting how Mrs. Wilkens bristled, I rushed ahead to answer. "No. We came last week for Fannie Porter's funeral and met Dr. Alex when my cat was poisoned."

"Oh my," her voice held sympathy. "The Reverend was just telling me about his cat. I think they're trying to scare people."

Reverend Walter took her hand. "Who do you think 'they' are?"

She pressed her lips together. "I've heard rumors. At first, they were saying Dr. Alex was deliberately poisoning pets to build up his business."

Mrs. Wilkens frowned. "And people believed it?"

The woman shrugged. "I don't think so because the next thing I heard was that it was some kind of satanic ritual from those people at Pottersville."

I sighed. "There's certainly is a lot of finger-pointing at the folks there. What do you think?"

"I think the rumor people should lay off blaming everything on Pottersville. Those are hardworking people, and I'm getting tired of all the bad-mouthing."

Reverend Walter grinned. "Ida, you are a credit to the community."

She blushed. "I'm not the only one. We don't speak out, though, because bad things happen to the ones who do."

"Like their pets get poisoned?" I asked.

She nodded.

"Well, Ida, we plan to get to the bottom of this."

She smiled at him. "You are a true man of God, not like that slick evangelist. You know, some of us are sure he's only after our money. What happened to the decent churches?"

I thought about the church that had Fannie's funeral and the kind minister who was also a volunteer EMT and spoke up. "Maybe you should check out the little church by the park. The minister strikes me as a woman of God."

Alex walked out of the surgery wearing his white lab coat, carrying a little black poodle. "All set, Ida. He's looking good for a senior citizen. Whatever you are doing, keep it up."

We watched as she attached him to his leash and walked to the door. Before she opened it, she turned, "Ravens Valley used to be a good place to live. Don't believe all those signs with happy people and happy chickens.

The devil has taken over."

Chapter Thirty-Four: Organic Chickens

Reverend Walter was the first to speak after Ida left. "It's time to cast the devil out. Let's get to those files."

While they set themselves up behind the empty reception desk with Alex's laptop, I showed him the article from Lorrie's bedroom.

As he read it, he kept shaking his head. "This does not sound like something Dad would be involved in. We've had numerous discussions at the dining room table about the labor laws. Dad always said the last thing Santos Brothers needed was trouble with the Department of Labor and ICE over immigration issues."

I realized that as much as I liked Alex, I didn't totally trust him. I remembered the conversation I'd overheard with Annalisa about money. Alex wanted to fix up the wreck of a house next to the clinic, and he wanted to purchase back acreage that his grandfather had lost. Could he somehow be involved in an illegal but perhaps lucrative scheme?

I hoped Mrs. Wilkens would be too involved in the poison records to tell Alex I was going to show up at Santos Brothers and ask about their personnel policies. Fortunately, Alex was called away almost as soon as the computer was set up. "Sorry, I'm going to have to leave. Sheep emergency."

I refrained from asking what kind of emergency a sheep could get into. As soon as he drove away in his van, I told Mrs. Wilkens I was going on a little investigation of my own.

She hardly looked up from the computer as she exclaimed, "There! What about that cat?"

I left as Reverend Walter was giving her the history of the family the cat belonged to.

The bright, clear skies had grown cloudy as a front moved in from the west. My phone told me thunderstorms were expected this afternoon. When I arrived at the Santos Brothers estate, two landscapers were working on flower beds. They spoke to each other in rapid Spanish. I was able to discern a couple of words that indicated someone inside the office was not happy.

I walked into a small reception area of the office to find a couple of upholstered chairs and motel-quality artwork on the walls. I was surprised they hadn't used any of Lily's paintings. The reception desk was empty, and a desktop computer screen saver floated images of colored Easter eggs. Behind the desk were several four-drawer file cabinets. I wondered if they were personnel files and if I could sneak back and take a peek.

While I pondered how I could take a surreptitious look, voices rose from one of the offices. "Damn it, Elvis! What were those boys thinking? You need to get them under control!"

I accidentally banged my knee into the metal desk trying to ease around to the files. Annalisa peeked out from one of the offices. "Yes? Can I help you?"

I waved at her and tried to fashion my lips into a friendly smile. I knew I would be lying when I talked with Annalisa, and my face was not cooperating.

You look like you just ate a lemon.

"You're not much help."

"Excuse me?" Annalisa joined me at the desk. "Did you say something?"

"Sorry. Was I talking out loud? Bad habit."

"Can I help you?" She studied me for a moment. "You're Alex's friend."

"That's right. Although I wouldn't say we are friends. More like acquaintances after he saved my cat from getting poisoned to death."

Annalisa put one hand on her hip, studying me. "What can I do for you?"

Here's the part I hadn't rehearsed. How could I ask her about using children in poultry processing without having her call Trey to have me arrested? I stumbled through the sketchy reason I'd come.

"Uh, kids," I stuttered. "Um, I'm a teacher in an inner city school, and I wanted to do a lesson on farming." Pinocchio would have been proud of me. "I…um…saw your trucks with the girl with the eggs, and it sparked an idea. Maybe we could do a field trip here, or maybe you could come to my classroom?"

Fat chance with a field trip. No funds for it, and I couldn't ask the parents for the money. Like Pinocchio, I felt my nose growing.

Annalisa wrinkled her brow as I spoke. I'm guessing she was wondering if I was making this up or was sincere. She must have decided because she smiled, showing beautiful, straight teeth. "That's exactly why we are setting up the education center here. To get kids interested in organic farming."

I thought about the kids in my classroom. For many of them, food was scarce, and they wouldn't care if it was organic or made by a chatbot as long as it filled their empty stomachs.

"We aren't quite set up yet, but we're working on a video about how we raise our chickens. And we're hoping to have a demonstration site behind this building where we show them how the chickens are raised according to the standards set up for certifying as organic."

It sounded like an elevator sales speech. I nodded. "I read about how you have to use organic feed, and you can't use antibiotics or synthetic pesticides. Sounds complicated."

"But worth it. We have more orders now than we can fill."

Elvis stepped out of the office and joined her. "What are you talking about?" He smelled faintly of leather even though he was wearing jeans and a short-sleeved shirt. I noted the muscled and tattooed arms. Between his good looks and the hint of leather, I felt a faint fluttering in my stomach.

Shame on you!

I can't help my hormones.

Annalisa looked at him, and I was sure her eyes softened. Or maybe I was projecting.

Annalisa introduced us. "Liza is a schoolteacher in Minneapolis. She was wondering about bringing her class here on a field trip when we've got it all set up." She smiled at him. "See, I told you this would be a good idea."

He did not smile back. "Ah, yes, Chicken University."

She frowned at him, "Dad agrees with me that education about what we are doing is important. We can bring smaller independent farmers into our co-op."

I didn't know Santos Brothers was a co-op. "Do you get your chickens from other places?"

"Some of them. As I said, we have more orders than we can fill."

Remember what you came here for? Child labor?

Good point.

"I'm thinking if I brought my class here, we could also talk with them about the workforce. I mean, many of my kids are immigrants, and some of them come from rural areas. It would be nice to show them…uh…people like their parents working in the field of organics. I've heard…ah…younger immigrants can get jobs around here." My voice trailed off as I saw the expression on Elvis's face darken. He moved near enough to me that the faint leather grew stronger. For a moment, my body wasn't sure if it wanted to get even closer or flee possible danger.

When he spoke, his voice had a tightness to it: "We hire only documented *adults* if that's what you are getting at." He glared at me. "Are you really a teacher or are you one of those journalists looking for a big scoop?"

Me? A journalist? I took one journalism class in college and dropped it after a week when I discovered I didn't like to write.

I laughed. It was the most genuine sound I'd made since showing up at Santos Brothers. "No, really, I teach fifth grade in Minneapolis. I can show you my ID, if you'd like."

He stayed close enough to me that I felt his body heat. "Curious that you show up here. I heard you were friends with Fannie Porter."

It sounded like he was accusing me of a bad thing. I decided to play dumb. Or maybe I didn't have to play at it.

"I'm confused. What does Fannie have to do with your workforce?"

Annalisa looked daggers at Elvis before she spoke. "I apologize for that comment. It's just that we are continually scrutinized about our employees, and we do get a little touchy about it."

Elvis scowled. "I'm suggesting that some people in this town want to smear Santos Brothers, and Fannie was…inquisitive."

Inquisitive? I was surprised he knew the word.

I smiled as insincerely as I could, "If you want to know, I met Fannie over a Zoom call. She was helping me with a class I'm taking." I attempted to look rueful. "I interviewed her because of the book-banning movement here. Once I got here for the funeral, I saw all the signs for Santos Brothers and thought the organic farming would be an interesting topic for my kids." I inched away from him. "You know, because of their backgrounds."

I was instantly ashamed of my words. They stereotyped my students in a way that was not fair.

Elvis appeared to be satisfied with my explanation. As I looked at him, I realized that contrary to my initial hormonal reaction to him, he had a weakness to his chin and a way of carrying himself as if he spent a lot of time in front of a mirror, preening.

A rooster who can't crow.

You said it. Now go away. You are distracting me.

I was so busy talking with Charlee that I missed the beginning of Annalisa's sentence.

"…perhaps a tour later?"

Outside, the sky had darkened, and thunder rumbled in the distance. The last thing I wanted to do right now was tour a barn full of chickens, knowing they'd soon be on someone's barbecue grill. Recovering, I thanked her for the offer. "Sorry, I really need to get going before the storm hits. It's a long drive back to the cities." I held my hand out to Annalisa, "Well, thank you for your time. Perhaps you have a card, and I can contact you during the school year to see if you're set up for visitors yet."

While she opened a drawer in the reception desk for her card, I turned to Elvis. "The education center is a great idea. Good for you, looking after the community like this."

"Sure." His eyes were hard as he strode down the hall. I guessed I didn't pass muster with him.

Annalisa handed me a card and spoke in a low voice. "You have to forgive him. He's from Texas, and you know, the border crisis and all. He's kind of touchy."

"No problem. I'm sure you also have to fight off rumors all the time. Even though I've only been here a couple of days, I've heard it mentioned that some of the people who work for you live in a place they call Pottersville, and it's filled with drugs. I'm sure it's all poppycock."

Poppycock? I was beginning to sound like Mrs. Wilkens.

To my surprise, Annalisa's cheeks turned red. "I…uh…think it's terrible what people say." She turned abruptly and walked away.

Outside, thunder rumbled in the distance. I walked out as a bolt of lightning streaked across the sky.

I'd hit a nerve bringing up Pottersville. Something was clearly wrong here. If only I could get at those personnel files.

Chapter Thirty-Five: The Cats

By the time I reached the clinic, big drops of rain splatted against the windshield of Mrs. Wilkens's Geo. I discovered that she needed new wiper blades and wondered if we could find them for such an ancient vehicle here in Ravens Valley.

Mrs. Wilkens barely looked up when I walked in.

"Hello? Finding anything?"

Reverend Walter wrinkled his brow. "Not sure. Alex has treated ten cats, including yours and mine, in the last four months."

"We haven't found anything before that, at least in Alex's records." Mrs. Wilkens held up a piece of paper with the names of the cat owners.

"Any pattern?"

Outside, lightning lit up the sky, followed by thunder. The lights in the clinic flickered.

Reverend Walter rubbed his forehead. "I don't see a pattern except my foggy brain tells me there's something I'm missing."

"Any similarities among the cat owners?"

Mrs. Wilkens looked at the reverend. "We've been pondering it. The cats are from a variety of people—schoolteachers, one of the nursing home nurses, even one of the sheriff's deputies."

"So maybe we have a psychopath in the making who is randomly going after cats".

Another flash of lightning and a closer crash of thunder. It reminded me of how lightning struck a tree that then fell on my old Toyota. I blinked away the image of my beloved car squashed beneath an oak tree. Peeking out the window, I made sure I hadn't left Mrs. Wilkens's car under a tree. The wind whipped through the trees as rain pelted down.

Mrs. Wilkens raised her voice above the din. "We'll have to talk with Alex, but we know Lucy wasn't an outdoor cat, and we know we left Goldie in the motel room. I don't believe it's random. Someone had to know where to find the cats."

Suddenly, it all seemed far more sinister. "You mean like the cats were lured outside and targeted?"

Reverend Walter patted Mrs. Wilkens on the hand. "We don't know. Lucy did have the tendency to sneak out, although she never went far."

But I'd left Goldie in the motel room. As I recalled, she'd refused to come out of the cat carrier as if the musty motel carpet was beneath her dignity. She was a smart cat, but not smart enough to open the door and let herself out.

Alex's van pulled up, rain streaming down the windshield. He ran from the van into the clinic, holding his medical bag over her head. "Whew, it's wet out there!"

While Mrs. Wilkens and Reverend Walter filled him in, I stood by the window watching the rain and thinking about my visit to the Santos office. I'd sensed sparks between Elvis and Annalisa—both sparks of attraction and sparks of anger. Who were "the boys," and why did the temperature in the office drop to below zero when I mentioned Pottersville? I needed to get back and see if I could find anything in the personnel files.

"…it looks like it began in late spring." Mrs. Wilkens was speaking as the three gathered around the laptop.

Alex scratched his head. "I think I treated the first one in May before I understood what was happening." He spoke in a husky voice, "I lost that one."

I sensed the sadness in his words. "Was there anything significant that happened around the time you treated the first cat? New people moving to town? Controversy of some sort?"

Reverend Walter spoke in a thoughtful voice. "Well, for me. That's around the time when the church 'retired' me and brought in Vogel."

Mrs. Wilkens regarded him. "I don't suppose you took your revenge by poisoning the cats?"

I nearly gasped at her words until Reverend Walter chuckled. "It wasn't cats I wanted to poison back then."

In my limited experience with religion, I didn't see ministers as having a sense of humor. They were either preaching fundamentalism from the pulpit or forming a cult. I quickly shook off the thought of the short time Mother and I were part of Josiah's Household of Faith.

Best to stay away from that topic.

Yup.

By the way, Mrs. Wilkens appears to be charmed by the minister.

I'd hardly noticed until I saw the rosiness of her cheeks and heard her giggle. Mrs. Wilkens giggling? Really?

Alex squinted up at the ceiling with a thoughtful expression. "Wasn't it May when vandals broke into that abandoned fertilizer warehouse near Pottersville and set it on fire?"

"They said some of those poultry workers from Pottersville were living there and accidentally set it on fire."

"Could it have had rat poison?" I asked.

Alex shrugged. "A lot of those old storage places had chemicals and poisons. I hate to think of what went up into the atmosphere when the place burned."

I sat down in one of the chairs and rubbed my eyes. This wasn't adding up. "Pottersville was blamed again for something bad happening. It doesn't make sense to me. I'm guessing some of the poultry workers are undocumented. The last thing they'd want is to break the law and get sent back."

"I agree." Reverend Walter settled next to me. "I know those folks, and they are hardworking, decent people who have been dealt a nasty hand. And this town has not done much to help them."

I tried piecing the little snippets of information together. "We know someone started poisoning the cats around the time the warehouse burned. We think that the poison is probably an old, banned rat poison. We also know the church fired you around that time, and Reverend Vogel took over."

I put my hands up in surrender. "It doesn't add up to anything."

"Wait," Alex stared up at the ceiling. "Something else happened around that time. Something at the processing plant." He looked at Reverend Walter, "Do you remember?"

"Rumors." The Reverend rubbed his temple, "As I recall, rumors of an accident at the plant. But it was hushed up quickly. Didn't make the papers—not that the local paper would dare print anything bad about the Santos Brothers." He raised his eyebrows at Alex. "No offense."

Alex shrugged. "I'm not part of the business."

"What were the rumors?"

Reverend Walter closed his eyes, his lips moving as if trying to remember. "Yes, now I think I have it. This was before my 'retirement.' I used to go to Pottersville and have an evening service once a month. Those poor folks who wanted to worship were hardly welcomed into the church here in town. That last service before the end of my 'service,' I sensed a great deal of agitation. Unfortunately, my Spanish is limited, but I got the impression someone from Pottersville had gotten hurt, and they were worried the feds would come in and close the place. They needed their jobs."

"Poisoning the cats might have been revenge?" I felt stupid as soon as the words were out.

Reverend Walter raised his eyebrows. "You never know if someone would go that route. I didn't see it."

"And the poisoning goes on."

"Walter, when did the book banning start? Was it around the same time?" I noted how Mrs. Wilkens had already dropped the "reverend."

He took a deep breath and looked at Alex, "What do you think?"

"Fannie started getting harassed later in May. She told me the first encounter with Protect Our Children was after she proposed setting up a bookmobile for the kids who live in Pottersville."

I took it all in. "May seems like the beginning of several things, but I don't see how they tie together." I ticked off the poisoning, the beginning of the book banning, the possible incident at the chicken processing plant, and Reverend Walter's sudden loss of a job. "And then there's the unsolved hit-and-run and arsons going on now."

"Not to mention Felix hanging from my door." Alex scratched his head.

Mrs. Wilkens's eyes opened wide. "What?"

Alex explained about the stuffed cat. "Nasty little prank. I suspect cousin Josh had something to do with it. However, I'm not going to Vince—yet."

We were all silent for a few moments. Outside, the rain had stopped, and a little ray of sunshine poked through the clouds. The change in the weather didn't change the atmosphere of perplexion and worry in the clinic.

Reverend Walter looked down at the floor, shaking his head. "I'm going to have to meditate and pray on all of this."

Mrs. Wilkens's phone rang with an annoying lilt. "Yes, this is Ginny Wilkens." She said very little other than "ohs" and "uh-huhs" as the person on the other end spoke. When the call ended, she sat heavily on one of the waiting room chairs with a distressed expression.

"That was the hospital ICU. It seems he has a brain bleed, and they might have to do surgery." She ran her hand through her hair. "They wanted to know about advance directives and whether Lorrie had ever said anything about resuscitation." She looked at Reverend Walter, "I don't know what to say. I kind of lied about my relationship to him."

Reverend Walter gazed at the ceiling before speaking. "Lorrie wasn't much of a church-goer, although I knew his mother. She was…well, difficult, I think. But I hardly ever talked with him except about Pottersville. We might have to leave the decision-making in the hands of the hospital."

"Wait," Alex raised his hand like he was in a classroom. "Lorrie spent time with Fannie." His voice faded out. Fannie would not be able to help us.

Mrs. Wilkens rubbed her hands, "I really should go to the hospital. Poor Lorrie."

Reverend Walter put his arm around her shoulder with a brief hug. "Let me take you. With my clerical collar, I can usually get by all the guardians at the hospital."

"It's time we brought the sheriff in on this." I said it with little conviction. I doubted he would do anything more than fill out a form, but at least it would be on record.

I remembered the snippet of conversation between Annalisa and Elvis referring to the boys. Was she talking about the Blackmers and how they'd attacked Lorrie? Is that what Annalisa meant? Picturing Lorrie's battered face, I felt the anger grow. He was a decent, harmless guy.

You need to find out what happened.

I didn't argue with Charlee. Ravens Valley not only felt dark but also dangerous. Time to do something about it. Except, of course, I was a schoolteacher whose best skill was teaching children.

Poe's Raven came to me, "Darkness there and nothing more." Time to check out the Nevermore.

Chapter Thirty-Six: Pamela

I had it in my head I would burst into the Nevermore and demand answers. Charlee had a different idea.

Wait.

What do you mean, wait? You're the one who said I should do something.

Not stupid things, you dope.

You just called me a dope?

This conversation might have gone on except Mrs. Wilkens interrupted me. "Liza, you look like you're seeing a ghost."

"Ah, just thinking through everything that's gone on."

"Well, Walter is going to drive me to the hospital in Mankato. I'll meet you back at Lorrie's this evening if…if everything is okay." She choked up on the last few words.

I hugged her, "Tell him Henry is fine."

After they left, I turned to Alex. "We have to do something. The person who beat Lorrie should be in jail, and I don't think Trey or the sheriff are going to help us."

"I hope you're not suggesting we find this person and do a citizen's arrest."

Of course, I hadn't thought it through. "Maybe if we can identify who did it, we might get the sheriff to do something more than plan for retirement."

"First things first." He pointed to his watch. "I need to check on my patient and make sure she and her lamb are doing okay. I doubt whoever jumped Lorrie has skipped down." He lowered his voice, "Probably one of the Blackmers or their wannabes."

I sighed. Vets and their animals. Speaking of animals, it was time to make sure Goldie was all right before I went to the bar for answers. "Care to meet me for a drink when you are done with whatever it is you do?"

"Sounds good. There's a nice little bar just off the square in downtown. If we go there, it will be fun to watch the people whispering about us." His eyes twinkled with amusement. "I'm considered eligible here in town."

"Um. I don't know what to say to that."

He blushed, and in that moment, he looked like a teenaged boy.

"I can save you from the town talkers because I'm thinking we should go to the Nevermore."

His eyes widened. "That's a place to stay away from—especially you."

"Meaning a single woman without an escort?"

"Meaning you've already been targeted by Trey. Word travels fast."

"Well, I'm going to see how much fruit they put in their Mai Tai."

He sighed heavily. "Listen, wait for me, and I'll go with you. Do you by any chance have a gun?"

"You're kidding…aren't you?"

He smiled. "Maybe."

We agreed he would pick me up at Lorrie's as soon as he was done tending the new mother and baby.

* * *

When I let myself into Lorrie's, the sun was pouring through the dirty windows. I guessed they hadn't been washed since Mama died or even before. Goldie did not greet me. I looked around upstairs before going into the basement. For some reason, I felt like I had to be extra quiet, as if I was sneaking up on someone. I stepped lightly on my way down. In Lorrie's bedroom, nothing had been disturbed, and Goldie, who maintained her place on Lorrie's pillow, barely acknowledged me.

"Don't you care that I'm back and in one piece?"

Apparently, Goldie didn't care much. I walked over and gave her a little stroke. She raised her tail but did not move.

"Are you okay?"

She didn't answer.

I walked to the dresser with Henry's box. Maybe I could find more clues. Goldie stretched and leapt softly off the bed. She stood by my feet and watched as I picked up the photos on the dresser and studied them.

One of them was a black-and-white snapshot of a couple and a little boy. I guessed the boy was Lorrie. He wore a button-down, short-sleeved shirt and shorts. He squinted into the camera, holding his parents' hands. Lorrie's mother looked stern with her lips pressed into a firm line, and his father looked uncomfortable in a suitcoat and tie. If Lorrie hadn't been in the photo, I would have said his parents were the model for American Gothic.

"Nothing here, I guess." Reaching down, I picked Goldie up. "Come and have something to eat."

While Goldie ate her wretched tuna cat food, I sat at the kitchen table with a beer, trying to sort everything out.

Lorrie had been critically injured for saying something about the Santos Brothers. Fannie had been hit by a car for unknown reasons, but had told us in the Zoom meeting that she was afraid. She'd never mentioned the Santos Brothers in our Zooms, but she'd said something to Lorrie. Protect Our Children started making noise around the time the first cat was poisoned. Pottersville was blamed for everything bad in the county.

"Oh yes, Goldie, let's not forget someone burned down Fannie's house and tried to burn down the library. What the hell is happening?"

To my total surprise, she jumped up on my lap, settled, and when I stroked her, she purred. Maybe Alex had done a cat brain transplant. This wasn't the old Goldie.

We enjoyed a few minutes of communion before Alex pulled up in his van. He came around to the back door and let himself in.

"Are mother and baby doing okay?" I continued to stroke Goldie, and she continues to purr.

"Not only that, but I think I'll actually get paid for my services." He sat down, and Goldie immediately transferred her affections to him.

I offered him a beer, and we made plans for our visit to the Nevermore. "If this is such a bad place, why did Lorrie hang out there?"

Alex cracked open the tab on the beer can. "I've only known Lorrie since I came back to town, but I think he liked to be with some of the regulars there. Old vets…military vets, not animal vets."

"Is it really a bad place? Like a biker bar in the movies? You know, guys wearing leather and chains and opening bottles of beer with their teeth?

He laughed. "I would say it's got a rough crowd. Definitely not upscale. The Nevermore has a long history of ups and downs in Ruston County, going back to the days of Prohibition. My grandfather told me it was the 'in' place to go in his time. For a while, it was called the Nevermore Supper Club. By the time I was a teenager, it was the one place in the county where someone with a fake ID could get a beer. Then it got closed down. A couple of years ago, the new owners advertised it as a working man's watering hole."

"Really?"

"Grandpa told me that back in the 1920s, a local schoolteacher built the bar and decided to make money on the side by calling it a literary society. Thus, the name 'The Nevermore' from the Poe poem. If they got raided, they had tables with books of poetry and novels."

"What? Here in rural Minnesota?"

Alex sat up straighter in mock indignity. "What? We can't live on farms and be educated?"

"Humph."

Alex stroked Goldie, gently probing her neck and her belly. "She's doing well."

This reminded me of Henry. I beckoned him to come with me back down in the basement. In Lorrie's room, I showed him the box. "Henry, or what we think might be the remains of Henry, was sitting on top of the magazine."

"Curious."

Goldie took the opportunity to settle in once again on Lorrie's pillow. As I watched her, I was overcome with the thought that Lorrie might never be back.

"Shall we head to the bar?"

Alex stopped me. "Wait. We need to talk about this escapade." His voice had changed from an earlier hint of humor to something tight, almost unpleasant.

"I thought we'd go in, see if any of the regulars knew what happened to Lorrie and why."

Alex laughed, but there was no mirth in it. "When I turned twenty-one and was back from college, a couple of old high school buddies challenged me to go to the Nevermore."

"And you got beat up? Were you scared?"

He shook his head. "No. Not at all. I was disappointed. The place was only half-full, the jukebox broken, and someone had thrown up right by the bathroom door. It was downright depressing. But worse, the conversation at other tables was filled with ugliness. N-words, disparaging remarks about the Spics taking over the county. We stayed for a couple of beers, but I decided when I was done with school, I'd stay in the cities and away from the small-town racism."

"You aren't making the place sound dangerous, just odious."

Odious?

It just slipped out.

Ask him to tell you more. He's trying to get at something.

"Excuse me?" Alex peered at me. "Did you say something?"

"You decided not to come back to Ravens Valley? Yet here you are." I raised my voice as if I was repeating the question and silently wished Charlee away.

"Dad was unhappy when I told him. Said he'd paid for my education so I could be the company veterinarian. Instead, I made another bad decision— my wife."

The sun began to set, glowing bright yellow through the dusty window. "You told me she died?" I prompted.

He pressed his lips into a grim line. "While I was doing an internship at a small animal clinic in Minnetonka, I met a veterinary tech. She was so different from the girls I'd dated before. You know, kind of 'out there.' Loved animals and trying dangerous things like skydiving. We started dating and eventually married. I inherited money from Grandpa, and I used it to buy a small practice where I'd treat the pets from the wealthy suburbs. It was

Pamela's idea and dream."

Where was this going? I simply nodded.

"Frankly, I struggled with the owners and their pampered pets. In truth, I've always liked large animals. Maybe growing up with chickens did that to me."

"You do well with cats."

His lips curled into a slight smile at my remark. "What I didn't know was that Pamela's thrill-seeking included experimenting with drugs. For a year or two, things went well, then the books stopped balancing, and my drug inventory didn't add up. Pamela got more demanding." He let out his breath with a whistle. "Long story short, she was an addict who was plundering the pharmacy and also stealing from the clinic. I was so busy treating FiFi and Fluffy that I didn't notice until it was too late. I ended up losing the clinic and Pamela…she overdosed before our divorce was final."

I held back from touching him. I heard the pain in his voice, but a part of me wondered how he hadn't figured this out. I guessed there was more to the story.

I took a deep breath, "Let's go solve this crime." As soon as I said it, I felt stupid. This wasn't a cute little game of Clue. People were getting hurt—and possibly killed.

Alex's phone rang. "I have to take this." He stepped outside, and I watched him pace in the backyard as he spoke. When he finally slipped the phone back in his pocket, he came back in with brow furrowed.

He spoke in a tight voice, "I have a crisis at home I need to take care of."

"Can I help?"

He shook his head, "I'll explain later. How about if you wait here, and when I'm done, we'll go to the only bistro in town for supper." He regarded me. "Not the Nevermore—okay?"

I crossed my toes like a good little fibber. "Sure. Give me a call."

After he left, I turned to Goldie, who was busy licking her paws. "Don't tell anyone, but I'm off to check out the Nevermore Bar. 'So faintly came the tapping…'" Apparently, Goldie wasn't impressed that I could quote Poe.

Shouldn't you wait for reinforcements?

Probably, but I need to talk with those friends before someone gets to them and tells them to shut up.

Why I thought it should be me was a question for the ages.

Chapter Thirty-Seven: The Nevermore

The Nevermore was located a mile outside of Ravens Valley on a paved county road. It stood alone among a stand of cottonwood trees. Their leaves shimmered in the fading light. The gravel of the parking lot crunched under the wheels of the car as I pulled up as close to the front door as I could. The bar had a porch with several white plastic tables and chairs and ashtrays for the smokers. The porch was empty when I stepped out of the car.

Two middle-aged men in blue jeans and t-shirts stood by a pair of motorcycles and talked in loud voices. Both of them had ruddy, weathered faces that spoke of outdoor work and too much alcohol.

"Stupid &!$#% nearly killed him. Boy, is he mad now!"

"Big blow up. Hope we get our money—you know?"

A truck with a bad muffler pulled in, and I couldn't hear anything more. By the time the truck parked and turned off its engine, they'd mounted the motorcycles and ridden off.

For a moment, I hesitated walking through the door. Then I pictured Lorrie's injuries. Someone had to stand up for him.

Great thought, sis, but be careful.

Careful is my middle name.

Hah!

As soon as I opened the door, I smelled stale beer and an odor of unwashed humanity mixed with a pine-scented cleaner. Looking around, it was hard to think this place was once called a supper club. Directly opposite the door was a bar with six wooden stools. To the left of the bar, which might have been the dining area at one time, were three pool tables.

The bartender was a slight woman with a pixie haircut and heavy black eye makeup. She wore a nametag that said, Cyd and she appeared more goth than biker babe. Hanging behind the bar was a framed photograph of Edgar Alan Poe. Judging by the smeared and dusty glass, it hadn't been washed in many years. Propped up next to it was a dusty stuffed raven with one of its eyes missing.

Patrons sat at wooden tables talking over the country-western music in the background. Most of the drinkers were men who looked like they'd come in from a day in the fields or road construction. The Nevermore struck me as a working man's bar rather than a biker dive. On the other hand, I only knew about bikers' dives from watching a few B-grade movies.

I walked up to the bar, "Hi. Wondering if I could get a beer?"

My voice was so tentative, I think she considered carding me before asking, "Tap or bottle?"

"Got Summit?"

"Got Bud Light."

"Good enough."

She flipped off the cap and handed me a cold bottle.

I settled on a stool. "Do you know Lorrie?"

She snorted, "All the time he's spent here, he could probably own the place—like my no-good husband who loves to play pool and stays away from real work."

"Yesterday, someone beat Lorrie up. He's in the hospital, and I'm wondering who did it."

Her eyes narrowed. "Who are you?"

Good question, sis. Better come up with a believable answer.

I decided to be honest. "I met Lorrie this week. He helped me when my cat was poisoned. He seems like a decent person, and someone hurt him. I want to know who." I added, "I don't get the sense you have much in the line of law enforcement around here."

She rolled her eyes. "No one wants to rock the boat. Jobs at stake—even mine."

"Were you working when Lorrie got hurt?"

"You're pretty nosy, aren't you? No, I wasn't here. I was home with that no-good I married, trying to talk him into getting a job."

"Did you hear about it?"

"Yup."

I tensed, wondering why she was being so evasive. I glanced at a table near the bar and noted that the two men sitting at it were watching us.

She leaned close enough that I could smell the slight perfume of her shampoo. "Blackmer's involved. Best stay out of it."

"Who could tell me more?" I persisted.

She sighed, pointing to a round table in the corner. Three men sat with beers, rolling dice. "Those are Lorrie's regulars. They were probably there. You might ask them. But I'd stay out of it, if I were you."

A man with a gruff voice at another table held up an empty glass, "Hey, barkeep. You working?"

"Gotta go. Wouldn't want to miss a fat tip." She made a face.

I took my bottle and walked over to the table with the dice players. I was aware that other patrons were staring at me. What came to me was the old plot line for a novel—a stranger comes to town.

The three guys at the table looked to be about Lorrie's age. Two were bearded and scruffy, like they'd spent the night before in a homeless shelter. The other was clean-shaven. What they all appeared to have in common was a world-weary expression. I saw it in the sagging chins and dark shadows under their eyes as if they'd lived a hardscrabble life.

Getting literary, are we?

I ignored her as I formulated what to say. Outside, two motorcycles roared to a stop.

One of the scruffy-looking men watched me before turning to his companions. "Incoming trouble."

As I approached, it seemed the three men shrank back at the sound of the motorcycles. They kept their eyes on the door until the two riders walked in. They were men in their early twenties wearing blue jeans and windbreakers.

I sensed a collective sigh of relief from the table as the two settled at the bar.

I introduced myself, "I'm Liza. Lorrie is a new friend of mine, and I'm looking for information on what happened to him."

The man closest to me held out his hand, "Lorrie told us about you and your old lady friend. Pleased to meet you. I'm Jed, and this sad-looking guy to my right is Mack. Over there is Karl. He's the clean-cut one." He gestured to the empty chair next to Karl. "Have a seat."

Once I settled in, he told me what had happened. "You know Lorrie's a good guy, but common sense hasn't been his strong suit." The other two nodded. "We were just shooting the breeze when his friend Mannie walked in. Mannie is…uh…outspoken. Served in Iraq and thinks he knows everything. He started on his usual rant about the Pottersville people taking over jobs."

Mack nodded, "Never ask Mannie a question about anything because he'll tell you—over and over."

"Anyway," Jed continued, "He got into it with Lorrie and the next thing we knew, Lorrie was standing up and shouting at him about how those folks in Pottersville had been 'used' and he had the proof." He paused, placing his hands on the table. "Our rule here at the Nevermore is to never raise your voice because someone will hear you."

"Yup," Mack agreed. "Raised voices bring trouble."

"Well, things calmed down, and we sat chewing the fat for another half hour or so when Lorrie says he needs to leave. Says the oddest thing." He turned to the other two. "Remember what he said? I quote, 'Fannie had the goods on them, and Henry is keeping it safe.'"

Karl, the clean-shaven one at the table, rubbed his forehead before speaking. "We'd been so busy talking, we didn't notice the Blackmers walk in. Shoulda been paying attention."

Jed sighed. "Shoulda gone out with Lorrie instead of sitting here like a bunch of stooges. We didn't hear the fight at all. One of the Blackmers came back in muttering, 'Damn dumbass should have told us what he knew.'"

Karl closed his eyes for a moment. "We got out of here as soon as we could. Found Lorrie bloody and beat up, but he wouldn't let us take him home. Said he was fine."

I pictured him staggering to his car and winced. "Were they trying to find out what he knew about Pottersville?"

Jed stroked his beard, "That would be my guess. We didn't want any trouble with the Blackmers, so we headed home. Shoulda made sure Lorrie was okay."

I filled them in on what I knew about Lorrie's health and added, "He's not in good shape. Might appreciate a visit."

I got the sense these guys were bar friends only. I doubted they would be visiting Lorrie anytime soon.

While I finished my beer, the trio told me about how things had changed in Ravens Valley over the last several years. For them, the change came when Elvis Gates was hired to run the new poultry processing plant.

"Before that, they shipped the birds off to Worthington to that plant. Santos raised them but didn't do the slaughtering and the packaging." Mack frowned. "I used to work for them. Heck was a decent boss, and Vince—well, Vince was always carping about cutting down on expenses."

Karl nodded, "Sure managed to cut down on paying people by bringing in the Mexicans on that guest worker program. They were willing to do the work folks around here didn't want to do."

I knew about the guest worker program, which recruits temporary workers mainly from Mexico to work in the fields and, in some cases, to work domestic jobs that can't be filled locally. The parents of some of my students came here under the program. I also knew that despite the rules in place for the workers, like guaranteed housing and transportation, many of them were exploited.

"Annalisa told me they are careful to not do anything illegal with the people they bring in."

"Hah!" Jed looked around after he'd spoken. His eyes widened as the door of the bar opened. "Incoming. Blackmer spotted," he whispered.

I watched a burly man in a brown leather jacket lumber over to one of the guys sitting on a stool. He had the upper body of a wrestler but the bowlegs of a cowboy. He clapped the younger man on the back.

"I suggest it would be a good time for you to leave. Blackmer doesn't like anything out of the ordinary. And you are out of the ordinary," Jed continued in his whisper.

"What? You think he's going to beat me up for sitting with you?"

Karl, who had been the quietest of the three, threw the dice. "Best leave. Now."

The three became instantly involved with the dice game as if I didn't exist.

Part of me wanted to stride over to Blackmer and ask him if he'd hurt Lorrie and why. And part of me wanted to flee. I compromised, sort of, and made my way to the bar ready to confront this burly man with biceps the size of my thighs.

Careful. If you end up in the morgue, so do I.

Cyd looked up from wiping the bar; her eyes widened. For a moment, I felt like the squirrel in the middle of the road deciding whether to go back or run in front of the truck. Fortunately, good sense prevailed, and I opted for the door.

Outside in the warm evening air, I took a deep breath. What had I been thinking? Was I going to approach the bully and bash him over the head with a beer bottle? Hardly.

My phone pinged with a text from Mrs. Wilkens. **Where are you?**

Just leaving Nevermore. Trying to stay out of trouble.

She didn't text back.

While I was texting, the door to the bar opened, and Blackmer strode out. "You got a problem with me?"

Really? Was that the best he could do? Hackneyed lines from a bad movie?

"Excuse me?" I decided to play dumb.

"I heard you were asking about Lorrie."

"I was. Seems someone beat him up, and he's in bad shape. I wanted to know a little more so I could report it to the police." I smiled sweetly while the sweat poured down the sides of my chest. I hoped he didn't see how my hands shook as I gripped the phone. "Maybe you know something?"

He took a step toward me. I'm sure it was meant to be menacing, but it struck me as overly dramatic. I felt a giggle bubbling up. I'm not sure if it was mirth or hysteria.

"You're not from around here, are you?" In the waning light, his eyes had an unhealthy gleam to them as he eyed me up and down.

Another motorcycle roared up. The man on it looked like Blackmer but more simian. I guessed they were related.

Blackmer called out to him as he dismounted. "This gal wants to know what happened to Lorrie so she can report it."

The ape man smirked before he spoke, "Hey, I've seen you around town, haven't I? With that old lady."

I hated the disrespect in his voice. I felt my temper rise. "Really? I think I saw you tearing away from Fannie's house after you set it on fire."

Careful. You don't need to bait the grizzly.

If he beat up Lorrie, I want to take his head off.

Blackmer moved in close to me. He smelled of sweat and stale cigarettes. "Hey. What's your problem?"

"Someone hurt my friend Lorrie, and I want that person in jail. Would that be you?"

Ape man approached and stood beside Blackmer. Both had the same close eyes and heavy brow. My survival instinct told me I was in trouble. I looked around to figure out options. I could break for the door of the bar and hope someone would help me, or I could try to get to the car.

The car keys were in my pocket, and I guessed that by the time I got them out and got to the car door to unlock it, the apes would be on me. I tried option three, keep them talking until either they got bored or someone else showed up.

Unfortunately, I wasn't as skilled as Scheherazade, but I tried. "Listen, I don't want trouble. But Lorrie was badly hurt, and if you know something, you should tell the sheriff. And if you do, I won't report seeing you at the fire at Fannie's."

Blackmer looked at his cousin, "What? You know anything about that fire?"

Ape man glowered at me, "What makes you think it was me?"

I pointed to the motorcycle. "Recognized it."

His face darkened, and he made a fist. "You lie."
It was time for me to flee.

Chapter Thirty-Eight: Mrs. Wilkens to the Rescue

If I could get inside the bar, I could call 911. As if the goddess of the universe read my thoughts, the door to the bar opened. I glanced back to the porch and saw the younger men who had been sitting at the bar. One of them shouted out, "Hey, got a light?"

When Blackmer reached in his pocket, I took off toward the men on the porch. Ape man grabbed my arm as I tried to zip by. I jerked away. "Let me go!" To the men on the porch, I yelled, "Help!"

Blackmer quickly seized my arm. "Nothing to worry about, boys. Husband wants her home and not roaming the bars. We'll take care of it."

"No," now I was screaming. "They want to hurt me!"

Almost in step, the two men turned and hurried back into the bar.

Blackmer laughed, "They know the real law around here."

Boy, was this turning into a bad movie.

Relax and charm them.

"I don't have charm."

Sure you do.

Blackmer pulled me to him and wrapped an arm around my chest. He squeezed until I could barely breathe. "What did you say?"

"Talking with my dead sister," I rasped, trying to get a full breath.

"Hey, Len, the broad's crazy."

In the moment of panic, Charlee had managed to calm me down.

Something clicked in my addled brain. Len's reaction when I'd accused him of burning down Fannie's house.

"You didn't start those fires, did you? Someone else is horning in on your business."

The arm around me loosened enough that I could cough. I hoped all my ribs were still intact.

"What do you mean, 'my business'?"

Careful.

Careful was not a word that I understood in these circumstances. These guys had the strength and the power and the desire to hurt me and worse. "Guys, everyone knows you're the enforcers. But someone else is doing it, too."

Blackmer whirled me around so I was facing him. "Who's burning things down?"

Time to be clever.

"You know I've never been good at 'clever.'"

"What?" Blackmer glared at me. His eyes told me he was a man of little patience.

"My dead sister says that you know who the arsonists are if you think about it."

Wild guess. Would this slow them down?

He yanked me so close, my nose was nearly buried in his cheek. Someone looking on might have thought we were having an intimate moment, not a brutal one. He released a few F-bombs before he whispered in a voice that sent a cold shiver down my back, "We have a nice little place out in the woods for people like you. My boys like skinny, and you are a bag of bones."

No one, not even my worst enemy in high school, had ever called me a "bag of bones."

"Really? Is that the best you can do?"

The way he crushed me against his chest said he meant business. No wonder people were afraid of him.

"Charlee, now what do I do?"

Faint.

I can't faint on command.

You can feign a faint. He can't take you anywhere on a motorcycle if you are unconscious.

Ah! Hah! Charlee was pretty smart.

"Can't breathe. Things going black." I let my body crumple against him, hoping I was more convincing than I felt.

Blackmer was startled, but not startled enough to ease me down. He let go, and I landed with a thud and really did feel like fainting. Fortunately, I didn't land on my bad shoulder. In that millisecond, as the black blobs were floating in front of me, I chided myself for not getting the surgery on the shoulder. Blackmer's voice pulled me out of the faked faint.

"Goddamn bitch! Can't haul her on a motorcycle like this. Get me some water or something!"

We might have played out the scene where someone throws water in the face of the unconscious person, and they immediately wake up, except the sound of a car tearing into the lot interrupted Len from running into the bar for a glass of water.

The car stopped with a screech. I kept up my faint because I wasn't sure who was in the car.

"What have you done?" Mrs. Wilkens's voice rang out like a school vice-principal. "Liza, are you okay?"

Right behind her, Reverend Walter yelled into a phone. "Unconscious person at The Nevermore. Send an ambulance and the sheriff."

I rolled on my back like I was waking up. "He tried to…assault me."

Blackmer held his hands in a surrender motion. "I didn't do anything. We were just talking. Isn't that right, Len?"

Mrs. Wilkens bent over me. "Are you alright? Did he hurt you?"

"Well, he did smell bad." I tried to laugh, but my brain didn't cooperate. It came out as more of a whimper.

Reverend Walter stood close to Blackmer. "Stanley. It's been a while."

"She's crazy. I didn't hurt her."

"Seems she's on the ground. How did that happen?" Reverend Walter's voice had a sternness to it that he'd probably honed after years of wrangling altar boys.

By now, a crowd had gathered on the porch, including the trio of Lorrie's friends. Cyd, the bartender, brought me a glass of water. When she leaned down to give it to me, she wore a little smile. "Most who tangle with Blackmer and Len don't get up on their own."

The first emergency person to show up was my friend Trey. I insisted he call off the ambulance. "I'm fine. Just a little faint." I scowled at Blackmer, "That guy needs a shower and a better deodorant."

Trey failed to see the humor and opened his mouth to say something I assumed would be stupid. Mrs. Wilkens jumped in before he could speak. "You need to arrest this man. He assaulted Lorrie and needs to go to jail."

I sat on the gravel and watched this, thinking that Mrs. Wilkens had accomplished what I could not. Blackmer would go to jail.

Except, of course, Trey turned to Blackmer. "Did you assault anyone?"

Blackmer shrugged. "This crazy woman accused me of burning down the library."

It was clear to me, to Mrs. Wilkens, and to Reverend Walter that this would be going nowhere.

After about a minute of back and forth between Blackmer, Trey, Mrs. Wilkens, and me, Trey motioned me to his vehicle. "I'm thinking of arresting you for creating a nuisance."

Great, Blackmer nearly kills someone, and I'm arrested?

Reverend Walter stepped in. "Now, Trey, you know she didn't start this and didn't do anything. I'd hate to have to visit your mom at the home and tell her what you did."

Trey's jaw dropped.

The Reverend kept talking, "You know how proud she was when you put on the uniform. You wouldn't want her to hear you've been harassing young ladies, would you?" The kindness in his voice was laced with steel.

In the end, the party broke up with no one arrested. I knew, though, that I now had a target on my back.

Mrs. Wilkens insisted that she drive me to Lorrie's. Reverend Walter followed in his car. As we sped down the highway, I kept glancing back, looking for a motorcycle. Silly, of course. If Blackmer wanted to come after me, he knew where to look.

"How did you know to come to the bar when you did?"

"Walter, who knows everyone in this town, called Jed. Jed told him what was happening, and we came to the rescue."

We sat outside on Lorrie's patio. It was a warm August night with enough of a breeze to keep the mosquitoes at bay. Mrs. Wilkens filled me in on Lorrie.

"He's doing better. They had to drill a hole in his skull to relieve the pressure from a subdural hematoma."

She spoke as if I had any idea what a subdural hematoma would be. If she hadn't been watching me, I would have taken out my phone and googled it.

Reverend Walter chuckled, "The doctor explained that it's a clot that forms between the brain and the skull. Once they fixed that, Lorrie was better."

"Did you talk with him?"

Mrs. Wilkens shook her head. "He's still very sedated. But we did talk with a sheriff's deputy and filed a report."

I didn't see this going anywhere. They'd send it on to Ruston County, and Sheriff Wayne would let it sit on his desk, hoping nothing more would happen before his retirement.

Uncanny how the Reverend seemed to read my thoughts. "I still have friends and some clout in this town. It's time to light a little fire under the leadership. Blackmers have ruled for the last few years, and I think we've had enough."

My phone rang, and Alex's name popped up. He said he was sorry; he got tied up with a family crisis, and could he take a rain check on dinner? It reminded me that I was hungry.

Mrs. Wilkens watched me with raised eyebrows. "How's it going with the doctor?"

"Family issue," I mumbled. "And, I haven't had dinner." I sounded like one of my whiny students.

Mrs. Wilkens leaned over to Walter, "Why don't we drive into town and get a pizza. I think Liza needs a shower and a beer."

By the time they got back, I'd showered off the gravel and the smell of Blackmer. Instead of pizza, they brought back broasted chicken and a big salad. I nearly choked on a chicken bone, I was so hungry.

Imagine...killed by a chicken.

Not funny.

"Liza?" Mrs. Wilkens peered at me. "Are you okay. You have that look like you've gone into a special place."

I refrained from telling her my dead sister was bothering me. "Sorry. Just trying to piece all of this together."

Over chicken that could clog the cleanest of arteries, I filled them in on what I'd learned from the trio in the bar. "It sounds like Lorrie told his buddies that Santos Brothers were mistreating the guest workers, and Fannie had proof. Blackmer wanted to know where the proof was." I stopped for a moment. "Jed said Lorrie mentioned that Henry knew."

Mrs. Wilkens sighed, "Are we going down the wrong track with Henry. Maybe he isn't a dead cat." She turned to Walter. "Do you know any Henrys?"

He scratched his head. "Well, there's old Henry who lives in the nursing home. I doubt that's who he was talking about. Old Henry is deaf and 98 years old."

"Maybe Henry is a nickname?"

Goldie, who had been in Lorrie's room in the basement, came up the stairs, looked at her empty dish, and issued a soft meow.

"She's usually not so polite," I commented before I opened a can of food and put it out for her.

We were quiet as we watched Goldie eat her food. Unlike me inhaling the broasted chicken, Goldie ate with a certain delicacy and sophistication. I wouldn't want to go so far as to say I admired her, but she did have her own style.

Come on. You've always liked the cat.

Pah!

Mrs. Wilkens was the first to speak as Goldie took a lap of water. "I think we need to go to Pottersville and find out if they are being used by Santos."

I pointed to the dark sky. "I think we need to sleep on it."

Reverend Walter stretched before standing up. "Time for this man of God to commune with Morpheus. I'm intrigued by all of this, but I have duties tomorrow."

"I thought you were retired." I stood with him.

"Food bank duties. Since they threw me out of my church, I decided to do God's work elsewhere. I'll bid you both good night." Before he opened the door, he added, "Stay away from Blackmer and his gang." He winked, "At least for the time being."

After he left, I commented, "Nice man."

Mrs. Wilkens looked at me with an angelic smile. "Agreed. Now get a good night's sleep because we have work to do."

Listen to her sis. I think you are in for an interesting day.

"I like boredom," I grumbled on the way to the bedroom.

Chapter Thirty-Nine: Pottersville

I awoke in the deep of the night with Goldie settled on the pillow next to me. For a moment, I wasn't sure where I was. The odor of the musty curtains reoriented me. I was in Lorrie's spare bedroom in a bed that hadn't been aired in thirty years. I resolved to hang the bedspread and blanket on the line in the morning.

Goldie stretched and meowed. I was immediately alert. Goldie was a champion sleeper and never awoke in the middle of the night. I sat up and listened. The house was quiet except for the hum of the old refrigerator. In the distance, a semi ground its way up the hill out of town. Otherwise, everything seemed quiet. Yet, I felt spooked. I waited for Charlee to give me advice, but she was silent.

Then I heard what sounded like a low whisper, followed by a giggle. A giggle? I threw the covers off so quickly, I startled Goldie, who jumped to the floor and scurried out of the room. The voice and giggle came from the back door. In the kitchen, I snapped on the light in time to see the back door slightly open, and something stuck between the door and the jamb. It appeared to be a lump of canned tuna. Goldie raced toward it. I had the sense to grab her by the scruff of her neck and pull her away from what looked like a spoonful of canned cat food.

"Oh no, you don't!" I picked her up just before she got to the food.

Outside, someone huffed as they ran away. Still holding Goldie, I sped through the doorway in time to see a shadow moving toward the road.

"Hey!"

The running person was wearing a hoodie. He turned to the sound of my voice and stumbled. I made a dash as Goldie scratched to get out of my clutches. "Oh no, you don't." If she got away, she'd make a beeline back to the lump of food.

A streetlight at the end of the block gave out a sickly glow, but it was enough to see the person pick up a bike that had been tipped over at the bottom of the driveway. The bicyclist pedaled away, and I watched, knowing I'd never catch up.

"I think it was a kid on the bike!"

When I returned to the house, Mrs. Wilkens stood in the kitchen blinking in the light. There are things in life that you don't want to see. Mrs. Wilkens, in the middle of the night in a sheer nightgown, was one of them. Thank God she didn't sleep in the nude.

I pointed to the food on the floor. "I think it's poisoned."

She found a plastic bag in one of the drawers and carefully scooped it in. Once it was cleaned up, Goldie gave me a disappointed look and headed down to Lorrie's bed. "Hey," I spoke softly, "I just saved you. You should be purring on my lap, thankful to be alive."

The first call I made in the morning was to Alex. "I think I've spied the poisoner."

"Excuse me?"

He sounded like I'd awakened him. Then I looked at the time on my phone. Six in the morning.

"Sorry, Alex. I didn't sleep much last night." I told him about the food left in the doorway and how much Goldie wanted it. "We put it in a plastic bag. Can you get it tested or something?" I told him about chasing a kid on a bicycle.

"I'll come and pick it up after I've gone for my run. This is curious, indeed."

Over a cup of very old Maxwell House coffee, Mrs. Wilkens and I talked about last night.

"You're sure it was a kid?"

I shrugged. "It was late, the person was short and wore a hoodie. Could have been a girl, I guess."

"Humph! Girls don't poison cats."

Really? Nothing would surprise me in this town,

We sketched out a plan for the day. I wanted to check out Pottersville since so many things pointed in that direction. Mrs. Wilkens thought it was a fine idea. "I'll see if Walter wants to join us."

She said it with such a lilt in her voice that I raised my eyebrows. "You seem to get on well with Walter. I thought you were an atheist."

"Agnostic. Not sure what to believe," she shot back as a little pink color rose up her neck.

Walter insisted on taking us to Pottersville. "They know me there. If you have questions for them, they are more likely to talk if I'm with you. Plus, I'm guessing my Spanish is better than yours."

Indeed, I had discovered that my mediocre command of Spanish was no match against my fifth graders speaking Spanish at bullet-train speeds.

When he arrived, he was wearing his clerical collar, a blue short-sleeved shirt, khaki shorts, and sandals with socks. Mrs. Wilkens also wore shorts and sandals with socks. I refrained from asking them if they'd called the "what to wear hotline" before getting dressed. It was time to be serious.

On the way to Pottersville, Walter filled us in about the encampment, as he called it. "When Santos Brothers decided to do their own poultry processing, they knew they wouldn't find enough local workers to run the plant. Despite the hype about Mexicans taking all the jobs, Minnesota relies on migrant workers and still can't fill about half the agriculture jobs available."

"When the guys at the Nevermore complain about losing their jobs, it's a myth?"

Walter nodded as he signaled and turned onto a paved two-lane country road. On either side of the road were acres of tall corn swaying in the breeze. Overhead, a flock of birds swooped down and then rose again. It was an idyllic scene.

Walter continued, "In order to run the plant, Santos Brothers became involved with the guest worker program. Part of the agreement to bring the workers in was to provide housing. That was the beginning of Pottersville. Except, of course, it wasn't called Pottersville. I think they called it the Elm Park trailer court."

A pickup truck pulled out of a side road and followed us. I glanced back a couple of times, noting how it carefully kept its distance, neither getting closer nor falling back. "It looks like we are being followed."

Walter glanced at the rearview mirror. "Could be. You two seem to attract attention."

My phone rang, and Alex's name popped up. "Hi, I'm back from my run. You can drop the…uh…sample at the clinic later this morning, if you'd like."

"We are on our way to Pottersville to ask a few questions. Did Fannie ever say anything to you about it?"

Alex hesitated. "Ah, no. Other than her plan to put together a bookmobile for them." He paused. I thought I heard a female voice in the background. "Um, I would caution you to take what anyone says with a certain amount of skepticism. Some migrant organizers have been stirring things up in the past weeks." The call abruptly ended.

I stared at the phone, expecting him to call back. When nothing happened, Mrs. Wilkens, sitting in the front seat, turned to me. "You look puzzled."

I didn't want to tell her that I detected a chill from Alex when I mentioned Pottersville and that his voice had a hint of a warning.

You like him, sis. Yet this is odd.

No kidding.

I might have reflected on it more except Walter turned onto a rutted gravel lane that bumped through a stand of oaks and birch and ended with trailers sitting on land that had once been a dump. I had pictured a trailer court with regular lanes and little yards. Instead, about eight single-wide trailers were set up in a row. Behind them, several more camper trailers were parked at various angles.

"Not exactly luxury living," I commented.

Several young children splashed in a plastic kiddie pool in front of one of the trailers while a group of men sat at a picnic table under a tree, smoking and drinking from coffee mugs.

Walter waved at them. "*¡Hola! ¡Hola!*"

A woman stepped out of the trailer where the children were playing and stared at us. Mrs. Wilkens walked up to her, pointing to the children.

"Beautiful children."

She continued to stare at us without speaking. I squatted next to the pool and spoke in my rudimentary Spanish. One of the children frowned and said in perfect Midwest English. "We speak English, you know."

"Good," I replied, "Because my Spanish is terrible."

He nodded solemnly, "Yes."

Mrs. Wilkens tried speaking to the woman again. "Do you work for Santos Brothers?"

The little boy answered for her. "Mama don't speak much English, and Papa says not to talk to strangers."

We didn't get any further in our communication because the pickup truck that was following us pulled up next to Walter's car. Len, the ape man from last night, stepped out. Immediately, the woman spoke in clipped Spanish to the children, who quickly got out of the pool. She wrapped them in towels and hurried them inside.

Once again, I felt like I was in an old west B-grade movie where the bad guy gunslinger and his gang show up, and everyone scurries inside.

The men at the picnic table stopped talking as Len approached me. "What are you doing here? It's private property. Didn't you see the sign?"

"Good morning to you, too. And, by the way, what are you doing here? We were invited."

Mrs. Wilkens said in a firm voice, "Yes, we were invited."

Len licked his lips and kicked away a stone, "There's been agitators here, and I've been hired to protect the residents."

I doubted by the look on the woman's face when he arrived that she felt protected.

Walter walked over and extended his hand. "Len, so we meet again."

Len was clearly taken aback by Walter's friendliness. "Uh…yes. I'm just making sure everything is okay here."

Walter smiled. "Looks pretty serene right now. You're security for the owners?"

"I make sure no one bothers the people here."

"Who is it you work for? I know you told me before, but my elderly brain doesn't work like it ought to."

He blinked in confusion. "AP properties. I keep an eye on things."

"Ah, yes. AP, that's right. Well, we'll be on our way. We wanted to see if the folks here still wanted a church service on Wednesday night. You know you and your brothers are invited anytime."

Len stood his ground until we settled in the car and backed away.

"Should we come back later when that ape guy isn't tailing us?" Mrs. Wilkens kept her eyes on the rearview mirror.

"No, I think I found out a few things. Let's not bother them right now. We'd bring more trouble than those poor folks need."

"What a dismal place." I glanced back to see the pickup following me.

"Let's have some lunch, and I'll tell you what Mateo told me about Fannie." Walter pulled out onto the paved road and turned back to Ravens Valley. "I think I have an idea of what she uncovered."

"Should we call Alex and have him join us?"

Walter was quiet for too many seconds. "I think we should leave Alex out of this for now."

The pickup truck followed us all the way into Ravens Valley.

Chapter Forty: White Vans

Walter took us to the diner with the wonderful coffee and the broasted chicken. Heads turned when he walked in, and several people greeted him. I noted the puzzled expressions when they eyed Mrs. Wilkens and me.

The server brought us coffee with a big smile. "Reverend Walter, it's nice to see you out. Where have you been hiding?"

He laughed, "Nestled in my man cave."

She laughed. "Oh, you!"

As she walked away, he commented. "I baptized her, confirmed her, and did her wedding. The baptism and confirmation stuck—the wedding did not."

When she came back with our food, she bent close to Walter and whispered, "A lot of us are fed up with Vogel. We're on a campaign to get you back."

Walter winked at her. "Keep campaigning."

"We don't like Vogel and that Pru Santos huddling together all the time and telling us what books we can read. Plus, my daughter said his son, Jasper, is a real creep."

As she walked away, I remembered Jasper from the festival parade and how he bullied those little boys. The kid had given me bad vibes from the moment I first saw him at Ravens Nest Inn.

While I ate the chef's salad, complete with iceberg lettuce and two hard-boiled eggs, Walter filled us in on his brief conversation with the men at Pottersville.

"They said a few weeks ago Fannie came out to talk with them about the bookmobile. Except she asked a lot of questions about what happened to Paulie. Everyone got nervous, and no one wanted to talk to her. When I asked about Paulie, they stopped talking to me. That was when Len showed up."

"Paulie? The kid at the motel?"

Walter nodded. "He stays with Big Mike at the motel now since he got hurt."

Mrs. Wilkens dabbed ketchup off her lips. "Why did Fannie want to know about Paulie? That's strange."

I thought back to my interactions with him. He seemed smart.

Didn't he tell you he signed some papers?

You are on the ball. Where have you been?

Sleeping?

Mrs. Wilkens stared at me until I realized I was having a conversation with myself. Recovering, I said, "I heard he signed some papers about the time he moved in with Big Mike."

Mrs. Wilkens wrinkled her brow. "Walter, do you know what happened to him? He has these scars and walks with a limp."

Pushing his plate aside, he leaned on his elbows and kept his voice low. "Rumor was that he got hurt at Pottersville. Some kind of a fight or something."

"But you don't believe it."

He drummed his fingers on the table. "People tell me things in confidence. I can't reveal much, but let's say the employment practices at the processing plant are a bit shady."

I remembered the article on Lorrie's dresser about food processing plants using teenagers under unsafe conditions.

"You mean, like he worked for Santos Brothers?" I pictured Annalisa's insistence that they obey all the laws and regulations. "He's underage. I can't think that Annalisa would put up with that." I filled Walter in on the article Lorrie had. "Could this be the same thing?"

"I don't know."

"In the article, the child who was hurt was working for a cleaning contractor, not the processing company."

"That's what I hear." Walter's voice turned vague.

Mrs. Wilkens caught on to it. "What aren't you saying?"

He pushed himself back from the table. "Let's go for a drive. It's a nice summer day."

Mrs. Wilkens responded with a quizzical expression.

I remembered I'd promised to drop off the bag with possible poison in it to Alex. "Can we stop at Alex's clinic so I can give him what was left for the cat?"

To my surprise, he answered, "Let's take a drive first."

Pieces were falling into place, but the puzzle still didn't reveal a picture. I was about to say more when the server came back with the bill. Mrs. Wilkens immediately took out her credit card. "On me."

I hoped she had more in her retirement account than I had in my savings account.

Walter drove us in the opposite direction of the park where Mrs. Wilkens and I had met with Jessica from the library. He turned onto a gravel road that wound down to the river. As we neared the line of trees that banked the water, he pulled off onto a rutted, bumpy drive that ended in a closed gate with a bullet-riddled sign that had once said, "No Trespassing."

"Is Trey going to find us here and arrest us?"

Walter laughed. "Although there are no signs to tell us, we are no longer in Ruston County. Trey has no jurisdiction here." He let himself out of the car and opened the gate.

At the bottom of the drive was a small, well-kept, one-room cabin. An open wooden porch with Adirondack chairs faced a clearing down to the river. As soon as I stepped out of the car, I smelled the water mingling with the scent of green leaves and pine.

"My little heaven. When Jenny, the server, asked where I'd been hiding and I told her my man cave, I was here contemplating nature and the meaning of life."

The setting was such that I could understand spending days on the porch listening to the gentle flow of the river. I felt the serenity for about twenty seconds before a wasp landed on my arm. Ah nature. Another reason why I live in the city.

We settled on the porch. Turning to Walter, I spoke, "I sense you have been evasive about letting Alex know what we were up to."

Walter rubbed his neck. "Mateo said something about 'that doctor with the long hair' being involved. When I tried to get more information, he simply told me the doctor visited with the blonde woman."

"Annalisa?" I brushed away an ant that was crawling up my leg. The prickly sensation I experienced was something other than an insect. Was Alex involved in the evil happening in Ravens Valley?

Keep an open mind.

Mrs. Wilkens sat quietly while a jay scolded something in the distance. When she spoke, it was in a thoughtful tone. "Walter, do you think Alex is part of what's going on? I can't see him involved in cat poisoning and book banning."

He wrinkled his brow. "I can tell you, after all these years of ministering to my flock, I still can't always read people. Frankly, I don't know. I just know Mateo was clear about a doctor being involved."

I had a bright idea. "What if I ask Alex?"

You sound desperate. Tread carefully.

Mrs. Wilkens, not always the voice of reason, put her hand on my thigh. "Perhaps that wouldn't be a good idea."

We discussed everything that had happened in the past week, from Fannie's death to the possible re-poisoning of my cat. Nothing fit together.

Walter stood and gazed at the river before taking a deep breath. "I am wondering about the poisoning. When we look at whose cats were targeted, it seemed random. But I'm not sure it was."

"What do you mean?" I peered at him. In his youth, he must have been a handsome man with a square jaw and green eyes. Even now that he had acquired jowls and a paunch, he stood tall and straight.

He took a list out of his pocket, slipped on his reading glasses, and studied the list. "I think that everyone on this list has spoken out at some point against the book banning." He sat down again and pointed to the names. "Here's one I remember speaking at a library board meeting. Here's another who wrote a letter to the editor of the paper. And this one volunteered for Fannie at the library."

Mrs. Wilkens squinted at the list. "I can't see Pru Santos, as sanctimonious as she is, killing cats."

I thought about the person on the bicycle. "It definitely wasn't Pru on that bicycle."

"Maybe someone directing a kid to do it?"

We sat in silence, thinking about it, while a couple of squirrels scampered up an oak tree in front of the cabin.

Our silence was interrupted when my phone rang. Alex was calling back.

"Hey," I tried to sound upbeat. "Sorry, we got waylaid."

"Well, I'm at the clinic now. I'll be here for a couple of hours because I'm doing paperwork. Bring it when you can." He ended the call abruptly.

I stared at the darkened phone. It seemed to me Alex had suddenly done an about face from the friendly, even flirty guy who handled cats so gently to an impatient, irritable middle-aged man.

You need to check this out. Either he's a good guy, or he's not. Just don't let your hormones speak for you.

I had no reply for the voice in my head.

We needed a plan, and I suddenly felt restless. I turned to my companions. "I have to take the possible poison to Alex. Maybe you two can find more connections with the poison list. Or better yet," I raised my eyebrows at Mrs. Wilkens, "find out who is employing Blackmers and who the doctor is that comes to Pottersville." I didn't add, and please don't discover it's Alex.

We agreed on a plan. Mrs. Wilkens was going to contact her librarian researcher friend to find out about AP Enterprises. The two of them were then going to drive to Mankato to check up on Lorrie. I would go to the clinic and gently probe Alex for information.

It all seemed like a reasonable plan until we found Trey standing in Lorrie's driveway waiting for us. The door to Lorrie's house was open, and one of the other deputies walked out wearing blue vinyl gloves. She shook her head.

I jumped out of the car. "What's going on? And dammit it you better not have let my cat out."

Trey stood with his hands on his hips. "We got a tip about drugs."

Walter had to restrain Mrs. Wilkens from striding over to wallop him. "You damn well better have a search warrant."

Trey shrugged, "All worked out legal, I'm sure."

"And have you found any?" Walter spoke in a neutral voice.

Trey suddenly became very interested in his foot as it kicked a little pebble down the drive. "Not yet."

As the neighbors gathered, Walter took out his phone and made a call. Ten minutes later, the sheriff showed up. By the red color of his cheeks, it was clear he was not happy. He stormed up to Trey, grabbed him by his arm, and led him far enough away that we couldn't hear the conversation. Three minutes later, Trey and the other deputy quietly got into their vehicles and drove away.

Sheriff Wayne sputtered, "Goddamn. I wanted to fill out my term and be done." He apologized and tried to explain that it was another of the swatting calls and that Trey overreacted. I doubted much of what he said was true, but I didn't want to stand in the yard and argue. I wanted to make sure Goldie hadn't escaped.

I hurried in through the wide-open front door, calling to the cat. Of course, Goldie didn't respond because she never responded when I called. What cat ever did?

She wasn't in the bedroom, and the door to the backyard was closed. If she'd gotten out, it would have been through the front.

"Goldie? Here, kitty kitty?" I felt stupid using those words, but I was in a near panic thinking that if she got out, I'd never find her.

Downstairs, I approached Lorrie's neat little bedroom and found nothing but chaos. They'd overturned his drawers, pulled out his clothes from the closet, and completely ripped apart the bedding.

"Goldie?"

I checked under the bed and saw nothing but dust balls. I looked in the closet that was now a heap of clothes. No Goldie.

Keep looking. She's here.

What do you know? I snapped. "You're an irritation inside my head."

Keep looking.

As I scanned the room, I noticed that the box with Henry's ashes had been tipped to the floor. It didn't appear that the deputy had opened the box—probably didn't want to deal with the remains of an old cat. I stooped to pick it up, and Goldie suddenly appeared. She looked up at me, and I thought I saw distress in her eyes.

I tried to pick her up, but she wriggled out of my grasp and put her paws on the box. "My God, Goldie, are you trying to protect old Henry?"

Except, she wasn't. In one very catlike movement, she swiped her paw and knocked the box over. The contents spilled out. My jaw dropped. The spilled box contained a small cloth bag that might have been Henry's. It also contained a couple of very grainy photos of two white vans taken at night from a distance. And, it had a flash drive.

Lorrie's words slammed into my head. "Henry knows."

This is what Trey was trying to find.

Chapter Forty-One: Henry's Secret

I slipped the flash drive in my pocket as Mrs. Wilkens walked down the stairs. She found me holding Goldie, who was now contentedly purring in my arms.

"Thank you, cat," I whispered to her. "But this doesn't mean we like each other."

"Well, this is a fine mess."

I agreed. I'm not sure why I didn't want to share the flash drive. Sometimes our decisions are not rational. I pointed to the photos on the floor next to the open box.

She picked them up. Taking the photos over to the basement window for better light, she scrutinized them. "These are dark and grainy, but it looks to me like the trailer behind the van is the one at Pottersville."

"Remember Lorrie saying something about white vans?"

"Clearly, this is evidence." She pressed her lips together.

Evidence of what, I didn't know. Maybe Santos Brothers picked up their employees and shuttled them to the processing plant.

Still cradling Goldie, I walked up the stairs with Mrs. Wilkens. Walter was in the living room putting cushions back on the sofa and sneezing. "Accumulates a lot of dust over the years."

Mrs. Wilkens showed him the photos, while I explained where I'd found them. He studied them until another sneeze came on. After wiping his nose with a crisp white handkerchief, he looked at them again.

"Hmmm."

I suggested my theory that it was a shuttle to the processing plant.

His expression remained puzzled. Sniffling, he pointed to the backyard. "Let's go outside. Can't handle the dust." He took an inhaler from his pocket and used it. "Ah, better."

We settled on the patio. "I think Lorrie was on to something." He put the photos down on the table. "See this?"

"You mean the tree?"

He nodded. "These photos were taken in the dark. I know the shift at the plant doesn't start until seven in the morning, and they do twelve-hour shifts. I'm guessing this is the middle of the night."

"Vans picking up people in the middle of the night?" I spoke as Goldie followed the movements of a nearby squirrel. I almost wondered if she was shaking her head to tell me to think harder.

Listen to your cat.

She's your cat, too.

Don't argue.

I turned to Mrs. Wilkens, "Do you remember if Lorrie said anything else besides talking about vans in the night?"

She slowly shook her head. "Maybe…when we see him…he'll be alert enough that he can tell us what he saw and explain his suspicions."

I was anxious to talk with him, too, but the flash drive in my pocket was calling to me.

You should show them the drive.

I know. But I want to look at it first in case…

In case what?

I caught the tail of the discussion between Walter and Mrs. Wilkens. "Let's keep to the plan. I'll get hold of my librarian friend while Walter and I see Lorrie in Mankato. You take the tuna to Alex and see if he says anything suspicious."

"I'll be sure to make note of any clues he drops."

My words came out in a bratty way that caused Mrs. Wilkens to give me the vice-principal look. "Don't let his charm fool you." If Alex was indeed her grandson, her tone hardly showed it.

As soon as they left, I took out my laptop and plugged in the flash drive, praying it didn't have a virus on it that would blow up my summer's worth of work on the final paper.

Of course, the drive was password-protected. "Aargh!" I glared at the screen. I didn't know Lorrie well enough to make an educated guess about the password. First, I tried the simplest 1-2-3-4-5. Then I tried his name. The third time, I typed in Henry. All I got back was a gray area with shaking asterisks.

Goldie sat at my feet. I looked down at her. "What could it be?" I spent a half hour going through Lorrie's house looking for clues like mother's maiden name and family birthdates.

What's missing?

My brain.

No. What's missing?

I stopped and stood in the middle of the early 1970s living room. "There's no computer in this house!" I said it so loudly that Goldie scampered into the bedroom. "This isn't Lorrie's flash drive. I'll bet he was hiding it for Fannie."

Duh.

Well, thank you for your confidence.

Back at my computer, I tried typing in "Fannie." Again, the shaking asterisks. What did I know about her? What had she said to me that might be a clue to a password? Or was I on a mission impossible? In the movies, the heroes always have access to a computer hacker who can get into anything. I had a cat.

I thought back to what Mateo and his friends had said to Walter. Fannie had asked a lot of questions about Paulie. Had she ever mentioned him to me? I couldn't remember.

I typed in Paulie. Same result. I thought about his name. He was Latino, and Paulie must have been an Americanization of Pablo. I tried it, and instead of wiggling asterisks, the drive opened up.

"Voila!"

I clicked on a file entitled Photos. Inside were jpegs of the grainy van photos and a photo of Paulie's leg. Wincing, I studied the photo. His leg was a mass of burn scars, including areas where the skin had been grafted.

"This wasn't the result of a fight unless someone attacked you with a blowtorch," I said aloud. Charlee didn't respond. She was probably as appalled as I was.

Closing the file, I was about to open one called AP documents when I heard a car pull into the driveway.

Quickly, I closed out the file, disconnected the flash drive, and closed the computer. I barely had time to slip the drive into my pocket before Alex knocked on the back screen.

"Come in," I called to him, willing the shakiness out of my voice. What if he knew something about this?

He looked pleasant in a button-down, short-sleeved shirt and khaki shorts. "I thought you were bringing me some poison."

I forced a laugh. "We had a little setback when Trey decided to raid Lorrie's house for drugs."

He scratched his head. "Trey did what?"

I sighed. "Take a look." I beckoned him down into Lorrie's bedroom, where chaos reigned. "I'm guessing Lorrie could sue or file a claim, but I doubt he will—assuming he recovers."

Alex picked up the spilled Henry box. "They even dumped out the ashes?" He set it on the dresser with a shudder. "What's wrong with these people?"

He put his arm around me. "I'm sorry this is your introduction to Ravens Valley. It's really a decent place."

If you don't count the Blackmers, cat poisoning, arson, and Protect Our Children.

I gently pulled away. "Listen, let me give you what the kid left for Goldie last night, and you can see if we have seen the devil in Ravens Valley."

Upstairs, I took the bagged sample of cat tuna from the refrigerator and gave it to him. "Are you able to check it yourself?"

"My toxicology skills are pretty poor. I'll have to send it into the lab." He studied the tuna in the bag. "Did you say a kid left it for you?"

"I saw someone in a hoodie ride away on the bicycle. It looked like a junior high-sized kid to me."

The flash drive in my pocket tingled against my thigh. I was tempted to take it out and show it to Alex. Walter's warning held me back. However, I did mention the photos. "In the mess that Trey and his friend made, I found a couple of really odd photos. It looked like white vans parked in front of a trailer. Would you know anything about them?"

Alex hesitated a moment too long before speaking. "Photos of vans. Seems out of character for Lorrie. Do you have them? I doubt they mean anything."

"Mrs. Wilkens and Reverend Walter have them. I think they were going to ask the sheriff about them."

He shook his head. "I doubt Wayne would be much help, but maybe I could figure them out."

Before I could reply, his phone rang.

"Sorry, the herd can't wait." He stepped outside to take the call.

He's too interested in those photos.

Maybe. I'm keeping an open mind.

When he walked back in, he pointed to his phone. "Got to go out on a call. Why don't you come to the clinic when I get back, and we can do some sleuthing?"

"Sure, Sherlock."

He returned my comment with a tight smile. I detected worry in his expression. Worry about what?

After he backed out of the driveway, I called Mrs. Wilkens. "Alex was here. He seemed strange when I told him about the photos. He said he's going out on a call so I'm going to go over to his place and look around. Maybe I'll find a white van."

"Careful, dear. We'll check in after we've seen Lorrie."

After I hung up, I quickly opened my laptop to the AP file. It appeared to be legal documents of incorporation for AP Enterprises. I scanned it, not understanding what it all meant.

"I need a name. Who does this company belong to?"

The documents named an agent and a Minneapolis address for the company. I googled the address and found it located in an industrial park. Nothing that tied it to Ravens Valley—at least that I could figure out.

You should have gone to law school instead of teaching.

Hush. I never wanted to live a life of billable hours.

Goldie interrupted my conversation when she jumped up on my lap as I tried to make my way through the legalese. I closed that file and opened another. It was a contract between Santos Brothers Farms and AP Enterprises to provide cleaning services for the processing plant. My eyes widened at the cost of the service, but what did I know about cleaning up chicken parts?

The next file included a scan of a deed. It listed the buyers as AP Enterprises. I wondered if this was the property Pottersville was on. AP Enterprises owned land here, contracted for cleaning services, and paid Blackmer for security. Who exactly was AP Enterprises?

I had a headache and still didn't know much. I was about to close the computer and take a break when one more file grabbed by attention. It was labeled NDA. The file opened to a scanned document with "confidential" stamped in red on it. It was a legal agreement between Mike Anderson as legal guardian of Pablo (Paulie) Sanchez and AP Enterprises. Mike Anderson must have been "Big Mike" from the motel.

I read it twice, and each time, I felt more of a chill. It appeared that Paulie had been injured when he worked as a night cleaner for AP Enterprises, and this agreement paid him a six-figure amount plus college expenses, and he, in turn, would not sue AP or discuss the cause of his injuries. At least that's what I gleaned from it.

One of the signatures at the bottom of the document was Annalisa Santos.

Holy Hannah, Charlee. What have we uncovered?

Charlee stayed quiet. I suspected she was as stunned as I was.

I gathered my purse and told Goldie to guard the house. It was time to have a chat with Alex.

Chapter Forty-Two: The Shed

I had driven as far as the park by the river before common sense told me to slow down and think about what I wanted to say to Alex. Pulling into the park, I noted the blue of the cloudless sky and the rustle of the leaves as a breeze blew gently toward the river. I sat at the same picnic table Alex and I had eaten on just days ago. How could all this beauty become so malevolent in such a short period of time?

I reflected on the little I knew about Annalisa. She struck me as being driven to succeed. I guessed she had a relationship with Elvis, the smarmy Texan. I thought back on the short interchange between Annalisa and Alex at the Santos party. I suspected he wanted money, and she wasn't excited about helping him.

What else did I know? She claimed to be careful about meeting all the regulations about the farm workers. And one last thing. She felt left out because Lily favored Alex. None of that information told me why she'd be signing an NDA on a child who'd been horribly scarred in an industrial accident.

And AP Enterprises. Was she the sole owner, or were other people involved? Did AP exploit the workers by renting them trailers and campers at Pottersville? Did they employ underage illegal workers? And where did Alex come into this?

I shook my head, remembering how tenderly he had cared for Goldie and how carefully and lovingly he had spoken to his mother. "No, he can't be part of this. Can he?"

I knew he was in financial trouble because of his late wife. I also knew he desperately wanted to restore his grandfather's veterinary business and horse farm. Could he be part of AP Enterprises? Maybe he let something slip to Fannie that started her looking into Paulie and Pottersville. Maybe he knew more about Fannie's death than he was telling me.

And what about the cats?

"A diversion?"

As I was talking to myself, I didn't notice that Trey had parked in the distance and how quietly he approached me.

"Who you talking to?"

Startled, I turned to him. "What?"

"I heard you talking to someone."

Oh, just my dead twin.

"I…uh sometimes talk to myself. Bad habit."

He stood over me, a bead of sweat rolling down the side of his face. "Seems to me you should be heading back to the cities now that your cat is okay."

I wanted to ask him about AP Enterprises and Annalisa. Sometimes, when I had to get the truth out of one of my kids, I'd use distraction to take them by surprise. I tried it with Trey.

"You know, actually, the truth is that I was talking to my sister. She can be annoying, but she's smart and figures things out."

Trey's jaw dropped as he looked at me in confusion. "I don't see her."

I shrugged. "We're twins." As if that would mean anything to Trey. "She was asking me who owns Pottersville." I shaded my eyes and looked at him with an expression that I hoped showed puzzlement. "Why would she ask me that?"

"Uh…"

"She says Annalisa Santos owns it."

Careful. You are heading out on a limb.

"What? A bunch of people own Pottersville. She just runs it."

"Oh, like it's a corporation with shareholders and such? Pretty smart to have made that investment."

Trey blinked, "Sure, I guess."

"She wondered if you worked for them, too. You know off-duty stuff."

You are hanging by a thread now.

I might have fallen and knocked myself out, but Trey's radio squawked. He turned away from me to answer. I took the opportunity to grab my bag and walk to the car. I stepped carefully so he didn't think I was fleeing.

Before I reached the car, he called out. "Who told you all of this?"

"Charlee," I shouted. "She's dead, of course."

Thanks for getting me in trouble.

You're welcome.

I checked my rearview mirror to see Trey with his hands in his pockets and his mouth hanging open. I hoped he wouldn't follow me.

The parking area at the clinic was empty. Alex was still out on a call. When I tried the door, it was locked. I decided to explore the grounds while I waited. The deteriorating house with its sagging porch and peeling paint appeared more like a horror movie set in the backdrop of the bright sky and the afternoon light. A couple of hardy roses grew near the foundation. I guessed at one time they were part of a larger flower bed. Clearly, though, it had been a long time since they'd been tended.

I walked beyond the house to the old barn. A crow landed on the hip roof and cawed at me. The door was slightly open, and I peeked inside. It appeared the same as before, except the car was no longer there. I walked to where I'd seen it the other day and saw no evidence it had ever been parked in the barn. In fact, the concrete floor had been swept. Had Alex's father decided to have it fixed? Or had they moved it to another hiding place?

Nothing in the barn told me that Alex was a part of AP Enterprises or Pottersville. I saw no evidence of any tire tracks that would indicate a white van was housed here.

Maybe I would find the "evidence," as Mrs. Wilkens called it, in another outbuilding. An old chicken coop with a rotting roof stood collapsing into the earth. Beyond it was a shed about the size of a double garage. Big enough to hold a white van? It appeared to have more recent tire tracks since the rain. It was a newer building, not part of the original farmstead. The double doors were padlocked shut.

What had Alex said? He kept extra clinic supplies in the shed, and that's why it is locked. "Even in Ravens Valley, we have thieves."

Perhaps it contained a white van.

I walked around to a small dirt-smeared window and peeked in. The dim light filtering through the window was hardly enough to see inside. On tiptoes, I pressed my face against the glass and let my eyes adjust. Overhead, a small plane buzzed, its sound fading.

There it was, the car from the barn. An SUV with the windshield shattered and the front end dented. A car that could have hit Fannie Porter and left her for dead. They'd moved it after I'd asked Alex about it.

Suddenly, I wanted out of this place. Out of Ravens Valley and back home with a cat that didn't love me and an elderly neighbor who irritated me. I wanted home with a classroom of fifth-graders whose main purpose in life was to "get Ms. Johnson."

Van tires crunched on the gravel drive as it approached the parking area. Alex had returned.

I quickly scrambled around to the back of the shed. He would know I was on the grounds because of the car. I only had seconds to figure out what to do.

Go to him.

He'll know where I've been.

Go to him.

I remembered an incident in my life where the best defense had been a good offense. I trotted as casually as I could down the rutted drive toward the clinic. Alex stood by the van watching me. I waved at him. "Alex, I saw the car in the shed. Did you move it?"

When I neared him, he slowly shook his head. "Curiosity either killed the cat or the cat's owner. What were you doing looking in the shed?"

Alex was between me and my car. Could I sneak by him and make a run for it? I used to be a decent athlete until I wrecked my shoulder playing softball. For a second, I pictured myself doing a quarterback scramble. Alex must have read my intentions because in a quick motion, he grabbed my arm, wrenching me close to him.

He didn't know about my unstable shoulder and how easily it could cause excruciating pain. Fortunately, I'd instinctively braced it. Still, the pain was enough to cause my legs to weaken. I stumbled, pulling him off-balance.

I jerked away while he was off balance and took off toward the barn. "Hey!" Alex called out. "I'm not going to hurt you! We need to talk!"

I didn't feel the need to talk right now. I felt the need to get hold of Mrs. Wilkens, and Walter, and the National Guard.

Behind me, a motorcycle approached. I doubled my speed, paying little attention to where I was going as long as it was away from Alex. Beyond the shed was a tangled area of brambles that might have been a garden at one time. It became a wooded area, and on the other side of the woods was the road back into town. If I could reach the road, I might have a chance.

"Stop!" Alex shouted. "Don't go in there…"

The roar of the motorcycle drowned out his next words. If I'd been able to hear him, I would have known that the area I thought was a garden was actually the location of the original farmhouse, including an outhouse that had fallen away, leaving the hole which had been covered by the bushes for years. I would have known to skirt the "garden" instead of racing through it.

I heard Alex's breathing as he closed in on me. I tried to speed up, knowing he was a runner and I was a jogger. Still, I might have outrun him because I have long legs and I had a burst of adrenaline racing through my veins. Except, my foot landed on something soft that gave away and instead of reaching the woods and safety, I tumbled into the hole that had once been the outhouse.

Merde!

At least that's what I think she said before I landed among old tin cans, bottles, and the compost of Alex's ancestors. My ankle twisted, and the pain that shot up my leg caused the world to fade. When it came back into focus, Alex squatted on the edge of the hole with a puzzled expression.

Chapter Forty-Three: The Ankle

I groaned, blinking and spitting dirt out of my mouth. For a moment, I wasn't sure where I was, except wherever it was, it had an earthy scent to it. Maybe I was dead, and this was what being buried smelled like.

Except, Alex called to me. "Liza, are you okay?"

"Not dead yet."

"Let me get you out."

It wasn't easy because I was still woozy from hitting the rock and my ankle felt like I'd ripped out all the tendons. At least my shoulder still worked. Alex was able to grab my arm and hoist me up.

Behind him, voices approached. One was female, the other was male. At first, I thought it might be Blackmer and one of his biker babes. Then I recognized her.

"What's going on?" Annalisa stared at me as I sat among the tangle of weeds next to the hole, massaging my ankle.

Lots of thoughts went through my mind, but Alex had the jump on me. "Liza was looking around while she waited for me. I forgot to tell her about the pitfalls of walking near the old homestead. Looks like she found the outhouse." He didn't mention that I was running away from him.

Head over heels into an outhouse. Classy, sis.

Oh, go away!

Elvis accompanied Annalisa and stood with his arm draped around her shoulder. They both wore black. Even in my distress with the pain in my ankle and the fear in my heart, I recognized them.

Don't say anything.

But…

Hush.

"Elvis, why don't you help me get Liza back to the clinic. Maybe I can take a look at her hoof."

He sounded a bit too hearty for the situation.

Between the two of them, they hoisted me up and helped me limp back to the clinic. Once in the waiting room, I sat on one of the molded plastic chairs while Alex gently slipped my shoe off. I smelled earthy but couldn't get past the fact that all the compost came from an old outhouse. I choked back the urge to gag.

Hey sis, settle down. It's just old-fashioned dirt now.

Easy for you to say. You're dead.

After probing my ankle, he patted my knee. "I don't think you'll be running the Kentucky Derby, but it's not broken. We'll ice it and wrap it and have you back in the parade in no time."

I was not amused by his folksy approach until it occurred to me he was playing a game for Annalisa and Elvis, who stood like drill sergeants with impatience written all over their faces.

"Alex, we need to talk. Some things have come up. Maybe she can go to the *medical* clinic instead."

They wanted me out of the way, and I wanted answers.

"I'm good. Alex seems to know his…uh…hoofs."

Alex beckoned them into the surgery. Before closing the door, he looked at me with an unreadable expression. "I'll just be a few minutes. Keep the ice on the ankle and keep it elevated."

Thoughts raced through my head as I heard the low rumble of voices inside the surgery. First, this would be a great time to hobble out to my car and take off. Second, why would Annalisa burn down Fannie's house? And third…I was interrupted by my phone before I could come up with the third thought.

Mrs. Wilkens's face popped up. With no salutation, no "hello, how are you?" she said, "We have the story, and we think you should meet us somewhere out of Ruston County. Lots of people mixed up in it."

"Can't. I'm at the clinic with Alex, Annalisa, and Elvis. Sprained my ankle and they're having a hell of a fight behind closed doors."

"What?" Her voice faded, and the call dropped. She must have hit a dead zone.

Meanwhile, Annalisa's voice rose. "Do something, Alex. You want the money, then get rid of her."

Might be a good time to leave.

I groaned as I set my foot on the floor. "Not sure I can do this."

Pffft. Go! Leave your shoe.

With effort, I made it to a standing position before the world started to swirl, and the nausea rose.

Go!

I made it all the way to the door before Elvis came bursting out of the surgery and grabbed me. "Oh no. You're staying here." He dragged me back to the chair. "Sit!"

I was surprised he didn't point a gun at me.

Annalisa came out, followed by Alex. Alex's expression reminded me of my kids when I caught them cheating.

"You know something, don't you?" Her blue eyes were like ice as they bored into me.

I answered with a question, "What? You mean the cats? I don't understand poisoning them."

She wrinkled her brow, glancing at Elvis. "What cats?"

"The ones you've been poisoning. Does this have anything to do with Protect Our Children?"

Good job leading them away.

"Protect Our Children? Pru's little hobby?" She nearly spit out the words. I suspected Annalisa had little time for her aunt.

"Isn't that why you're interested in me? Because Fannie was helping me with a project to stop such nonsense?"

Annalisa's face turned pink as she sputtered, "You're here only because of the book banning?"

And maybe the murder of Fannie Porter, plus the abuse of children.

I groaned just enough for Elvis to loosen his grip on me. "Do you think I could get something for the pain?" I appealed to Alex. "Maybe a horse tranquilizer or something?"

"I have something in the back. Let's try that."

Annalisa pulled up a chair and sat by me as I rested my ankle on another chair. "So how come you've been asking questions about Pottersville?"

"Because Fannie wanted to set up a bookmobile there and was getting pushback. I wanted to know why."

Elvis interrupted. "Annie, she's lying. She knows all about it."

I feigned confusion. "You mean I know about how Pru and the library board were against it?" Please, Mrs. Wilkens and Walter. Get here before I run out of stories to tell.

Alex came back with a couple of pills and a glass of water. "This should help."

I swallowed them as the ache in my ankle rose up my leg and into my hip. Elvis continued to hold on to my arm as if I might bolt. I worked on coming up with a more plausible story for my time in Ravens Valley.

Alex helped me out, "I don't think Liza has any of the information you are looking for. Everyone here knows Santos Brothers runs a clean, legal operation. Mom wouldn't be associated with Heck if not."

Annalisa stared at him. "Alex, what kind of BS are you spewing here?"

This led to a conversation I was having a hard time following. Something in the realm of "Mother always liked you best."

As I watched them, their faces went in and out of focus. My body gained weight and pulled me down. The pain disappeared, and my eyelids wouldn't stay open. "Mush be the horse tranquiller." At least that's what I think I said.

* * *

I woke up to the musty smell of mold and dust. I was on my back with my ankle elevated. My mouth was so dry my tongue stuck to the roof, and when I pried it away, I coughed and gagged. I was on a sofa covered with a once-white sheet. Low light from the setting sun inched its way through dirty windows.

"Where am I?" My voice was a croak.

Look around you.

I raised myself up onto my elbows and surveyed a room where all the furniture was covered in sheets. "The house next to the clinic?" My body felt bone tired like I'd run a marathon without practicing. "Drugged?"

Sounds right.

Why?

Listen.

Outside, people were on the porch speaking in low voices. I recognized Annalisa, Alex, and Elvis. When the fourth person talked, the sound of his voice jarred me.

"Fannie thought it was safe to come to me." Sheriff Wayne coughed before continuing. "She said she had all the information on her computer. Except we couldn't find it. I wonder if that woman in there and her geriatric friend came across the computer."

"We didn't find it in the house. If it was there, it's burned to ashes now." Elvis snickered. "Same with the library. If she had anything stashed there."

"Nothing at Lorrie's, although I doubt that dumbass would know an apple from an apple," Wayne replied.

A shiver ran down my spine. These voices, these people were evil, and I had the key to all of it in my pocket. I reached around to make sure it was safe, only to find an empty pocket. Had they taken it from me?

Alex cleared his throat before he spoke. "I didn't find anything in her bag or on her. I don't think Liza has what we're looking for."

Traitor!

I'm not so sure. He could have anesthetized you to death.

I groaned as I sat up. Blood rushed to my injured ankle, and the ache was worse than when I had dislocated my shoulder the last time. I needed water, pain pills, and an escape plan.

"How much longer will she be out?" Annalisa's voice took on a sharp tone. "We have to decide what to do with her."

Alex muttered something I couldn't understand. Enough of this. I surveyed the shadowed room and figured the kitchen would be in the back. It must have a door to the outside and maybe some potable water. Although at this point I could have taken anything wet—potable or not.

I stood trying to put weight on my injured foot. When I gasped, I was sure they could hear it all the way to the Ravens Nest Inn. Holding on to the arm of the sofa for balance, I stood straining to hear movement from outside.

The four of them continued to talk. Part of me wanted to continue to eavesdrop to get the rest of the story, but the other part of me—that being the practical Charlee urged me to hobble as quietly as possible down the dark hallway.

Go and quit groaning and squeaking.

You'd squeak, too, if you had to put weight on this foot.

Go!

I broke out into a cold sweat as I slowly made my way down the dark and dank hallway. By the time I reached the kitchen, I was drenched and both hot and cold.

Don't pass out!

Trying to stay conscious.

The evening light showed through the kitchen window facing west. In front of the window was an aluminum sink. I ever so carefully nudged the spigot, not wanting to risk making noise. Nothing happened. The spigot knob spun in my hand; the taps had long ago been turned off. A cool drink of water would have to wait.

To the right of the sink and counter was a door. It looked like it led to a back porch.

Go!

Just as I reached the door, Annalisa called out from the other room. "Hey! She's not on the couch. I thought you said she'd sleep for another couple of hours."

Damn. Despite the pain that shot up my leg, I ran for the door and twisted the knob. Nothing happened. The knob wouldn't twist, and the door wouldn't open. Panicked, I took in the rest of the kitchen. Did it have another exit door?

This would have been a good time to hear Mrs. Wilkens's voice demanding to know where I was. This would have been a good time to have stayed home and written a paper on something else—like world peace.

I spied another doorway. By now, I was lightheaded, and the pain was nearly intolerable. Before totally collapsing, I slipped down onto my hands and knees and crawled to the darkened doorway, praying it would lead me to safety.

Footsteps pounded in my direction.

Chapter Forty-Four: The Flash Drive

I scrambled through the doorway to find a closet underneath a back staircase. For a moment, I was frozen as the footsteps rushed into the kitchen. Could I make it up the stairs without passing out?

Hide!

I slid into the closet and pressed myself under a shelf. It rattled when my head hit the corner of the shelving, and I thought my days as a schoolteacher or even a living human being were over.

"Where's the goddamn light?" Elvis yelled, muffling the sound of the shelf.

"Electricity is turned off," Alex called back. "She wouldn't have come this direction. There's a side door out of the parlor. I'm sure that's where she went."

Footsteps retreated, and I made my way warily out of the closet in time to glance at Alex. He looked directly at me, then turned and followed the others. He knew I was here, and yet he didn't tell anyone.

Time was running out, and I had to get to my car or to the road and summon help. I heard the ringtone of my phone from the living room. I must have dropped it when I got up off the couch.

"Her damn phone is ringing. What should we do?" Elvis swore in a high-pitched twang.

"Leave it." Annalisa's voice rose. "We have to find her. She might have overheard us."

I could try to get back to the phone and call 911. Except the sheriff was in on all of this. Better to get to the road.

While my pursuers headed into the twilight, I slowly made my way upstairs to the second floor. If I could get to one of the rooms, I could see where they were and plan my escape. I inched up the stairs, stopping at every riser to listen. No one was in the house. By now, I was beyond thinking about the pain in my ankle and the thirst in my throat. This was survival mode.

After what seemed like hours, I reached the top stair and crawled into the first room. It had probably been a bedroom at one time, but now it was stripped bare. At the window, I peeked through a rotting lace curtain. The sheriff stood guard at my car, holding my laptop. Annalisa and Elvis patrolled down the driveway. I didn't see Alex, but I assumed he'd gone back to the old farmstead area. With all of them fanned out, it didn't seem possible that I could get out of the house without being detected.

Back door. Go to the river.

Would they expect me to cross an open field? Probably not. "Good idea," I whispered. "You go, and I'll stay here and nap."

Now, while they're all in front!

With a shaky sigh, I inched my way back down the stairs. I was tempted to try to retrieve my phone until I heard the creaking of the porch. Someone was out front. Probably the sheriff.

Back in the kitchen, I tried the door handle again. It wouldn't turn, and I wasn't sure I had the strength or the motivation to try to get it open.

Tug on it.

You're getting to be awfully bossy.

Charlee didn't reply. I held my breath, clenched my jaw, and gave it a tug. With a cracking sound, it opened. I didn't wait to find out if the sheriff had heard me before rushing through the back entry and out a rusted screen door. I was immediately hit with the smell of newly mown hay and the light of the full moon.

I stared at it for a moment, willing clouds to cover it. The sky was clear, and the moon lit up the night. Everyone could see me stumbling through the fields and pastures. I longed for the big city where people hardly noticed if you were stumbling down the sidewalk.

The lawn, now overgrown with weeds and tall grass, sloped down to a patch of bushes. Behind them was a tired wooden fence and the open field.

"Charlee, I can't do this. They're going to find me one way or another."

Charlee did not reply. Perhaps she felt the same way. I crawled under one of the bushes and collapsed. The adrenaline had worn off, the pain had intensified, and I was in surrender mode. They'd find me, figure out how to run me over, and continue with their business of employing children to clean their factory.

I closed my eyes and felt a tear dripping down my cheek. This would be the end, and I had nothing to show for all of this. The flash drive was gone—probably at the bottom of the old outhouse and I knew the killers and couldn't prove a thing. By the time they found my body, the car in the shed would be long gone, and AP Enterprises would continue to exploit the children.

Voices came from near the back of the house. Elvis sounded angry. "How could she have gotten away!" He used a few four-letter words that were not allowed in my classroom.

Annalisa answered, "Do you think she went into the field? Would she be that dumb?"

Dumb? She was calling me dumb?

"I don't see anything. Let's try the road again. She couldn't have gotten far with that ankle and all those drugs in her."

I held my breath, straining to hear sounds of them moving away. I wanted to crawl out from under the bush, stand up, and yell at them. Better sense prevailed. After what seemed like hours, the voices faded. It was time to go.

Except my body didn't want to move. Why bother hiding when I'd lost all the evidence? My ankle hurt, my head hurt, and I was tired and thirsty. On top of that, I had to pee. What heroine ends up hiding under a bush, worrying about finding a bathroom?

Should have taken advantage of being in the outhouse hole.

I'm in no mood for joking.

Sorry. I thought a little levity would get you off your butt and out of here.

Either I needed to try to sneak down to the river through the open field or find my way back to my car. Or get my phone and call Mrs. Wilkens.

A cloud finally obscured the moon, and I bathed in the darkness. Time to go.

The phone was my priority after I figured out how to empty my bladder without peeing down my leg. Thank goodness for the cloak of darkness and my ability to squat mainly on one foot and not fall over.

By the time I was done, the moon was again in its full brightness. I didn't care as I hobbled up the incline to the back door of the house. At the door, I stopped to listen but heard nothing. I felt a surge of optimism. I would get my phone, call for help, and this nightmare would be over. I'd be home by morning, tucked into my own bed with my indifferent cat shedding hair on the pillow beside me.

Moonlight through the kitchen window guided me to the dim hall. My ankle shrieked when I tried to put weight on it. I dropped to my knees and crawled along the musty hall runner. When I reached the room where I'd been dumped on the sofa, I stopped and listened. No voices on the porch, no sounds of people in the house. Perhaps I was home free. I slipped as silently as I could to the sofa and felt around for the phone. It wasn't there. Maybe it had fallen under the old piece of furniture. I was down on my belly, swiping my hand around when the floorboards creaked.

A soft voice spoke, "Missing something?"

Alex squatted down by me, holding the phone.

The words that flew out of my mouth were definitely not allowed in my classroom.

Chapter Forty-Five: AP Enterprises

He helped me onto the sofa and used a dusty throw pillow to elevate my ankle. "Looks like it hurts."

"Why are you being nice to me when you're planning to run me over?" I was beyond understanding human behavior at this point.

He handed me the phone along with the flash drive that had fallen from my pocket.

"What?"

"Listen, I am not the finest human being around, but I don't murder people."

I stared at his shadowed face and repeated, "What?"

Alex was in financial straits and was friends with Fannie. She probably told him how she'd uncovered the AP Enterprises and had proof. He needed to protect AP in order to get the money he needed to pay off his debts and fix up the farm. Alex knew Fannie's running route since they trained together.

"Alex, I saw the car in the shed. You ran over Fannie and hid it."

He rubbed his eyes and sighed, "No. Like I told you before, Dad asked me to hide it. He said he thought Mom had gotten the keys and accidentally hit Fannie. He said they found the car the day Fannie died, after Mom had gotten away from her caretaker early in the morning. He said he would report it when everything died down."

Did I believe the repeat of the story he'd told me before? In the shadowy living room with the furniture covered like sleeping ghosts, I wasn't sure. Charlee stayed quiet.

Perhaps we would have stayed at an impasse except voices rose as people neared the house. "We haven't found her yet, but she couldn't have gotten far with that bad ankle. I have Trey and Blackmer on alert."

The name Blackmer sent a chill down my back. I grabbed Alex's wrist. "If what you say is true and you didn't have anything to do with this mess, then you need to get me somewhere safe so I can report it."

If he hesitated, I planned to hobble out of the house screaming, "Fire!" Perhaps I could distract people enough to get to the car and make a run for it.

Except Alex didn't hesitate.

"I have my motorcycle in the barn. We'll take it."

"What?"

He patted my arm. "I'm not going to hurt you. Just don't fall off when we take the corner onto the road."

The next few minutes were a blur. He half-carried me out the back door, while I gritted my teeth to not scream in pain. By the time we got to the barn, I was soaked in perspiration and shaking. He grabbed a helmet and silently pointed to a motorcycle. I found some assurance in that he'd given me a helmet. If he was planning to throw me off the speeding vehicle, I doubt he'd care if my head was protected.

With herculean effort, I climbed onto the back of the motorcycle while he revved the engine.

"Hold on!" he commanded, taking us through the barn doorway, past my car, his van, the sheriff's car, and another motorcycle. I clung to him, braced for the moment he would kill me, or we'd die in a real accident.

Within minutes, we were out on the highway, the wind tearing through my t-shirt. I leaned in closer to him for warmth. I couldn't see the speedometer, but the way he passed cars on the two-lane highway told me we weren't obeying the law. Perhaps this was a suicide mission. I wasn't sure if we were being followed, and at this point, I didn't care. Instead, my brain cycled through a long list of things I wanted to do before I died.

Hey, sis, you'll get there.

Easy for you to say!

A few miles after we whipped by the Ruston County line, I heard the siren. Trey or the sheriff had probably caught up to us. Alex didn't speed up. Instead, he slowed down and, on the outskirts of the little town down the road from Ravens Valley, he pulled over. A state trooper stopped behind us.

I was shaking and cold and partially out of my head when the trooper approached. "Do you know how fast you were going?"

He wasn't talking to me, but before Alex could answer, I spoke in a shaky voice. "I think you should arrest us."

"Great idea," Alex added. "I'm drunk, and I was speeding. And I don't have a license."

The trooper rubbed his chin. "Not often I get a confession like this."

"We're in trouble," I whispered.

Behind us, another set of flashing lights approached. When the car stopped, Trey stepped out wearing his full deputy sheriff regalia. "I can take it from here." He tried to sound officious, but he came across as Trey the Stupid.

I noted the frown on the trooper's face. "Not your jurisdiction. I'll take them in, thank you."

That's how we ended up in a cell in the jail of the next county over from Ruston. I didn't even catch the name of the county. I laid on a cot with my leg propped up on a pillow and an ice pack on my ankle. I closed my eyes and drifted off.

Sometime later, I was awakened by Mrs. Wilkens demanding to speak to the prisoners. She came charging into the cell, which wasn't locked, her eyes on fire. "They can't arrest you! We'll find a good lawyer."

Alex sat on the other cot and raised his hand. "No need. We aren't under arrest. We're waiting for the FBI or the DEA or some other acronym to show up."

For a moment, her mouth dropped open. "Well!" She sat down next to Alex with a stern expression. "Young man, we have some business to take care of."

He's in for it now!

Hush.

Alex's eyes opened wide at the vehemence in her voice. "Yes?"

Mrs. Wilkens sat up straight as if composing her words. "It's possible you are my grandson. In which case, I don't like the idea of a relation of mine being a criminal."

I watched agape. Was she going to send him to bed without his supper?

A little smile twitched at Alex's lips. "First of all, I'm not much of a criminal, and second, we don't know for sure about my biological father."

"Well, we should find out."

He nodded politely, "How about if we deal with this later. Right now, we have a few legal entanglements to sort out."

Spoken like a true adult.

Can I go home now?

Hopefully not in handcuffs.

Mrs. Wilkens and Alex continued to talk in low voices. I strained to hear, but eventually my eyes drifted shut. When I opened them, it was morning and time to sort it all out. In a far more comfortable conference room complete with coffee and donuts, we shared our stories. The flash drive sat on the table in a plastic evidence bag.

Alex confessed that he knew about the AP Enterprises scheme to use undocumented workers for contract cleaners in the processing plant. He knew that Annalisa and Elvis were part of it, but didn't know about the sheriff. He suspected his dad might be involved, but again, had no proof. As for the car that hit Fannie, he kept quiet because he thought he was protecting his mother.

Mrs. Wilkens and Reverend Walter had more to say. They'd been able to talk with Lorrie, who was on the mend. Lorrie told them Fannie had learned about the AP Enterprises when Paulie got hurt. During his recovery, he spent a lot of time at the library and eventually talked about how he had been sent to Pottersville from his home village through an "agent." He was told to claim to be 18 and given false papers. The work in the processing plant was dirty and poorly supervised. He was hurt when the hose to a steam cleaner came off and burned him. Elvis, who was the contact for the mysterious agent on the other side of the border, talked him into signing the non-disclosure agreement in exchange for living with Big Mike and getting his education paid for. They even promised him citizenship.

I shook my head, thinking about the photo of his scars and what he must have gone through. "They were employing other children, weren't they?"

Walter spoke. "It goes deeper than simple employment. They were taking most of the wages in payment to the 'agent.' The kids were barely getting enough to pay for food." He paused, shaking his head. "And I didn't see it."

Mrs. Wilkens continued to relay what Lorrie had told her. "Fannie suspected that the Protect Our Children movement was a ruse by Elvis and Vogel to divert attention away from Pottersville. It started shortly after Paulie was injured. Pru was being used by them, too."

Alex tsked, "I doubt anyone has ever 'used' Aunt Pru. I'm guessing she was happy to take on the role of protector of the Ravens Valley morals."

The pieces were falling into place, but I still didn't have a full picture. "What about Blackmer and Trey and the sheriff?"

A man who had been standing at the door wearing a short-sleeved shirt and a loose tie walked in. "We've had our eyes on the sheriff for some time. You aren't the first to complain about his poor performance."

"Who are you?" I asked.

He shrugged. "An interested party."

I turned to Alex. "The Pottersville man…Mateo said there was a doctor involved."

Alex's expression turned hard. "I think it was the veterinarian Dad hired for the chickens." He raised his eyebrows, "Not me. Really. I'm guilty of knowing some of this, but I didn't have anything to do with it."

We spoke more about the scheme to make money off the backs of the children and the workers. It was clear to me that the dark clouds I'd noted in my first trip to Ravens Valley were real. After a lot of words, explanations, and conjecture I finally asked the question that had brought us to the funeral in the first place. "Who killed Fannie?"

The room was quiet for a few moments before Walter answered. "Heck Santos ran Fannie down."

By the drop in Alex's jaw and the widening of his eyes, it was clear he had no idea. "What?"

"I spoke with him this morning. He's going to turn himself in." Walter walked over to Alex and placed a hand on his shoulder. "It wasn't part of the AP Enterprises scheme or any kind of conspiracy. Your dad was drunk, he didn't see her, and he panicked."

"He put the blame on his wife?"

We sat in stunned silence. We'd turned over a rock and found ugliness under it, but Fannie died because of a drunk driver.

Chapter Forty-Six: Lemonade and Oreos

Several days later, with my ankle taped up and Lorrie home from the hospital, I sat with Mrs. Wilkens, Walter, Alex, and Lorrie on his back patio. Instead of beer, Walter had mixed us powerful gin and tonics.

Mrs. Wilkens took a sip of the drink and nodded with pleasure. "We're in contact with a nice lawyer who thinks we can nullify the NDA that Big Mike signed for Paulie. I doubt if we hadn't cracked the case, whether the poor boy would have seen a nickel of the money." She turned to Lorrie, "Tell Henry thank you for keeping the evidence."

Lorrie grinned back at her.

Goldie watched us through the screen, her eyes alert. I knew she wanted to leap through the door and roam the prairie. "Too bad, cat. You've cost me a lot of money, and your punishment is to go home with me." I'd been thinking over the past couple of days about the cat issue and had a theory that I wasn't quite ready to share.

Instead, I got up, hobbled away from the group onto the lawn, and beckoned Walter to join me. We quietly discussed my theory and then engaged the rest of the group. By the time I'd gone through my explanation, they were on board and ready to help.

After several phone calls to the owners of the poisoned cats, I enlisted Walter to set up a meeting. With it taken care of, we enjoyed the gin and tonics as the sun set over the cornfields.

The next day, a humid and sticky southern Minnesota August day, we gathered outside the church on the hill. Norman Vogel was the first to arrive.

His face was reddened from the heat, and he appeared to be exceptionally harried. No surprise considering his association with Elvis and the growing scandal. Jasper stood next to him, slumping as only a fourteen-year-old, slightly overweight teenager can.

Next, Pru arrived with her son Josh. He peered at us with a look that said, "I hate you all." Vince Santos followed behind his wife and son. His face was creased, and he had a nervous eye twitch. He, too, appeared to be exceptionally harried.

Walter walked up the steps of the church and opened the door with a key. Immediately, Vogel protested. "You aren't supposed to have a key. Remember? That was part of the deal." Walter ignored him and ushered us inside.

The church provided shelter from the heat outside. Walter flipped a switch, and several overhead fans moved the air around.

He led us to the front of the church and beckoned people to sit. I stood next to him and, without any preamble, held up the book *To Kill a Mockingbird*.

"It's one of the most banned books in the United States. It's been taken out of libraries, hidden behind the counter, and burned. I'm not sure why, but I'm sure Pru and the pastor have their opinions." I was tempted to ask if they'd ever read it, but that wasn't why I was talking about banned books to them. "This is a book about justice that wasn't served. Today, we are going to talk about justice served."

Wow, you are eloquent.

Not a good time for you to pop up.

I'll be quiet.

For a moment, I lost my train of thought. Jasper wiggled in his seat, and Josh muttered something under his breath.

"Here's the deal. Someone has been poisoning and murdering cats in this town."

Pru frowned, "You brought us here to talk about cats?" Her indignant protest echoed through the empty church.

Walter spoke up. He had a beautiful, deep, resonant voice. "Indeed, that's why we are here. Liza, please continue."

I noted that Jasper had become very interested in his shoes while Josh continued with a sneering expression.

"It seems that in your desire to determine what books children can and cannot read, you also made it a point to disparage those who advocated for the books."

Pru stared at me, "We most certainly did not!"

I took a piece of paper out of my pocket and read it from one of the last library board meetings. The minutes included, "And chairman Santos noted that people who allowed their children to read such filth should be 'punished on earth and damned to hell.' Reverend Vogel, who was in attendance, agreed."

Pru continued to stare without taking in what I had read.

"It is my contention and my friends here back me up on this, that you incited innocent children to punish those who spoke up by poisoning their cats."

Pru's jaw dropped. "What kind of nonsense is this?"

I put on my fifth-grade teacher armor and peered at Jasper first and Josh second. "Boys, do you have something to say about this?"

The sneer dropped from Josh's face as he, too, became very interested in his shoes.

Vince barked, "Wait, are you telling me my boy is responsible for poisoning the cats of my friends and neighbors?"

Walter nodded. "We talked with some of Josh's friends, and they told us how both Josh and Jasper bragged about putting the poison in canned cat food and giving it to the cats. They said it was punishment for promoting books filled with filth."

The room broke out in a cacophony of protests, except the two boys looked quiet and guilty.

I didn't want to get involved in the recriminations. I simply said, "I leave it to you and to Ravens Valley to do the right thing." Did I expect that to happen? I wasn't sure. I was sure I wanted to go home to my garden apartment, finish my paper, and get ready for the next school year.

* * *

In mid-September, with the leaves turning and the smells of autumn in the air, I visited my friend Ed, the retired janitor. We sat in his back yard drinking warm lemonade and eating Oreo cookies as I filled him in on my summer adventure. He listened, and when I was done talking, he tossed a bit of cookie to the crow cawing from the wires to the house.

"Those people, the ones who stayed quiet and let it happen, they're guilty, too."

I nodded. Ravens Valley and Ruston County had made a lot of headlines, including national attention over the last month or so. The library was being rebuilt with local and foundation money. Elvis, Annalisa, Wayne, the chicken vet, and several other people were under indictment.

Ed could read my mind. "And that animal doctor? What about him?"

Yes, what about him?

"She's talking to you, isn't she?" He studied me. "Not a bad thing, you know, having someone else to talk to."

"She's a pest, and I would make her go away except it would involve beating myself over the head."

Ed tittered. It was an odd sound because Ed hardly ever laughed.

"I don't know about Alex. They decided he wasn't involved other than knowing or suspecting what was going on and hiding the car."

"That isn't what I asked. What about him?"

I pictured how gently he'd taken Goldie from me the night she was poisoned. "Well, he's good with cats."

Hah! You know our father used to call you Liza-Cat.

Oh, shut up.

I turned to Ed. "What are the chances the Twins will be in the playoffs?" Best to change the subject.

Acknowledgments

First, I want to acknowledge my husband Jerome, who supported me through my years of writing. When he succumbed to the ravages of vascular dementia, I felt like I had lost a muse. Godspeed Jerome. Thank you to my wonderful family for being there when I needed you. To son-in-law Ted Scott, who planted the seed for this story. To Mark Roberts, my first reader and an editor extraordinaire. As always, thank you to Shawn Reilly Simmons and the crew at Level Best Books for your expertise in bringing Liza and Mrs. Wilkens to life. And a final thank you to the librarians of the world, please continue the good fight against book banning.

About the Author

Linda Norlander is the author of A Cabin by the Lake Mysteries, Liza and Mrs. Wilkens Mysteries and the Sheriff Red Mysteries. She is an award-winning author of short stories, humor and non-fiction. Before taking up the pen to write mysteries she worked in public health and end-of-life care. Norlander resides in Seattle, Washington.

AUTHOR WEBSITE:

http://www.lindanorlander.com

SOCIAL MEDIA HANDLES:

facebook.com/authorlindanorlander

Also by Linda Norlander